The Mother Keeper

A NOVEL

PAULA SCOTT

The Mother Keeper by Paula Scott
www.psbicknell.com

This is a work of fiction. Names, characters, places, and incidents are products of the author's imagination or are used fictitiously. Any similarity to actual people, organizations, and/or events is purely coincidental.

Cover Designer: Jenny Quinlan, Historical Editorial Cover Design
Editor: Jenny Quinlan, Historical Editor, historicaleditorial.com
Typesetter: Jeff Gerke, www.jeffgerke.com

International Standard Book Number (13): 978-0-692-88531-4

Printed in the United States of America

Amy,
This was written by a
sweet friend of mine who
loves Jesus and loves people
even in the messiness of life.
Love, Pamela
2017

The Lord is your keeper.

PSALM 121:5

Prologue

Snow wasn't in the forecast for New Year's Eve, but it came anyway, ending Jenny and Ken's evening of ballroom dancing at the Broadmoor Hotel. Of course, at nine months pregnant, Jenny did more sitting than dancing. Now, thanks to the increasing snowfall, they were headed home before midnight. When the baby rolled inside her, Jenny shifted in her driver's seat. Little Matthew, their future drummer, beat her ribs with his tiny fists. A breach birth. She drew in a deep breath.

It would be fine.

Her C-section was scheduled for January 6. It couldn't come soon enough for Jenny.

When the snowflakes settled on the FJ Cruiser's windshield, Jenny switched the windshield wipers on high and glanced at Ken in the passenger's seat. He hadn't wanted her to drive in the snow, but he'd had a beer at the Broadmoor, and she wasn't about to let him get behind the wheel.

"It's just one beer, honey," Ken had argued. "Hours ago. We've dined. We've danced. I'm fine."

"You shouldn't drink at all," Jenny said as they'd climbed into the cruiser with snowflakes in their hair.

"Come on. Jesus drank wine."

"You're not Jesus. And our church doesn't approve of drinking."

"The Bible doesn't say don't drink; it says don't get caught in drunkenness. I'm far from drunk, and our church has too many rules."

Jenny heaved a sigh as she turned on the car's heater. This was an old argument between them. It had been there since the day they'd wed. She believed Christians shouldn't drink; it led others astray. Ken thought otherwise. He said celebratory drinking was something Jesus not only approved of, but was something he did, pointing out the Pharisees of the Bible had called Jesus a drunkard and a glutton. Obviously, Jesus had enjoyed himself at parties. But right now, she was too tired to fight with Ken about it. And she wasn't so worried that someone would see Ken with a beer in his hand and tell their pastor. Soon she would no longer be running the church's children's ministry anyway. Matthew would be in her arms, and that's all she really wanted to think about tonight. Holding their baby, just being his mom. She'd taped all of Matthew's ultrasound pictures to the bathroom mirror. Every morning, she smiled at the photos while putting on her makeup, imagining Ken's blue eyes and her dark hair passed on to their little one.

Another punch from the baby's fist made her grimace.

She hated to admit it, but pregnancy had knocked her socks off. Jenny wasn't used to being sidelined by anything. She'd always been the first at whatever she set her mind to. First to get straight A's in school. First to take a break from a rising law career to take over their church's disastrous children's department and whip it into shape, always intending to place it in another's hands when it was thriving. First to decide she should transition over to Ken's law firm, where she could work alongside her husband every day righting the wrongs of the world. How sweet that would be for them to do it together.

But then she'd gotten pregnant, and all her plans had crumbled. This whole flat-on-her-back, growing a baby thing had surprised everyone, most of all Jenny. First, because pregnancy should come naturally, and it didn't for her. And second, because, while she and Ken wanted children more than anything in the world, they hadn't been ready to start their family just yet.

The children's ministry had fallen in her lap in the midst of it all. Not that she believed anything just fell into a person's lap. God ordered the steps of a believer, and above all things Jenny was a believer. She'd been a Christian since the first grade when a Sunday school teacher, Mrs. Berry, had led her to accept Jesus as her Savior. Maybe that was why she couldn't say no to ironing out their church's children's ministry issues. A lot of people got saved in Sunday school, and Jenny wasn't about to let such an important program fall by the wayside because the church couldn't find someone competent enough to get the job done. It helped that her brother Joe was a youth pastor in Tennessee and just full of ideas on how to rectify a children's ministry. Already her mind was on Sunday, what needed to be done in the Kid's Zone before she turned over the reins to the very capable Kathleen Trent.

Dancing at the Broadmoor for New Year's Eve had been Ken's idea. He was the outgoing one. "Maybe dancing will bring on Matthew's birth and we'll get that tax break for this year." Ken had winked when he'd said that yesterday. Jenny meticulously controlled their finances. Actually, she controlled a lot of their lives. Yes, she could admit she had control issues.

Keeping all her ducks in a row kept their world safe and sound, just the way she liked it. That's why she'd demanded the driver's seat tonight, to keep them safe and sound. She peeked at Ken, texting on his iPhone, probably wishing his parents out in California a Happy New Year, then she turned her attention back to the road.

An older model pickup truck roared out of the swirling snow, headed right for them.

Jenny's hands froze on the wheel as her scream merged with the sound of crushing metal and shattering glass—

And then her world went dark.

They say the truth will set you free, but what if the truth ruined your life? Today Ellie Ryan would know which way it would go. She was seventeen years old and scared to death. Her hands trembled as she opened the glass door of A Woman's Hope Crisis Pregnancy Center in Sutterville, Tennessee. Outside, the sky was clear and endless blue, the kind of sky Ellie liked to look up into for airplanes. She'd never been on an airplane, never been farther than Knoxville, Tennessee, using her thumb to get there, but she'd promised herself someday she'd do more than just hitchhike out of this town. She'd leave this godforsaken place forever and never look back. That's what she really wanted to do, never look back on what had happened here. Just put it in the past, if the past wasn't growing inside her.

After taking the free pregnancy test handed to her by the gray-haired lady at the front desk, Ellie settled into the reception area. As the time ticked by, she found it hard to breathe. A flat-screen TV mounted high on a wall ran the movie *Cheaper by the Dozen* with the volume turned down. The smell of microwave popcorn wafted through the building. This wasn't her first visit here. Two years ago, she'd sat in this same room with her sister, Jana, but on that occasion, they'd waited on folding metal chairs. The kind of chairs found in poor county clinics. And there was no TV. Today she passed the time on a leather couch like you'd find in someone's living room. Apparently, the clinic had been renovated by people with money. Popcorn-eating people.

Nobody else waited in the center, thank goodness. Soon either her fears—or her future—would be laid to rest. That was the thing about pregnancy; there was no halfway. You were either knocked up or you weren't. End of story. The woman who walked into the reception area to speak with her fifteen minutes later was not the elderly lady who had given her the test. This woman looked somewhere in her thirties, pretty and blond with fading freckles. She wore a name badge that read, "Patsy Klein."

The woman sat down beside Ellie on the couch. "Your test is positive. You're pregnant, Ellie."

So there it was. Just like that.

Closing her eyes, Ellie listened to her heartbeat unfurl in her ears, the sensation akin to putting a seashell up to your ear to hear the ocean. But she learned in school last year that it wasn't really the ocean you heard in the shell. It was the ambient sound from around you. Just the noise of your environment trapped in the shell. Ellie had never been to the ocean, but Jana had, and the seashell her big sister brought home for her became Ellie's most treasured possession. That and a 1960 Gibson Hummingbird guitar that had belonged to their mom.

Ellie liked to put the seashell to her ear while sitting on the frayed shag carpet in her bedroom in a single-wide trailer on the outskirts of Sutterville, where the grass grew knee high, put it close to her ear, just close her eyes, and listen to the sea.

When she learned the sound wasn't the ocean at all, that it was really Sutterville in her ear, she dumped that lying shell in the trash. The shell had betrayed her . . . just like her body betrayed her now. And the thing growing inside her was alive, like one of those little creatures that lived in seashells. Two years ago, after Jana's abortion, Ellie knew this to be true. It hurt to kill a shell creature. Once you killed the creature, the shell remained. And the shell was you. And you could pretend all day long to be the ocean, but in reality, you were only the noise from inside a trailer in a trailer park in Tennessee.

Struggling to keep control in the face of her worst fear come true, Ellie looked at Patsy Klein. The woman's face radiated goodness. Ellie just knew this woman was good all the way through. "Were you named after the country singer?" Ellie asked.

"Actually, no. Klein is my married name. But my mother was over the moon when I acquired the name. She loves Patsy Cline. I grew up listening to Patsy Cline's music."

"Me too." Ellie buried her face in her hands. The last time she and Jana came here, they'd been searching for a place to get an abortion. They'd taken to calling their dad "Clive" that summer, and, to their surprise, he seemed pleased with the arrangement. The crisis pregnancy center was new then, and they hadn't known Christians operated it. Like Clive, Jana's only religion was avoiding Christians and doctors. She despised both. When Jana figured out Christians ran the center, they got out of there as fast as they could, hitching to Knoxville to kill the little shell creature growing inside of Jana.

Hitchhiking back to Sutterville after the abortion—Jana vacuumed out and then filled full of pain—Ellie had decided she hated her existence. She'd never been to the ocean, had lived in a trailer her whole life, and now her sister had had an abortion while still in high school. But things improved after that. Jana ran off to California, and Ellie and Jamie grew closer. Jamie wanted the same thing Ellie did: to see the ocean. Actually, he wanted to live at the beach and surf when he wasn't playing football. Jamie Rivers could play football better than Sutterville had ever seen. He'd confessed to Ellie that he'd loved her since the first time she got on the bus servicing several trailer parks on the outskirts of town.

"You never let me in, not since that first day on the bus, and I've loved you this whole time," Jamie had told her a few days after Jana's abortion, though he didn't know anything about that. Ellie told no one about her sister killing the shell creature. It hadn't been hard. She'd learned the art of keeping secrets from Jana and Clive. The trailer itself was a lying shell too, making the sound of a family where there was only smoke, fried bacon, and booze. And the sisters trying to figure a way to escape—not just Clive and the trailer, but the whole Sutterville thing.

Now Patsy Klein's gaze reached all the way to Ellie's soul. She'd come here for a woman's help. A real lady who respected herself. Someone who didn't use her body to move up in a world where "up" was just a figment of your imagination. Nobody moved up in Sutterville. Girls either moved on or married a guy who played football in high school and then worked at the mill for the rest of their life. Their awful, dead-end life.

That first time Ellie and Jana walked into this center, a real nice lady had reached out to them. That lady had reminded Ellie of what a mother should be: a comfort. Of course, it had only been a moment before Jana put an end to it, but the little moment of solace stayed with Ellie. She sat here now because of that moment. "So . . . I'm pregnant." Saying it out loud sealed it for her. She'd judged Jana for getting herself pregnant, and now here she was in the exact same predicament, but without Jana's resolve to cut it out and make a clean getaway.

"Well, you have options. Let's talk about those." Patsy Klein crossed her legs, smoothing down her white linen skirt. "We have a program where the mother lives with one of our church families until the baby comes. Maybe we can do this for you. What are your plans for your baby?"

The talk of a baby stunned Ellie. She hadn't even adjusted to *pregnant* yet. "I don't know what I'm going to do."

"Adoption is a wonderful choice, Ellie."

"Do you arrange adoptions?"

"We don't here, but we will certainly assist you in contacting someone who does. Do you know how far along you are?"

"It happened on the Fourth of July."

Patsy took a little cardboard circle of dates out of her pocket and calculated the delivery. "Are you sure it was the Fourth of July?"

Ellie could still smell the Jack Daniel's from that night. Could remember the full moon reflecting off the lake in an eerie way as they left in Jamie's truck. The unease inside her with Jenner behind the wheel, and Jamie holding her close, drunkenly telling her he loved her.

She nodded, staring at her fingernails polished in blue.

"That places the baby's arrival when the dogwoods bloom. My favorite season. I was born in April."

Miss Patsy smiled in a reassuring way that softened Ellie down deep, down to the place it hurt the most, the place where she missed her mom.

"Really?"

"Your baby could come on my birthday." Miss Patsy put her hand on Ellie's knee. "If you accept refuge from Holy Mountain Church's Mother Keeper program, maybe you could stay with us." Miss Patsy smelled like lavender, the healing scent. Her teeth were bone-white and perfectly straight, and she talked with the soft Southern accent of the refined. Her nails were French manicured, and she wore a diamond wedding ring—a big rock to go with her expensive clothes. She probably lived down in the valley in a two-story mansion with shutters that never closed on windows surrounded by roses and a white picket fence.

"God has a new life for you, Ellie. A life where you can change. Please allow me to be a part of your future." Miss Patsy put her arm around Ellie, pulling her close. After a moment, Ellie leaned against her. "What about your mother? Will she allow you to live with us?"

A wave of despondency swept over Ellie. Normally, she would have pulled away, but instead she pressed her hot cheek against Miss Patsy's cool silk blouse. "My mom died when I was two."

"What about your father?" Miss Patsy gently stroked Ellie's back.

"My dad will be a problem."

"Nothing the Lord can't handle."

"You don't know Clive."

Chapter 2

A September wind whirled leaves down the street and tossed Ellie's long brown ponytail around as she walked from A Woman's Hope to the Sundowner Café across town. Johnson's Drugstore, with its old-fashioned soda fountain, beckoned her in for a strawberry milkshake, extra thick, but she kept walking. Under the circumstances, she didn't think she could stomach a shake. Besides, she was late for work. Clive would be mad, but she didn't care. She had waitressed at the diner for five years. Clive did all the cooking and cleaning. As long as she kept her hair in a ponytail, her apron clean and pressed, and politely served his customers, Clive remained content. Unless she showed up late. On the rare occasion this happened, Clive hit the roof, ranting and raving in the kitchen, vegetables flying in all directions as he chopped out his rage.

"Where have you *been*, kid? You know I rely on you to be here by 3:30. When you're not here by 3:30, I don't get dinner prepped the way I should and I drag hind-tail for the rest of the day. Dragging hind-tail riles me, kid. It riles the customers. You can't be late. It messes with my system."

Ellie knew his rants by heart. Clive's voice was gravelly from years of smoking Marlboros. He looked like a hundred miles of bad road but somehow remained handsome with his black crew-cut hair graying at the temples. His outfit of choice never changed: grease-stained blue jeans and a wife-beater T-shirt. Even in winter, when snow blanketed the mountains, Clive preferred his thin, sleeveless T-shirts. Sometimes he would throw on a worn flannel shirt, but as soon as he rolled into the diner's kitchen, the flannel came off. How he kept those white T-shirts stainless as he fried bacon, burgers, and chicken, Ellie didn't know. He often rubbed his grease-spattered hands on his pants, but never touched the shirts. Sometimes he wore an apron, but mostly not. Clive liked showing off his abs.

"A soft life makes a soft man. I ain't no soft man," Clive liked to say, fond of his lean physique.

Ellie often looked for herself in her father but never found anything she might have inherited from him. Jana had his coal-black hair and Cherokee cheekbones, but Ellie's hair was auburn brown and her face edged more softly.

"You're like your mother. Rose was a looker. Talented too. Don't ever drink or do drugs, kid. It fried your mom."

Clive had told Ellie this on her seventeenth birthday. A day off had been his gift to her. By then, Jana had made it all the way to LA, where she waitressed at night and auditioned for movies during the day. So far, the only thing she'd landed was a bra commercial, but it was a start, Jana said. A way to show everyone the great screen presence she had.

"We were born for the stage," Jana had told Ellie as far back as she could remember. "Mama had it too, star quality. It's in our blood." Jana wanted to become a movie star, the classic kind with a dark curtain of hair waving over one cheek. "You're gonna have to be the singer, like Mama. I didn't get the voice, you did." Elizabeth Taylor was Jana's favorite actress. "Liz lost herself in men and booze. I won't do that." Jana stuck out the chest she was so proud of, all the while talking about Elizabeth Taylor like she knew the woman personally. A dead woman, Ellie longed to remind her sister. Liz Taylor was dead. All the women Jana admired were dead. What could a dead woman do for you even if she'd once been famous? Death and fame were very much alike; both made a person seem better than they'd actually been.

Approaching the restaurant, Ellie spied Jamie sitting outside the diner on the bench that faced the mountains. He wore a new orange ball cap and was the last person she wanted to see today. She couldn't tell him about the pregnancy. Why wasn't he at football practice? Did Clive know Jamie waited for her? He had threatened to kill Jamie numerous times, but Jamie refused to take him seriously.

"Your old man secretly likes me," Jamie often said, grinning in that way that only he could grin.

"He spits in your burgers."

"That must be what makes them so good." Nothing in life fazed Jamie. Nothing but football.

He broke into a big smile when he saw her. "Hey, Ellie, where you been? I got great news!"

Ellie didn't answer until she could talk to Jamie quietly face-to-face. Quietness was her way. Jamie still hadn't figured that out. He was loud and likeable and as confident as an eighteen-year-old boy could be. Ellie craned her neck to meet his gaze. "I had an earache." The lie tasted bitter, but she swallowed it down with the rest of the lies ruling her life these days. She didn't want to lie, but she couldn't ruin Jamie's life too. And she did get earaches sometimes, just not today.

"You missed school. You never miss school. What's wrong?" For a big guy, Jamie had a little-boy voice. She liked that about him, liked most things about Jamie, but now that she was pregnant, everything had to change. She looked beyond him through the diner's picture window to where Clive talked with a customer. The customer stood with his back to the glass storefront. By the fierce look on Clive's face, she recognized the customer wearing the same orange ball cap as Jamie.

"Did you bring Jenner here?"

Jamie crossed his arms, the corded muscles in his forearms flexing with bravado. "Maybe Jenner will bust your dad's chops. I'd like to see that."

"You're so stupid."

"Why you gotta be that way?" Jamie stepped toward her, reaching out to touch her ponytail. "I got real good news, babe."

Ellie avoided his caress, hurrying around him. The bells jangled as she yanked open the diner's glass door.

Jamie trailed her into the restaurant.

"You keep away from Jana or bad things will happen." Clive glared at the beefy twenty-one-year-old standing in his business. Wearing a UT ball cap, Jenner looked a lot like Jamie, which made Ellie sick.

Clive spotted her. "Get to the kitchen and finish making the salad dressing." He glared at Jamie. "You, meathead, take your good-for-nothin' brother and get out of here."

"I'll leave after you tell me where Jana is," Jenner said.

Clive frowned at Ellie. "*Get* to the kitchen, kid."

Avoiding Jenner's gaze, she spun around and retreated behind the wall that separated the kitchen from the diner. She crouched below the pickup window shelf so she could listen to the men.

Bells jangled at the diner door once more. Ellie peeked over the pickup shelf as Red Perkins, the Spartan's defensive football coach, strolled into the Sundowner. "Jamie, you plannin' on sitting out our first home game?"

"No, *sir*!" Jamie rushed to his coach's side.

"Then why aren't you at practice, boy? We started ten minutes ago."

"I'm on my way, sir."

Red grabbed Jamie's arm, roughing him up a bit. "Sprint on over to the school. That should warm you up." He smacked Jamie hard on the rear, sending him on his way. "Hey, Jenner, what are you doing in town? I thought you were playing ball for Alabama."

"I came home to look after my mama and little brothers. I need Jana's address in California, but he won't give it to me." Jenner's eyes narrowed on Clive.

Red put his hand on Jenner's shoulder. He'd been Jenner's high school coach too. "Let that girl go. The only future you got's in football, son." Red turned to Clive. "You coming to the game this Friday, Mr. Ryan?"

"I'm not a football fan," Clive growled.

"You gonna let Ellie come?"

"She's got work to do."

"You won't have any customers. The whole town will be at the game. We're playing Mountain View. We're going to rub those rich boys' noses into the dirt. I'll tell you what, why don't you let Ellie come to the game so my boy Jamie plays well, and I'll bring the booster club on over here after the show?"

"I don't need your business."

"I know you wouldn't miss me, but my boosters are your best customers. They like my boys better than your old greasy burgers. If I let them know you were causing our boy Jamie to miss football practice, well . . ." Red pulled out a can of chew and tucked a lump of tobacco between his gum and cheek. "University of Tennessee offered the boy a full ride. He's now the town hero. If he screws up his scholarship because of your little girl, I'll make sure your best customers never darken that door again." Red pointed to the two rusty cowbells hanging from the entry handle. "There ain't much money in this old town. I'm not stupid, Ryan, and neither are you. My boosters keep you in business."

So *this* was Jamie's good news. He got the UT scholarship. Ellie should have known by the orange hats. Tears rushed to her eyes. *Good for Jamie.* All the more reason not to tell him she was pregnant. He needed to keep his head in football. If she told him, there was no telling what he would do.

Clive fixed Jenner with a hard stare. "I ain't givin' you nothin' on Jana. She's done with the likes of you." He turned to Red. "I'll see Ellie makes it over to the game. You make sure you escort her back here afterward—along with my customers."

Chapter 3

A gold tooth gleamed in Red's sunburned face when he smiled. "I've always liked that about you, Mr. Ryan. You're a reasonable man. If I was you, I'd think long and hard about how you treat our boy Jamie now that he's set for UT. If your pretty little girl can hold him, you can paper your diner with that boy's star. He's goin' somewhere."

"I'll *tell* you where he's goin'"—Clive showed Red and Jenner the door—"if he and his good-for-nothin' brother don't quit messin' with my girls, they're goin' to find themselves buried in these mountains."

On Friday afternoon, Ellie stepped out of her last period class, Creative Writing, her favorite, to find Jamie leaning against the old brick wall that held up the south end of Sutterville High School. It was a brisk autumn day with white puffy clouds building castles in the sky. Pushing off the wall to close the distance between them, Jamie pulled Ellie into his arms. Going after her lips, he hit her cheek as she swung away from his kiss.

He captured her chin and pulled her mouth back under his. "Hey, summer-rain girl," he said against her lips before kissing her.

Jamie liked to listen to "Summer Rain" since Ellie had first played it for him when she introduced him to all the old Johnnys: Johnny Horton, Johnny Cash, and Johnny Rivers. Jamie thought he was somehow related to Johnny Rivers because they shared the same last name.

When he released Ellie, she shook her head at him. "I've asked you not to kiss me at school."

"Where else am I supposed to kiss you? Your old man has blackballed me. I can't come to the trailer. I'm not allowed at the diner. I can't take you out anymore. When am I supposed to kiss you, Ellie?"

"I'm glad you got the UT scholarship."

"You don't look glad."

She slipped around him, walking toward the gate that exited the campus. Jamie fell in step beside her. "You headed for work already?"

"If I don't get the tables prepped, I won't be able to go to your game tonight."

Jamie took the books from her arms. "You gonna tell me what's the matter?"

"I can't talk now. I'm late for work. And don't ever bring Jenner around the diner again. Clive will kill him." Ellie took off walking.

"You better get back here and take your books. I'm not trailin' after you like some stray dog across Sutterville. The last thing I need is a fight with my girlfriend right now. I got a big game in a few hours, Ellie."

She spun around, strode back to him, and yanked her books out of his arms. Then she stared at him for a moment, biting her lower lip, knowing what needed to be said and the pain it would bring them both.

Jamie tried to caress her cheek with his fingers. "My UT scholarship doesn't change a thing between us. Remember that pact we made? We leave this town together."

She pulled away from his touch. "What's wrong has nothing to do with you." She turned and headed toward the diner, trying to escape the inevitable breakup with him.

He stood there for several seconds before jogging after her. When he reached her, he took off his UT ball cap and showed it to her. "This is my chance to get out of Sutterville. Jenner took a job at the mill yesterday. Says he's done with football. He wished me better luck. I'm not gonna waste my shot like he did."

"What about Jenner's scholarship?"

"He got kicked off the team for selling steroids."

Ellie stopped to look both ways before crossing the street. The last person she wanted to think about was Jenner. Jamie would have stepped in front of the white pickup speeding past had she not put her arm out to halt him on the curb. They crossed the road together before he said, "You gotta go to UT with me. Who's gonna get me through college if you don't come? After UT, we'll get married. When I make it to the pros, I'll buy you a mansion in Nashville. You'll have your own recording studio and everything."

A raven flew past, squawking loudly. Ellie watched the big, noisy bird. Two small blackbirds pursued the raven, which had raided their nest. Ellie hated ravens. She softly quoted the poem they'd just memorized together last week for English class.

> And the raven, never flitting, still is sitting, still is sitting
> On the pallid bust of Pallas just above my chamber door;
> And his eyes have all the seeming of a demon's that is dreaming,
> And the lamp-light o'er him streaming throws his shadow on the floor;
> And my soul from out that shadow that lies floating on the floor
> Shall be lifted—nevermore . . .

Jamie returned the ball cap to his head and shoved his hands deep into his pockets. "Edgar Allan Poe, huh? You're in a dark mood."

Ellie kept her eyes on the raven and blackbirds, watching the blackbirds fighting as if their lives depended on it . . . that was exactly how she felt right now.

Like she was in a battle.

For her life.

When the birds finally swirled into the distance, she turned to Jamie. "I want to break up."

His eyes widened, and his mouth hung open for a moment. *"What?"*

"You can have any girl you want. Wait until you get to UT and then pick a good one, someone like your mama, who takes care of you."

Jamie jumped off the sidewalk, cursing a blue streak and kicking the dirt in the field where the birds swirled in combat. Ellie's eyes burned with unshed tears and blurred on the number thirty-three on Jamie's jersey. When he finally walked back to her, tears glittered in his eyes. "Why?"

She swallowed the lump in her throat. She wasn't about to cry anymore, she'd cried enough already. "Have you ever listened to the ocean in a seashell?"

"What are you *talking* about?"

"When you put a shell up to your ear, you hear the ocean, right?"

"Right." He cracked his knuckles.

"So it's really the ocean you hear in the shell?"

"Yeah. Sure."

She stared at him, her heart breaking. "It's not the ocean, Jamie."

"What do you mean?"

"When you hear that sound in the seashell, it's not the ocean. It's just the sound that's around you. It's Tennessee in your ear."

Jamie clenched his jaw, folding his arms across his chest. "I have no idea what you're talking about."

"I've become a shell. There's something inside of me that needs to grow. I can't do this with you in my life. You're an amazing guy, but you've got your own road to travel."

"You're a shell? Like a seashell?" He cursed some more. "How am I gonna play ball tonight with you breakin' up with me for no good reason?"

"You'll probably play better than ever. They don't stand a chance with you riled up." She turned and walked away from him.

"Come on, Ellie! Don't do this to me! Don't leave me," he hollered after her.

Ellie walked faster, but she couldn't outwalk the words pouring through her mind.

Once upon a midnight dreary, while I pondered weak and weary,
Over many a quaint and curious volume of forgotten lore,
While I nodded, nearly napping, suddenly there came a tapping,

As of someone gently rapping, rapping at my chamber door.
"'Tis some visitor," I muttered, "tapping at my chamber door—
Only this, and nothing more."

Chapter 4

Shawn hated playing Sutterville. The football team was as rough as the town. Shawn's quarterback position made him the prime target for the other team's fury. The only thing that kept him from getting seriously hurt during this game was his speed. Most of the time the defense couldn't catch him. Still, he limped off the field in the fourth quarter after Number 33 finally got a hold of him. Sutterville then outscored Mountain View in the final two minutes of the game when their backup quarterback threw an interception. Kevin always threw interceptions. It was ridiculous.

Usually, Shawn would ride home on the bus with the team, but his mom insisted he ride with the family tonight, holding ice on his bruised knee. When his mom started in about the Sutterville girl with a full moon turning the winding mountain road white through the dark pines, Shawn only half listened.

"I walked into the bathroom when she walked out, and we practically ran right into each other," his mom was saying in the front seat of the Suburban. "Ellie was as surprised to see me as I was to see her, but she agreed to come by A Woman's Hope on Monday to make plans. Isn't that so like God, Samuel, to arrange this meeting for us?"

"I saw you talking to that girl," Stephen interrupted their parents' conversation. "Who is she?"

"Ellie Ryan. She's a Sutterville High School student," said Mom. "I met her at A Woman's Hope."

"She wears lots of makeup, and her fingernails are painted black," said Seth.

"You couldn't see her fingernails from the snack bar," Stephen argued.

"I saw her under the lights when we were leaving. They're black as tar," Seth insisted.

"Little girls with black fingernails who give their bodies away need Christ's love," said their dad behind the wheel.

"Didn't I tell you that, sweetheart?" His mom all but danced in her seat.

Shawn donned his headphones, cranking up his favorite band, Mumford & Sons. He had other issues on his mind—Jill for starters—and didn't feel like listening to his mom get all excited about a Sutterville girl she planned to help.

Mom always talked about A Woman's Hope; it drove him crazy, though he was kind of curious about the girl with the black fingernails. But not curious enough to listen anymore with his knee throbbing and his younger brothers bickering in the backseat.

When they got home, after Shawn had showered, his parents called him and his brothers into the living room to tell them the Sutterville girl was moving in with them.

"She'll be like your sister while she's here," his mom was saying. "After she has the baby, she'll have to return to

Sutterville, but until then we are going to love her and take care of her the way we take care of each other."

"She can have my room," Stephen offered.

"Sure she can." A grinning Seth elbowed Stephen, who gave it right back to his younger brother much harder.

"Are you serious?" Shawn moved the ice pack around on his swollen knee. "You're actually bringing a pregnant Sutterville girl to live with us? You're kidding."

His dad ran his hand through his hair as he always did when thinking hard about something. "Look, guys, the church is always talking about stopping abortion, but what do we really do to help these girls besides tell them not to kill their babies? If this baby's going to make it, the mother will need to be taken care of. We can do that for her here."

Shawn picked up the bag of ice, crunching it in his hand. "How old is this girl?"

"Seventeen," said his mom. "Look, Shawny, you don't know Ellie. She's a special girl, and I'm certain an innocent baby will die if we don't open our hearts and let her into our lives."

"My heart's open." Everyone turned to Stephen, his curly hair was disarrayed as usual, the look on his face so earnest. "I saw her, Shawn. She's . . . she's not what you think. She doesn't look pregnant at all."

"Stephen thinks she's hot!" Seth dove onto the floor when Stephen lunged across the couch at him. In the attempt to get away, Seth knocked the ottoman out from under Shawn's leg. Shawn sucked in his breath, grasping his knee with both hands.

Stephen tackled Seth, rolling him into an end table, cracking the table leg in half.

"Samuel, do something!" his mom cried.

Striding over to the boys, his dad grabbed Stephen around the waist and hauled him off of Seth, whose nose was bleeding. "Enough!" Dad ordered.

Mom hurried to the kitchen, and returned with a towel she pressed to Seth's nose. "Lean your head back," she said, the towel trembling in her hands as his dad squeezed Stephen in a fierce hug until his sixteen-year-old brother stopped fighting.

"I'm okay, Mom," Seth insisted, pushing her hands away to hold his own towel.

Mom went over to Stephen, running her fingers through his wild curls. "What on earth is the matter with you, honey?"

Stephen didn't answer. When their dad released him, he brushed past their mom and bounded up the stairs to his room. A door slammed, and an unnatural quiet filled the house.

"What's gotten into your brother?" his mom asked as if he had some inside knowledge of what made Stephen tick, which he didn't.

"You shouldn't bring that girl here." Stephen could be a hothead, but he'd never pounded on Seth like that before. Stephen and Shawn had always protected their happy little brother.

His dad came and sat beside him on the couch. "How's your leg?" Shawn could tell his dad was upset by the way he clenched his jaw

"It's fine." He locked gazes with his father. They had the same blue eyes, Shawn a younger version of the man sitting next to him. "Really, Dad, a pregnant girl from Sutterville?"

His dad took a deep breath, blowing it out slowly. "I believe God wants us to do this, son."

Shawn was silent for a long moment and then nodded his acceptance. He knew better than to battle his parents when they believed God was calling them to do something. Turning to Seth, he asked, “Is your nose busted?”

Seth grinned, proud of his bloody face. Usually, if the brothers took sides, Stephen and Seth ganged up on Shawn.

“Stephen needs to play football. Why won’t he play?” Shawn asked Seth. “Kevin is a worthless quarterback. Stephen throws a lot better. We could have won tonight if Stephen was our quarterback.”

“Because you play football. He hates living in your shadow.” Seth returned the towel to his nose when blood trickled into his mouth.

Shawn looked out the dining room window to the backyard where Seth and Stephen raked leaves together the following afternoon. Seth’s nose had received no permanent damage, and Stephen had apologized for exploding last night. The broken end table lay out by the trash cans waiting for the garbage man to arrive on Tuesday. Dad wasn’t a handyman. He could hardly change a coffee filter by himself.

Shawn knew his mom was pretty upset after Dad set the table on top of the trash this morning on his way to the country club for golf with Dr. Larson. The cherrywood end table had been Grandma’s. If Grandpa was still alive, he would’ve been out in his shop gluing the wood together, placing a screw on the inside for steady measure, doing a carpenter’s work, like Jesus, Grandpa would say. His mom’s dad had been a pastor too, not charismatic and wildly popular like Dad, but sure as the sun rising, Grandpa preached the Word of God every

Sunday morning for most of his life until he died of a heart attack in his sleep last year.

Grandma now lived in an old folks' home called Sunrise Estates. Aunt Vivianne resided there too, the sisters sharing an apartment, which made it more bearable that they'd placed Grandma in a home. It wasn't an old folks' place where elderly people just went to die. Sunrise Estates was a pricey assisted-living lodge beside the ocean. Aunt Vivi, a widow like Grandma now, had married money, and she was paying for it.

After limping out of the dining room, where he watched his brothers through the window, Shawn pushed open the swinging door and stepped into the kitchen with a smile on his face, smelling his mom's turkey dinner. He caught his parents kissing, which surprised him. He hadn't seen them kiss in a long time. They must have made up over Grandma's table. "We're adopting a sister, remember? No need to create one," he teased his parents. "Two pregnant people in the same house would be insane."

Embarrassed, his mom untangled herself from his dad, reaching out to stroke the buzz cut on Shawn's head.

"So you're okay with Ellie coming to live with us now?" Mom asked, directing Shawn's thoughts back to the pregnant Sutterville girl.

"Stephen seems to like her," he replied, knowing this would tweak his mom.

"She'll be a sister to you boys." His mom stressed the word "sister."

"Sure." Shawn pinched his mother's cheek and then, favoring his sore leg, walked across the kitchen to eat turkey off the white porcelain platter.

"Maybe I should make a doctor's appointment for you." His mom eyed his puffy knee.

He shouldn't have worn shorts so she could see the swelling. "I'm fine," he replied around a mouthful of meat.

"Don't talk while you eat," his mom returned.

"Listen to your mother, mighty Mountain View quarterback." His dad joined him at the turkey platter, stuffing a large piece of meat into his mouth, "Don't talk while you eat, boy," he exaggerated around the food.

"They get their manners from you, Samuel." His mom swiped the platter out from under the two of them. "Go call Seth and Stephen to the table," she told Shawn. "Wait, Samuel, you better do it. They're out raking leaves for me. Shawny doesn't need to be walking all over the place on that knee."

His dad winked at him, leaving the kitchen with a hunk of turkey meat he had swiped when his mom wasn't looking.

"I'm fine, Mom." Shawn took the turkey platter from her to carry to the dining room.

"I still think we should have Allen take a look at it."

"Dr. Larson's a surgeon."

"He's a doctor. He'll know if it's serious."

"It's not serious, Mom." Shawn walked as normal as possible to the dining room that looked like a page out of one of his mom's Pottery Barn magazines, trying to show her his knee was fit as a fiddle. And he knew fiddles. He played them from time to time. He stuffed another piece of meat into his mouth as his mom followed him through the swinging door with a steaming bowl of mashed potatoes. The smell made his mouth water. He loved mashed potatoes drowned in real butter.

"Allen will be happy to look at you. We won't go to his office. We'll ask him after church tomorrow."

"No way." Shawn sat down in his regular seat at the opposite end of the table from his dad. As the oldest son in the family, he always got this prime seat anchoring the other end of the long mahogany plank. When he was younger, it made him feel older to sit here. Today he was just happy it gave him plenty of room to stretch out his bum leg. He might even use the empty chair beside him to prop up his knee if his mom, sitting beside his dad, got to talking about the Sutterville girl and forgot all about him.

"I don't understand why you won't show Allen your injury. You're always with the Larsons anyway. At their house. At the country club. On vacation with them. Allen thinks you're his son. He'll want to see your knee."

"If it makes you happy, I'll ask Dr. Larson to check it sometime tomorrow. But not at church."

Mom smiled. "That didn't have to be so hard."

You make it hard. But Shawn didn't say that to her. He knew his mom badgered him because she loved him. He had great parents. An amazing family. Perfect, really, except his dad, the incredible Pastor Sam, who everyone thought walked on water, couldn't fix a thing. Not even a jammed toaster.

Chapter 5

Holy Mountain Church perched on a hill overlooking a picturesque valley. The city of Mountain View sat cradled in that valley, all fine brick buildings, massive maple and oak trees, and manicured lawns that kept the woods at bay. Even in times of drought, Mountain View remained lush and green, fed by wells tapped into an underground river beneath the town. "The River of Life," Pastor Sam referred to this limitless water supply, encouraging Mountain View's people to believe they resided in a land favored by God. This morning Pastor Sam preached on this very subject, adding that when much was given to God's people, much was required of them. "The Klein family has a new addition," he went on to say. "Seventeen-year-old Ellie Ryan will be coming to live with us, and we ask that our church family welcomes her to Holy Mountain with open arms."

Jill Larson sat upright in her seat. She'd been fighting sleepiness but now felt wide awake. A major head cold kept her from singing with Shawn and his brothers this morning in the worship band. The cold medicine made her tired, but it also cut her appetite down to zero, which she appreciated. She'd lost five pounds in the past four days. This morning when she put on her favorite Juicy skirt, it fit like a glove. Two weeks ago, she couldn't zip it up. Having a cold wasn't so bad, except she couldn't sing with Shawn. That was her favorite part of church, being up there on stage with the Klein boys, singing her heart out on a Sunday morning.

"As you all know, Patsy has been pouring herself into A Woman's Hope up in Sutterville. Because of your generosity, our little crisis pregnancy center and our Mother Keeper program has just saved a baby!" Pastor Sam paused to allow the congregation a moment for applause. The sound proved thunderous with over two thousand people clapping their hands. "I ask that all of you pray with me now for Ellie and her unborn child."

In an instant, a pin could be heard hitting the new carpet freshening the sanctuary. "Ellie is due in April. She will be living with us and joining all of you here at Holy Mountain until the baby arrives."

Jill leaned forward in her chair, her heart thumping in her chest, her cheeks hot with humiliation. Shawn hadn't said a thing about a Sutterville girl moving in with them. How could he not tell her about something like this?

"Dear Lord, we lift up Ellie and the child growing in her womb. Place your hand upon these precious ones. They are yours, Lord. We give them over to your care. You are the real Mother Keeper. Help us bless and keep these little ones as if they were our very own children. You are bringing them to Holy Mountain to be loved by us all. Show yourself faithful, Lord, in your care for Ellie and her baby. In your Son's marvelous name we pray. Amen."

The whole congregation echoed Pastor Sam's amen. Jill hardly heard the rest of the sermon. How could Shawn not tell her about this girl? They'd been together last night at the movies, and he hadn't so much as hinted the Sutterville girl was coming. Jill squirmed in her seat until she gave up trying to pretend she was unaffected by Pastor Sam's announcement. She rose from her chair well before the sermon was over.

Her mom, sitting two seats down the aisle, urged Jill with her eyes to sit back down, but Jill stepped over her sister, Lily's, feet and headed down the long aisle toward the rear of the sanctuary. It was the longest walk of her life. She could feel the stares cutting through her. Forcing herself to smile, she squared her shoulders and strolled to the ladies' room.

The bathroom was empty, the rows of stalls spotlessly clean. The tile floor gleamed snow white. A granite countertop cradled six sinks that felt wonderfully cool against Jill's palms as she leaned into the mirror searching her face for any sign of her inner turmoil. Fortunately, her features hadn't changed, and her makeup was perfect. A slight redness lingered around her nostrils from blowing her nose for the past four days, but other than that, Jill liked what she saw.

When women began filing into the bathroom, Jill tucked her lipstick back into her purse and went in search of Shawn. She was furious with him, but nobody would ever know that, including him. She found Shawn sitting at the piano in the sanctuary. He was goofing around with his brothers, Seth holding a guitar, Stephen on the drums. "Hey, guys," Jill said, fighting to talk normally with a plugged-up nose.

"Hey." Shawn smiled that smile she found so attractive.

"What's this about a Sutterville girl moving in with you?"

Seth and Stephen donned guarded expressions. Shawn remained as guileless as her two-year-old nephew, Tanner.

"I was surprised Dad announced it today. Weren't you guys surprised?" Shawn asked his brothers.

Stephen and Seth nodded in unison. Stephen swept his drumsticks across the drums, making the *ta-da* sound.

Jill stamped down her irritation, widening her smile. "So this Ellie Ryan, she's seventeen?"

The brothers nodded again at the same time, like those little fake dogs in the back windows of old people's sedans. Shawn's brothers were always polite, Seth more so than Stephen, but she felt they didn't really approve of her and Shawn's relationship.

"What did you think of this Ellie, Stephen?" Jill watched his reaction, trying to discern his true feelings.

"She's okay." Stephen gently tapped his drums.

The Klein boys were disgustingly musical. Jill struggled to shine when she performed with them. Again, she forced a smile, turning her attention to Seth. He was younger. A freshman in high school like Lily. "What did you think of her, Seth?"

"She's pretty, if you like black fingernails."

"So none of you have really met her?" she asked Shawn.

"Nope." The innocence of his reply grated on Jill's nerves.

She walked over and spread her fingers against his cheek. "You didn't shave this morning, babe."

"I slept late," he said.

She leaned over and kissed him on the lips.

Seth put down his guitar, and Stephen dropped the drumsticks. Both brothers appeared relieved to escape. They walked off together without talking, which made her all the more suspicious.

"What do you really think about this pregnant Sutterville girl?" She kept her hand on Shawn's cheek, liking the feel of his rough stubble.

Shawn took a deep breath just like Pastor Sam did when he was about to say something profound. "My dad says God wants us to keep Ellie until the baby comes—"

"So, this girl is going to be like your sister or something?"

"That's what my mom says."

Crossing her arms, Jill hugged herself. The sanctuary was always cold. She liked to wear summer clothes that showed off her tan but froze every Sunday because the church's air ran full blast summer or winter, it didn't matter.

Shawn reached down to the floor under the piano and pulled out a sweater. It was his, but he kept it there for her. Jill softened toward him as he handed it to her. She smelled the sweater before putting it on. Tide laundry soap assaulted her nose. "Have you run out of that cologne I bought you, babe?"

"Just about." Shawn grabbed the edges of the large sweater and tucked it around her. "Don't be upset about this Sutterville girl."

Jill felt like she might cry, but she didn't want to mess up her mascara.

"God will take care of all this." Shawn smiled.

"I know." She leaned into him.

He gave her a hug and then stepped away. "Hey, Mrs. Larson."

"Hello, Shawn." Beth Larson stood at the bottom of the stage waiting for Jill to turn around.

Jill rolled her eyes at Shawn before facing her mother.

"We're going to brunch at the club. Would you like to come with us, Shawn?" Slim, blond, and beautiful, Jill's mother looked like an older version of her daughter. Jill called her Beth most of the time instead of Mom because they liked people thinking they were sisters instead of mother and daughter.

"That would be great. Let me go ask my dad if it's okay." Shawn grinned at Jill and then headed for the side door off the stage that led down a hall to Pastor Sam's office.

Beth watched him stride away before turning to Jill. "You shouldn't have left the service early like you did. You showed your feelings by walking out."

"I had to go to the bathroom." Jill pulled Shawn's sweater more tightly around her.

"I didn't know Samuel and Patsy had decided to do this, or I would have warned you, honey."

"You're Pastor Sam's personal secretary. How could you not know about this Sutterville girl?"

"Sam didn't tell me a thing."

Jill could see her mom was hurt too about not being informed. "What are they thinking, taking in a pregnant girl?"

"I'm sure Sam's prayed this all the way through."

"It's Patsy's idea, no doubt."

"I'm sure this is all Patsy's doing," Beth agreed.

"So what are they going to do with the baby?" Jill walked off the stage, and she and her mom slowly made their way out of the now empty sanctuary filled with row upon row of padded blue chairs.

"I have no idea."

"You think Patsy's crazy enough to keep that Gutterville baby?"

Beth didn't respond.

As soon as they cleared the double doors into the lobby, a sea of people spread around them. Jill's dad stood talking with

Pastor Sam. The two men shared an easy rapport. Her father wasn't on call today, but because he was the best bone surgeon in Tennessee, he kept his phone on all of the time. When someone got severely injured in an accident, Daddy took the call. He'd saved so many mangled limbs they called him a miracle worker.

Jill was proud of her father. With him standing by Pastor Sam, she tried to decide which man was the more handsome. Pastor Sam stood taller, was still muscled like the athlete he used to be, and had all of his hair. But her father oozed success and wealth, and of course he dressed better. Pastor Sam preferred off-brand polo shirts and slacks from JCPenney's when he preached. Outside of church, Shawn's dad favored Levi's and simple T-shirts. He really needed to dress better.

"My beautiful girls," Jill's dad said when she and Beth arrived. "Jill, I was telling Sam that you're going to be Ellie's new best friend. Isn't that right, doll face?"

"Sure, Daddy," Jill said sweetly. "I'll tuck her under my wing like a baby bird. Will she be attending Mountain View Academy, then?"

"We appreciate that, Jill," Pastor Sam said. "I'm not sure if she'll be allowed to go to MVA. We're looking into it."

"Oh, right, she's pregnant," Jill made sure to remind everyone of that.

Her dad spotted Mr. Hartman, Mountain View's principal, and waved him over to join the conversation. "Here's the man of the hour. Josh, will you be letting our girl, Ellie, attend MVA?"

Mr. Hartman looked surprised to be put on the spot. He was in his early thirties, already balding, and had only been principal at the academy for a year now. He cleared his throat. "Well, pregnancy isn't allowed at our school—" he began.

Jill's dad interrupted him, "Come on, Josh, we aren't talking about one of our MVA girls getting herself in trouble. This is about practicing what we preach by rescuing the needy. Isn't that right, Pastor Sam?"

Rarely did her dad call Sam "Pastor." When he did, everyone braced themselves for the rant to come.

Pastor Sam put his hand on Daddy's shoulder to settle him down. Jill could see the affection he felt for her father in Pastor Sam's blue eyes. Shawn's eyes were that way too, windows to his heart. Such good hearts. She loved that about the Klein men. At least Shawn, his dad, and Seth. They were open books, so easy to read. Stephan proved harder to figure out. Jill decided she didn't like Stephan anymore. He'd become someone she no longer knew, even though they'd grown up together for the past ten years since the Kleins moved to Mountain View when Pastor Sam took over Holy Mountain Church. Making the church what it was today: amazing.

"Allen, why don't you, Josh, and I meet in my office tomorrow and talk this over? The ladies have been in their heels all morning. I'm sure they would like to slip into sandals and get something to eat."

Beth smiled at Pastor Sam, and he returned her mom's grin. Jill felt an uneasy twinge race down her spine watching them together. Daddy put his arm around Beth and pulled her to his side. Patsy crossed the lobby, and Daddy winked at her as she scooted under Pastor Sam's arm.

"Now all the prettiest girls in Mountain View are accounted for." Daddy earned a blush from Miss Patsy.

Jill studied the four adults together. They'd been best friends practically since the day the Kleins stepped foot in town. She knew their story well. Daddy found Pastor Sam preaching in some obscure little church in Richmond, Virginia. Holy Mountain's elders were so impressed with Pastor Sam they offered him five times what he was making there. At first, Pastor Sam surprised them all, declining the invitation to come to Mountain View, but after a year of Daddy's and Granddaddy's persistence, Pastor Sam finally caved, and now here they were, ten years later, with she and Shawn set to marry once they finished college. If Shawn went to medical school like they'd planned, Jill wondered where that would put their wedding date. Years away, for sure, which she couldn't take.

The thought of waiting so long to be with Shawn made her all the more determined to convince him it was okay to have sex before marriage. A lot of Christians did, and everything worked out fine. Her half sister, Jane, and her husband, Phillip, slept together before they married, and look at them now. Few knew their magnificent white wedding three years ago at Holy Mountain Church with Pastor Sam officiating wasn't as white as it appeared. Then they had Tanner, the cutest boy ever—aside from Shawn—and Jane was now expecting a little girl in January. Jane and Phil ran a popular preparing-for-marriage ministry at Holy Mountain. Sure, Jane and Phil had their problems. Phillip golfed every weekend, leaving Jane, sick again with her second pregnancy, to take care of Tanner, Mr. Handful, all by herself, but aside from little things like that, Jane and Phil led fabulous lives.

As if her thinking made him appear, Shawn, guitar in hand, rolled through the first set of double doors that led to the sanctuary. Eagerly, she stepped toward him. He usually played the piano and let Seth have the guitar, but today he and Seth did several songs together on guitars before Shawn returned to the piano to wrap up the final worship song. When he played the fiddle, on rare occasion, it melted her. He could play anything.

As he joined the group, Shawn draped his free arm around Jill's waist. His other arm held a guitar. She felt the muscles in his arm ripple against her back, though he held her lightly. He always held her lightly. She leaned into him, longing for more. That was the story of her life, always longing for more of Shawn Klein.

It was nearing sundown, the September night promising an early snowfall in Colorado. Jenny's arm felt like it was going to fall off after painting all day. But she wasn't about to quit until the whole damned wall was white. Before her breakdown, she never cussed, but now she said whatever bad word came to mind. Why not? Why the hell not? She wasn't good for anything else; she might as well get their house repainted and talk like that painter Ken had wanted to hire to do the job. Before the accident, they'd planned on paying a professional to repaint the house. They'd even gotten a written bid they'd both signed from a paint-covered man who cussed when they walked around the house with him so he could give them his honest estimate. Jenny hadn't wanted to hire him because of his foul language. "Who is honest when they talk like that?" she'd argued, which had upset Ken.

"Men cuss," said Ken, his face reddening with frustration because this was the fourth painter they'd talked to in a week and Jenny hadn't liked any of them. "What's the big deal, Jen? We aren't taking him to church with us on Sunday. He's painting our house, and he's affordable."

That's what really mattered to Ken. Affordable. But that written bid was out of their budget now, so the cussing certainly didn't matter. Everything was out of their budget, with medical bills draining them dry. She didn't know why Ken insisted on her still seeing that counselor every other week that cost two hundred and fifty dollars a session. Just yesterday, she'd told the counselor it bothered Ken that she had taken up cussing.

"It's just not you, hon," Ken said. "I miss your sweet mouth. Those words don't belong there." Jenny had mimicked Ken's funny facial expression as she told the counselor about it. Like Ken was confused or maybe even constipated when he announced that he didn't like her cussing.

"Does God care that I cuss? He doesn't care," she'd responded, standing there waving her white paintbrush at Ken. "This sweet mouth is long gone, along with other body parts between us."

She'd told the counselor this and then tried to breathe deeply from her core, like the counselor had taught her to calm herself down. It was no secret she was broken. There was no longer a uterus in her body to grow a baby. That had been taken in the accident too, along with their Matthew. Ken was missing several inches of his right leg. It was a wonder he could even walk like he did after the five surgeries he'd had so far.

She found it impossible to be the wife he wanted her to be now because she'd never be a mother to his children. She'd spent her entire life living to please God, blindly devoted to Jesus since she was a little girl, and now God had shattered their world. Before the crash, she thought God would give them the perfect family. First Matthew, then a daughter, Madison. She'd already chosen those names, all set to call Matthew's little sister

Maddy, but instead God gave them brokenness that went on and on. God really didn't care about them. At least they could live in a white house with charcoal trim like they'd always dreamed.

When she first started painting one Saturday morning this summer after drinking nearly a whole pot of coffee by herself, and then running down to the hardware store before Ken got up, her husband had called her crazy. He felt bad for saying it and shut up fast because she really had gone crazy for a while back in January. The Bible said God worked everything together for the good of those who loved him. If one more person told her this, she would lose it again. Just like she'd lost it on the one-year anniversary.

They'd gone to church to ring in the New Year with their church family. It seemed the safest place to be on that night. But it hadn't turned out to be safe at all. One too many people had told her God had a plan for her life. A plan to prosper and not harm her, to give her hope and a future.

"Do you call this not harming me?" Jenny had yanked up her black silk shirt to show Cherie Roper and Dawn Springer, standing with her in front of the dessert buffet decorated with silver streamers and glitter-covered stars, the scars on her abdomen. "God took my baby, and he took my womb. He might as well take my life because I'm sick of hearing how God has good plans for me! God doesn't work everything together for good! This isn't good!" she'd screamed as loud as she could, shocking herself and everyone else with her unexpected rage.

Ken had raced over from talking with Cherie's and Dawn's husbands, clueless men holding tiny appetizer plates, stuffing fried jalapenos into their mouths. When Ken had reached out to touch her, Jenny slapped his hand away with a fierceness that astounded everyone in the room. "And I'm sick of you telling me we need to move on! That we need to adopt a baby from China or some other godforsaken country that kills their babies! God killed our baby!" she'd wailed, losing all control, collapsing on the floor.

Ken had scooped her up and carried her sobbing from the church. Several doctors had followed them out. She hadn't calmed down in the car in the snowy parking lot, saying all kinds of god-awful things that made no sense to anyone, using profanity, which she never used, not even a "holy cow" or the word "crap," which she hated Ken using.

Ken had held her pressed against his warm body in the backseat of their BMW while Doctor Crutchfield, a friend of Ken's with a shiny bald head and big muscles because he spent all his free time at the gym, rushed them to the hospital.

At the ER, they'd sedated her, and she slept for two entire days hooked to IVs in a hospital bed. It was more sleep than she'd gotten in a month since she'd been on a jam-making roll, spending most nights whipping up pomegranate, strawberry, and peach preserves she'd planned to sell at the church's Christmas bazaar. But she never sold all that jam in December. Never made it to the church bazaar because she knew she was coming apart somewhere down deep inside, somewhere profoundly primitive, and she didn't want people to see that wild, haunted, primitive thing alive in her eyes. Alive in her heart, like an animal eating her from the inside out. That was nine months ago, the same amount of time it would take to grow a baby in the womb she no longer had. After her first day of painting, Ken had said, "It's going to take you forever to paint this house."

"I figure it will take about nine months," Jenny had retorted, covered in paint and kind of satisfied with herself because she was doing something useful for a change. "If I can't grow a baby for us, I might as well paint our damned house."

Ellie hid the two garbage bags filled with her clothes under the bed in case Clive came into her room before the Kleins arrived. Jana had taught Ellie about the trash bag suitcase when she left Sutterville with Mr. Dardy, a long-haul trucker headed for Bakersfield, California. Jana had tucked everything she owned into trash bags two years ago.

After packing her own stuff into trash bags that morning, Ellie cleaned the trailer, anticipating the Kleins' coming while Clive was out riding his antique pet. She called his Harley the "antique pet" because it was twenty years old and Clive never let them have the dog she so longed for, or any other pet for that matter. Ellie hated that motorcycle when she was young and wanted her father's love. Now the Harley was her greatest relief because it kept Clive busy outside of the diner, where they both labored six days a week, hardly speaking to one another. They had lived in the trailer for as long as Ellie could remember, parked beside Mr. and Mrs. Dunburger. "The Hamburgers" Ellie called the reclusive old couple because when she was little she thought that was their name. The Dunburgers rarely left their trailer. Others in the park kept to themselves as well.

It was an eerily quiet place, like a cemetery, which shouldn't surprise anybody considering most of the residents were well over retirement age. Clive was the only occupant who made noise in the park, but he gave his elderly neighbors free coffee when they came to the diner, so nobody complained about the antique pet.

A teacher at the elementary school came to complain once because Clive was always revving the pet in the parking lot while waiting to pick her and Jana up after school, and the teacher said two little girls shouldn't be on a motorcycle without helmets, but Clive ran him off with a gun. The pistol wasn't loaded, but the teacher didn't know that. "I ain't loading my gun for no sissy teacher," Clive said after the teacher sped out of the trailer park in his little blue Honda that sounded like a lawn mower. "What's that teacher gonna do to me?" he'd asked Ellie. She didn't answer Clive because she liked Mr. Langstrom and had watched him drive off with a lump in her throat that felt like a pinecone.

"You stay away from that sissy teacher," Clive had told her. "I don't want to have to bury him in the mountains." Clive was always threatening to bury someone in the mountains. Jana would laugh sometimes when he said it, but she admitted Clive's threats weren't funny. "I think he'll probably kill somebody someday," she'd told Ellie. Before the Kleins arrived, Ellie made sure Clive wouldn't find his gun, hiding the pistol behind the laundry soap in the cupboard above the washing machine.

Miss Patsy said Jesus would help with Clive. Ellie longed to believe Jesus could help her. Wanted to believe that more than anything in the world, but if Jesus was real, he hadn't done a thing for her.

For years, she'd knelt beside her bed and prayed to God at night, even when Jana told her not to. "Praying's so pointless," said Jana. "If God was real, we wouldn't be stuck in this stupid old trailer. Our mother wouldn't be dead and Clive wouldn't be ruining our lives every stinkin' day."

But Ellie sometimes watched religious shows on television, hearing how God gave people miracles. So she prayed for a two-story house, a mom and dad who loved her, and a dog. She really wanted a dog. At ten years old, that didn't seem like too much to ask, but by the time she turned twelve, Ellie decided she didn't need parents. She needed to take care of herself. And that was the end of praying beside her bed each night. She still planned on getting a dog someday, a golden retriever. She really liked golden retrievers.

Now she paused in her packing to kneel beside her bed one last time. It wasn't a mom and dad and a home she asked for now, it was help with Clive. He'd called Jana a whore after finding out about her abortion because she bled all over the bathroom. "A smart whore," he'd said. "You done the right thing getting rid of that, girl. Good thing your sister's a lot smarter than you. Ellie ain't about to get herself bred by one of these no good Sutterville boys. Ain't that right, kid?" Jana was always "girl," Ellie always "kid" to Clive.

But Ellie wasn't going to step into that conversation, and of course Jana wasn't about to give her a moment to do so either. "Unlike you, I'm willing to pay the price for real relationships," Jana had told Clive. "All your nasty girlie magazines in the bathroom make me sick. You wouldn't know what to do with a real woman if she bit you on the lip."

Jana and Clive had always butted heads, both being know-it-alls. Ellie had plenty of her own opinions too; she just kept them to herself. By the time Jana hit high school, living in the trailer with her and Clive was nearly unbearable. Fortunately, Clive spent most of his time at the diner and so did Ellie when she wasn't in school because she didn't have Jana's backbone to say no to Clive about working there. If they were slow on customers, Clive let her sit out on the back steps behind the diner and strum on her Hummingbird, writing songs in the shade of the old brick buildings lining the alley. Having to tell Clive she was pregnant was her worst nightmare come true.

Praying beside her bed, *God, if you're real, please help me,* was all she could come up with. It was five minutes to three, and Miss Patsy had promised they would arrive at three to pick her up. Ellie knew Miss Patsy would be on time. She was that kind of woman. After pulling out the garbage bags with her clothes, Ellie grabbed her guitar. The Hummingbird was her only valuable possession, and it was priceless because it had belonged to her mom. Jana said the Hummingbird called to Ellie back before Ellie could even play it. She wrote her first real song at ten years old, and Jana had said, "Make up another one. That sure was good, Ellie Jelly." That was Jana's special name for her. "You sounded just like Mama."

Ellie doubted Jana could remember what Mama sounded like since Mama died when Jana was five and Ellie just two, but Jana had all kinds of memories of Mama, most of which Ellie figured her sister just made up. Ellie wished she had one memory of Mama, but there weren't any. But she had the Gibson Hummingbird. That old guitar sounded like melting sugar when she played it nice and slow and soulful. Nothing calmed Ellie more than strumming her Hummingbird. Leaning against her bedroom door now, she cradled her Hummingbird like a baby in her arms, and began to play Johnny Cash's version of "Hurt" while waiting for the Kleins to come.

At their knock on the trailer door, Ellie quickly put down her guitar and rushed out of her room to turn off the TV and beat Clive to the threshold to yank open the trailer door. It made a big clank because it was old. He looked at her funny but stepped out of the way, careful not to spill the beer in his hand. The smell of alcohol and cigarettes lingered in his wake.

Ellie's heart pounded so hard she thought she might pass out. Her legs felt like butter left on the kitchen counter in summertime. "You're here," she said to Miss Patsy and her husband. Her voice sounded faraway and unfamiliar to herself, like someone else's voice, a surprised and hopeful voice. "Come sit down," she told the Kleins, motioning to the broken-down couch Clive had just vacated.

Clive moved farther down the wall, watching the Kleins make their way to the sofa where he napped on Sunday afternoons or sat drinking beer and watching television as he'd been doing before their arrival. Ignoring Mr. Klein's attempt to shake his hand, Clive placed his beer on the kitchen counter and hooked his thumbs in his wife-beater T-shirt. The Kleins went and sat down at the same time on the couch, matching smiles on their attractive faces.

"We've come for Ellie," Miss Patsy's husband, the pastor, said in a gentle voice that allowed Ellie to breathe again. He smiled at Ellie before turning his earnest blue gaze on Clive.

"You social workers?" Clive asked.

"My name is Patsy Klein. I run A Woman's Hope in Sutterville. This is Samuel, my husband. He pastors Holy Mountain Church down in Mountain View."

"Mountain View," Clive said, as if he understood something important now.

"I'm pregnant," Ellie said, unable to stand the tension building in the room.

Clive went still. He stopped running his thumbs along the edge of his T-shirt and dropped his hands to his sides. "Does Jamie know?" he asked after the longest beat of Ellie's life.

"No. This isn't Jamie's business." Ellie locked eyes with Clive. *Please, please, please just let me go.*

"All right," Clive said, and she could hear the sadness swelling in him. "So, kid, what are these fine people going to do about it?"

Clive had called her *kid* for as long as she could remember. An unexpected rush of emotion hit her. She hadn't felt anything for her father in a long time. Her eyes filled with tears, making his white T-shirt a field of snow before her. Miss Patsy stood up and put her arms around Ellie, pulling her close. The pastor rose too, stepping over to stand beside Clive like a friend.

"We would like to take Ellie into our home until she has the baby." The pastor's voice was reassuring. "We'll take good care of her. See that she visits a doctor regularly, and we'll pay all her medical bills. Our church does this through our Mother Keeper program that encourages adoption."

"She don't eat much," Clive said.

Pastor Klein smiled. "You're right about that. She's a little thing."

"She may be little, but she's got a real big voice. She sings like a songbird and writes her own ballads just like her mama, God rest her soul," Clive said.

Ellie began to sob without making a sound. Miss Patsy held her now as if she'd never let her go. Ellie had longed for this all her life, to have a mother's arms around her. Pastor Klein laid his hand on Clive's shoulder. Clive stood there stiff as stone. Ellie used every ounce of strength she possessed to pull herself together. She hadn't bawled like a baby since that night after the party at the lake when she got pregnant and hated that she did so now, weeping all over Miss Patsy's nice clothes.

"We'll take good care of your daughter. After everything is worked out with the baby, we will bring her back here with a few more pounds on her." To Ellie's utter surprise, Clive accepted this, though she couldn't fathom why. Pastor Klein took out a business card and handed it to Clive. "We're easy to find down in Mountain View. Come by Holy Mountain Church anytime. If you want to see Ellie, we'll arrange it."

Clive took the card, set it on the counter, and picked up his beer.

"Let's gather your things," Miss Patsy whispered in Ellie's ear.

Ellie turned and led the Kleins to her bedroom, where they grabbed the garbage bags as if they did this all the time, lifting trash bags instead of suitcases like normal folks owned. Ellie grabbed her guitar and led the way out of the trailer in utter silence, her face washed with tears. Clive stood by, holding his beer. He didn't drink from the can, only cradled the Coors in his hand for the comfort it gave him.

The Kleins had arrived in a big black SUV like the Secret Service used. Pastor Klein loaded the bags in the back and offered to take Ellie's guitar from her. She allowed him to place the Hummingbird in the back with the bags, though she would rather have had it on the seat beside her.

Clive leaned against the open trailer door watching them drive away. The Hamburgers stepped out onto their porch, watching too. Ellie noticed that several trailer doors swung open, neighbors all curious about the strange SUV departing the park.

Ellie was thankful for the SUV's tinted windows. Because they rarely came out of their trailers, it would take most of the neighbors a while to realize she was gone. Many of them might never know. Maybe the whole town of Sutterville would keep humming along, unaware she was pregnant. She wondered what Clive would tell Jamie. She knew he'd say nothing about her pregnancy.

"Did you bury her in the mountains?" Jamie might joke, but soon he'd figure out she really was gone. Then what would Jamie do?

Chapter 8

At four that afternoon, Shawn fixed himself two peanut butter and jelly sandwiches, though he'd only been home an hour from the country club, where the Sunday brunch was the finest in Tennessee. His brothers rested on the couch, Stephen at one end, Seth at the other, watching football. Empty potato chip bags littered the floor. "You better clean those up before Mom and Dad get home," Shawn warned.

"Ellie comes today," Seth said, kicking Stephen.

Stephen kicked back, keeping his eyes on the television. Seth grinned all the more.

"She's from Sutterville," Shawn said, as if being from Sutterville eliminated any element of intermixing.

"And she's knocked up," Seth reminded everyone.

Stephen kicked Seth hard enough to make him yelp.

Holding his plate of sandwiches in one hand, Shawn walked over and thumped Seth on the head.

Seth sat up on the couch, rubbing his head while holding his shin.

Shawn made himself comfortable in Dad's leather La-Z-Boy.

After eating his peanut butter and jelly sandwiches in front of the ballgame, he went back into the kitchen and pulled a carton of milk from the fridge. An uncooked lasagna covered with tinfoil waited in the fridge. On the counter sat a peach pie. That's what made the kitchen smell so good. He checked the freezer for ice cream. A vanilla tub was there, but upon pulling it out, he realized it was empty. Two spoons lay in the kitchen sink, the evidence of his brothers' feast drying on the un-rinsed silverware. Shawn threw the empty ice cream tub in the trash and washed the spoons. He returned to the living room and picked up the crumbled potato chip bags.

"Thanks," said Seth, keeping his eyes on the game. The 49ers were getting pounded, which probably pleased Stephen since the 49ers were Shawn's team.

Normally, Shawn wouldn't be missing a moment of this game, or any other Sunday showdown, but lately his heart hadn't been in football. Neither was Stephen's. At least high school football. "I don't know why you don't try out for our team. You'll come straight to varsity with me," he told Stephen.

Stephen ignored him.

"Stephen won't play because the team already has a quarterback. You." Seth threw an empty juice box at Shawn.

"You're a better quarterback than Kevin. You could have held the Sutterville game for us. We wouldn't have lost if you had quarterbacked," Shawn said.

Stephen finally turned his attention to his older brother. "I'm not as good as you."

"You're younger and you never practice. Who knows how good you are?" Shawn crushed the juice box.

Stephen returned his gaze to the television. Shawn knew by the look on Stephen's face that their conversation was over.

It hurt that he and Stephen weren't close like they used to be. There had been a time when Stephen followed him around like his shadow, Seth dogged them both, and the three brothers ran their own football games in the backyard. Dad had taught them all how to throw a ball, but Shawn was the one who worked with Stephen and Seth until his little brothers could blast the ball through the tire swing from the other end of the yard. The boys were all tall and well-muscled, like their dad. Natural athletes.

"Grandpa Klein quarterbacked himself out of the Kentucky coal mines," Dad would remind them. "You boys got quarter-backing in your genes."

Seth, a second-grader at the time, had gazed down at his pants. He'd put his hands in his pockets and then pulled them back out. "I've got nothin' in my jeans," he'd said in despair.

They all laughed that day, and Stephen spent the next five years throwing the football at the tire swing or at a running Seth, who, when he was little, caught the ball with his body, which sent him sprawling to the ground.

Stephen's bullheadedness bugged Shawn. He knew his brother could carry the team if he got injured in a game. Kevin couldn't carry a juice box. The pressure to perform in foot-ball weighed on Shawn. The only game they'd lost so far, the one with Sutterville, was because he got hurt. That big guy, Number 33, with the UT scholarship, was about impossible to outrun. When he'd hit Shawn, it felt like a truck plowing over him. At the end of the game, Number 33 came over and asked if his knee was okay. Shawn could tell the guy wasn't mean. Just a great ball player.

Shawn dumped the juice boxes in the trash, noticing six empty juice boxes already there. He lifted the nearly full bag out of the bucket, carrying it outside to the garbage bin. His mom had cleaned all day yesterday in preparation for the Sutterville girl's arrival. Their house always looked nice, but now it sparkled, and he wanted to keep it that way until his parents came home with Ellie. He tested her name on his tongue, trying to get used to it instead of "the Sutterville girl."

Going back into the house, he walked down the hall to the guestroom where Ellie would stay. His mom had even made new curtains for the room, a sunny yellow shade that matched the new daisy bedspread.

"She reminds me of a mountain daisy—you know, those little flowers you boys used to pick for me up at the lake?" His mom had said when she came home with the bags of new daisy bedding a few days ago. The room looked fancy now. The girl stuff appeared strange in their house. The only female who ever lived here was his mom, and even his mom and dad's bedroom was decorated in browns and earth tones, "classic colors," his mom explained.

This room looked pretty. He didn't go in, just stood at the door for a moment, making sure his brothers hadn't messed anything up in here. He heard thumping on the floor and realized what it was. "Duncan, this isn't your room anymore," he scolded the white-muzzled golden retriever crawling out from the other side of the bed on his belly. "Come on, boy, this room is for girls only now."

Duncan stood up and came to him, swishing his tail. Shawn knelt down and petted him. They'd had Duncan since they moved here. He was ten years old and no longer jumped around, except when you pulled out a tennis ball in the backyard. "You're going to have to find another place to sleep, boy." Shawn closed the guestroom door, and Duncan followed him down the hall. He let the dog outside and then returned inside, limping up the stairs to his room. All their bedrooms, even his parents', were upstairs.

He changed out of his church clothes and grabbed his wallet off his dresser before he left the house. It wouldn't take long to run down to get some ice cream to go with his mom's pie tonight. His silver truck needed a washing anyway. He plugged his iPod into the power outlet, playing Mumford & Sons as he drove first to Sal's Sud Shop, where he scrubbed the truck himself after feeding every quarter he could find into the machine. It was cheaper than driving through Rainsong Car Wash.

After finishing his truck, he cruised down Mountain View's scenic Main Street, noting the tourists were now mostly gone with September here. Some would be back for the fall colors come late October and then again at Christmas time, especially for the parade through town ending with the tree-lighting ceremony and placement of the nativity scene in front of the courthouse. He heard about other towns fighting to keep Christmas. Mountain View wasn't that way. Everyone said, "Merry Christmas," in Mountain View, and nativity scenes in people's yards were as common as streetlights. By December, football season would be over. This relieved him. It was a secret he kept from his family, from Jill, from Holy Mountain Church, from all of Mountain View. He desperately wanted to be done with football because he was sick of it and hoped Vanderbilt wouldn't offer him a scholarship.

He also didn't want to go to medical school, another one of his secrets. Jill would kill him if she found out. His parents would be disappointed too, and Dr. Larson would probably take back the truck. Shawn loved his truck. It had been the surprise of his life last year when Dr. Larson and Jill drove up in it after football practice on a hot October day that happened to be his birthday. Dr. Larson had said, "Get in, son. Let's go for a drive."

In the air-conditioned truck, they'd driven out of the parking lot and over to the car dealership on the highway headed out of town. "The truck is yours, Shawn," he'd said, giving Jill a big wink. Dr. Larson liked to wink, especially at the ladies.

Shawn hadn't been able to move. Jill had put her hand on his leg. "Babe," she'd said. "Daddy bought the truck for you. Don't you like it? You said this was your dream truck."

"It's brand new," Shawn had said in wonder.

"And it's all yours." Dr. Larson had smiled. "Keep making my Jill happy."

Now, drying off his side mirrors at the car wash, Shawn felt that tenseness in his neck he'd had for a while now. What would Dr. Larson do if he told him he no longer wanted to attend medical school? Or play football? Unless he was in surgery, Dr. Larson never missed a game, even when they played Willington Union, four hours away. The whole football thing would play itself out, Shawn supposed, unless the Vanderbilt scouts returned this year and recruited him. Then he had a real problem on his hands.

He could always go the "God is calling me to do something else" route. When you threw God into the equation, people backed off—at least most of the people in Mountain View did. Shawn doubted Dr. Larson would back off, though. And his parents had their hearts set on him becoming a doctor after he played college ball like his dad.

Was God calling him to do something else? God didn't seem to be saying anything right now. Shawn was working his butt off to please God and everybody else, and he was starting to feel like a drowning man in a sea of expectations he couldn't meet. He was doing his best to live up to being Pastor Sam's boy. The straight-A, athlete-of-the-year football captain, who, with a pure heart, led Holy Mountain in worship on Sunday mornings and youth group Wednesday nights. Keeping up with just this was kicking his butt. Being a worship leader, playing college football, and preparing for medical school, all the while being Jill Larson's boyfriend, would bury him. Forget the pure heart. He hadn't had a pure heart since he was twelve years old and found pictures on the Internet that made him blush and put a fire in him. He did his best not to look at those kind of pictures now that he was older and a worship leader.

At the Kroger around the corner from the car wash, he picked up vanilla and strawberry ice cream. His whole family favored vanilla, but when it was gone, which would be on the first round, his brothers would polish off the strawberry too, though both Stephan and Seth didn't even like strawberry. Shawn wondered what kind of ice cream Ellie liked. Then he wondered why he wondered such a thing. He didn't even know Ellie, but because of Stephen's reaction to her, he was pretty curious about meeting her. A girl hardly ever caught Stephen's eye. His brother was real picky that way.

After lunch at the country club, he and Jill had walked out and sat by the pool. It was too cold to swim now, but the pool held so many good memories for them that it remained one of their favorite places to just hang. Three summers ago, at the pool, he and Jill had realized they felt more for each other than just friendship. They'd been a couple ever since.

"Stephen doesn't like me anymore. I can feel it," Jill had said earlier that day. She'd kicked off one of her high heels and put a foot in the water, then jerked it back out. "That's friggin' cold."

Shawn had given her one of his I-don't-approve-of-your-language looks.

She'd laughed at him. "Lighten up, Francis."

"Why do you wear those shoes?" He'd seen the deep marks on her foot where the straps dug into her tanned skin.

"Beauty is pain; you know that, babe." She'd kicked off her other brutal shoe and joined him on the lawn chair. He'd scooted right over to make room for her, urging her to get off of him.

"Mmmm." The noise she'd made sent a bolt of heat to his belly.

He'd let her have the lounge, abruptly standing up.

"What's wrong?" She hadn't bothered to brush down her skirt, which had wrapped up around her thighs.

"Your parents are here." Shawn had looked worriedly toward the clubhouse.

Jill had laughed at him again. "They can't see us down by the pool."

"Half the golf course can see us." His face had felt like it was on fire, and a chill rushed over him. Lately, Jill had a way of making him feel hot and cold at the same time.

She'd made herself comfortable on the lounge, hiking her skirt even higher.

"Your tan's already perfect," he'd said, wanting to jerk down her skirt as he looked across to the first tee. Three men he recognized from church stood there at the hole, concentrating on their game. He'd turned back to Jill.

Smiling, she'd wiggled her hips. "I'm not working on my tan, Shawn."

Recalling the afternoon with Jill messed with his mind so much he redirected his thoughts to dinner with Ellie while purchasing the ice cream, then walking to his truck. His knee remained tender, but he wasn't going to limp any longer, no matter how bad it hurt. He was done being injured, done thinking about his problems with Jill. Ellie's problems began to distract him, like wondering who got her pregnant and what kind of personality she had. He sure hoped she wasn't a loud-mouth. Loud girls got on his nerves. He preferred quiet girls, even though Jill wasn't quiet at all.

The evening felt balmy, and the birds were singing up a storm. He loved Mountain View, with all its towering trees and the smaller dogwoods all over the place. The city employed a host of gardeners that clipped and combed every hedge and lawn in the town. Deer sometimes wandered through the streets and yards, and it wasn't strange to see raccoons at night wobbling down the sidewalks.

Feeling wistful about the place he'd grown up, Shawn drove home slowly. The Suburban was parked in the driveway. Entering the house, he found his family in the dining room, everyone but his mom sitting down. His mom carried in the steaming lasagna, placing it on the table as he arrived.

"We were going to eat without you," his mom said. He could hear the disapproval in her voice.

Holding up the ice cream, Shawn walked farther into the room. He had planned to deposit the ice cream in the freezer before meeting Ellie. No such luck. There she sat in the chair beside his mom's empty seat. She wasn't what he expected at all except for the dark eyeliner around her eyes. The harsh makeup couldn't hide how vulnerable she looked. Or how pretty.

"Ellie, this is Shawn," said his mom. Though she was displeased with him, a proud smile split his mom's face.

He crossed the room, tucking the bag of ice cream under one arm so he could shake her hand. "Hey, Ellie."

"Nice to meet you." She accepted his handshake. Her voice unfolded soft and melodious and a bit husky, as if she was really nervous. Her hand felt small and tentative in his grip.

"Nice to meet you too." He glanced down at her stomach. She didn't have one. In fact, she was really slender, wearing jeans and a yellow T-shirt. The T-shirt not too big, not too small, just right on her.

When she saw him checking out her stomach, the uncertain smile slipped off her face. His gaze slammed into hers, and he stepped back with the one rational thought that the ice cream was melting in his arms. His foot hit a soft, furry body. Duncan yelped in pain. Stumbling over Duncan in an attempt not to hurt the dog, Shawn nearly fell backward, holding tightly to the ice cream like he did the football when a play went bad.

His brothers about laughed themselves out of their chairs.

"Shawn, are you okay?" His mom took the crushed ice cream from his stumbling embrace.

"Ask Duncan if he's okay," his dad said, smiling.

"Duncan, are you okay?" His mom reached down and patted Duncan's head. The dog swished his long, feathery tail.

Shawn petted him too. "Sorry, buddy. Why were you lying under my feet?"

"He always sleeps there at dinner." Seth laughed some more.

"Take your seat. I'll see to the ice cream." His mom carried the ice cream to the kitchen.

Shawn realized Ellie was seated on his side of the table. He smiled at her as he settled into his chair beside her. She smiled back, but in her eyes—real pretty eyes—he saw fear. Looking at her, he had a premonition of sorts, a feeling that this small, ponytailed girl would change his life in a profound way.

Chapter 9

Jamie walked to the diner, determined to see Ellie. She hadn't been at school in three days, and he couldn't find her at the trailer. He strolled up the sidewalk with his orange UT ball cap on his head feeling like the king of the world—but missing his queen. Looking into the Sundowner Cafe's glass storefront, he didn't see Ellie anywhere. About this time, she was usually readying the tables for dinner, slaving away like his mama, always home cooking and washing and cleaning for him and his four brothers. Mama's whole life revolved around taking care of her family, even after Pop ran off with that woman from Abilene a few years back. Mama still waited for Pop to come home, looking out the window each night for his truck lights shining up Route 12, snaking up the highway past the trailer park, the lights hitting the window, then wrapping around the trailer's tiny living room when Pop's eighteen-wheeler made the turn into the park.

Jamie used to lie on his back with his brothers in the living room waiting for those lights to swirl across the walls. "Pop's home," Mama would say, and after the lights left the room, he and his brothers would all roll back onto their bellies to watch TV until Pop flung open the trailer door. Pop always had a pocket full of Jolly Ranchers for them and chocolate for Mama. Usually a Milky Way candy bar, her favorite. Mama had a sugar tooth, just like the rest of them. Jamie hadn't seen her eat a Milky Way since Pop left. It was Mama's way of grieving, he supposed.

Ellie reminded him of his mama, but a lot prettier. And talented too, writing all those songs she liked singing for him. He planned on marrying her after they escaped Sutterville together. What he didn't get was her breaking up with him for no good reason, but he intended to mend that today. They'd be back together like peas and carrots, as his Mama often said about him and Ellie. But he needed to do this fast. He had fifteen minutes before getting to practice. Straightening his ball cap, he opened the diner door, the cow bells clanking.

The diner was empty. Clive came to the kitchen window where Ellie picked up the food to deliver to the customers. When he saw Jamie, he walked off.

Jamie waited for Ellie's dad to come out of the kitchen, but he didn't. Frustrated, he walked through the row of tables and pushed through the swinging kitchen door. "Where's Ellie?" he demanded.

"She ain't here." Clive placed a white gallon bucket into a walk-in refrigerator.

Jamie crossed his arms, flexing his muscles in his short sleeve football jersey. When he did that, Ellie always teased him. He wished she was here to tease him now. "So where is she?"

"Taking care of family business," Clive answered.

"What kind of family business?"

"None of your business, meathead."

"Ellie is my business."

"Get out of here, boy." Clive picked up a knife.

"I'm not leaving till I know where Ellie is. Did you bury her in the mountains?" Jamie laughed at his own joke.

Clive didn't laugh. He raised the knife in a threatening manner and then brought it down hard on an onion, splitting it in half. "I'll bury you in the mountains if you don't show some respect, boy."

"Look, Mr. Ryan, I've respected you. You treat me like crap, and I've still given you your due as Ellie's dad."

Clive continued chopping onions without responding.

"I just want to know where she is. I love your daughter, and I plan on marryin' her."

"When you plan on marryin' her?"

"Someday."

"Someday?"

"Someday," Jamie insisted. The onions Clive chopped made his eyes burn.

"Someday," Clive taunted.

"Someday soon," Jamie said earnestly. "Where's Ellie?"

"She'll be back come summer." Clive used the knife blade to scrape the onions into a bowl. Then he gathered more onions to chop.

"Summer? What's up with summer?"

Clive remained silent, continuing to slice onions.

"Do people really eat that many onions?" Jamie blinked his burning eyes. They began to water.

Clive's eyes appeared unaffected by the onions.

"Can you chop something else for a while?" Jamie swiped at his stinging eyes.

Clive smirked. "Tell you what, Town Hero, you chop these onions, and I'll work on something else." He handed Jamie the knife and picked up another blade.

Jamie rubbed at his eyes again as he began to chop the onions. He waited for Clive to tell him where Ellie was, but Clive kept silent, slicing tomatoes now. A tear slipped down Jamie's face, then another and another. He pressed his face to his shoulder, but that didn't help. The onions were killing him. "When you gonna tell me where Ellie is?"

Clive acted like he didn't hear him.

"Mr. Ryan, come on, where's Ellie?" Jamie's cheeks were wet with tears. He felt like a freak.

Clive ignored him.

Furious, Jamie threw down the knife. "You don't plan on tellin' me a thing, do you, Mr. Ryan?"

Clive said nothing.

Jamie wiped his eyes with his hands, which set them ablaze. The onion juice nearly blinded him. He fumbled his way to the sink and splashed water on his face until he could see again. Using soap on his hands, he scrubbed his fingers, and then splashed more water in his eyes.

Clive kept cutting vegetables as if he wasn't there.

Jamie dried his face with a paper towel. He threw the wadded-up towel on the floor as he walked past Clive on his way out the door.

Chapter 10

Ellie ran her fingers over the Hummingbird's strings. The words seemed right, but the tune still felt wrong. A finch sang out on the branch above her head. To be a little golden bird full of songs you knew simply because it was your nature to know songs—she envied songbirds. It was so easy for them to create music. This week she'd worked on her songwriting every day. Miss Patsy said she hoped Mountain View Academy, MVA, as everyone called the private Christian high school, would soon allow her to attend classes there, even though she was pregnant.

"We want you there. It's a great school," Miss Patsy had said the first night when she came into Ellie's room to tuck her in. So strange to be tucked into a bed. "I still tuck my boys into bed," Miss Patsy had explained, kissing Ellie on the forehead. "I'm so happy you're here. Shawn now has somebody to eat strawberry ice cream with." Miss Patsy had smiled.

Ellie had returned the smile, remembering how Miss Patsy's oldest son did seem pleased when she said strawberry ice cream was her favorite.

"I could home school myself," Ellie had offered. "It might be easier than everyone having to look at a pregnant girl at that nice Christian academy."

"That nice Christian academy will make the right decision, and you will enjoy attending MVA." Miss Patsy had soothed the covers over Ellie's lap.

Ellie didn't want to tell Miss Patsy how much she dreaded going to that school, being pregnant and all. Before that first dinner with them, Miss Patsy and her husband sat her down in the living room, telling her that the Klein family didn't keep secrets.

"Secrets destroy lives," Miss Patsy's husband had said. Then he told her to call him Dad, like the boys, if she was comfortable with that. Or she could call him Pastor Sam, or just Sam, or Samuel Jackson as his mama used to call him when he was in trouble. Ellie liked Miss Patsy and Pastor Sam so much. Miss Patsy called him Samuel. She said Samuel with a Georgia accent that was so cute.

The Kleins were amazing people. Their house was amazing. Their Secret Service car, amazing. The golden retriever was amazing. Had she not been pregnant, all this would have been a dream come true. A Cinderella story where the poor girl moves into the palace and ends up marrying the prince. She squelched the notion that Shawn was the prince. She pictured him falling over Duncan at the dinner table and smiled.

"We've told our family and friends you are here to have your baby. They want to help you too," Miss Patsy had said.

Well, that was a terrible relief. Terrible in that now people knew she was pregnant. A relief because she didn't have to worry that her body would soon betray her and she'd grow a belly Shawn could actually see. When he'd looked down at her stomach upon meeting her, a fist had squeezed her heart. Life was so unfair. She knew who he was. The Mountain View quarterback Sutterville called "Sunshine." "I'm gonna take Sunshine out of the game," Jamie had said. Sutterville really only had one rival these past few years: Mountain View Academy, and that was because of Shawn Klein.

Good thing Shawn was fast. Jamie was probably faster, but Shawn had a way of rolling out of a play like a ghost, Jamie explained one day. If Jamie knew she was now living with MVA's quarterback, he would blow a gasket. Jamie wasn't mean, but he had a bad temper. One night he beat up a guy from Gatlinburg so bad the kid had to go to the hospital. It was someone's cousin on the football team. Ellie couldn't remember whose. The fight started because the guy grabbed her rear end at a party and Jamie saw him do it.

"You tell my girlfriend you're sorry for touching her," Jamie had warned the kid.

"Looking at a big, dumb jock like you, I can see your girlfriend needs some affection. I was just providing that. You should thank me," the drunk, stupid kid had retorted.

Jamie had gone crazy. It had taken half the football team to pull him off the kid. By then, the bloody boy had been unconscious. That night, seeing Jamie nearly kill someone, had scared Ellie. She never quite felt the same way about Jamie after that.

Everything happened for a reason. Maybe that fight occurred so she could let Jamie go now. She bit her lower lip and strummed her guitar. The song she'd written was about saying good-bye. Maybe she didn't feel sad enough over Jamie, and that was why she couldn't find the right tune for the song. She flattened her palm against the strings and slapped her guitar in frustration.

"You mad at that guitar?" Stephen walked toward her, smiling.

She was sitting out near Miss Patsy's prayer garden, a sprawling flower bed that smelled so good. A half dozen dogwood trees framed the flower garden, and lush green lawn soft as cotton blanketed the area. Birds and butterflies loved the place. It had become Ellie's favorite song-writing spot.

"You play music," he said. It was a statement rather than a question as he plopped down on the grass beside her.

"I do." She angled her head at him. "Do you?"

"Drums are my thing. Seth and Shawn play guitar. Shawn also plays the piano, drums, fiddle, and bazooka."

"Bazooka?"

Stephen laughed. "Not the bazooka, that's a bomb launcher, but Shawn plays everything."

Ellie noted he seemed kind of bitter toward his brother. "But does Shawn play everything well?"

"He does," Stephen conceded. "Shawn's perfect."

Ellie smiled. "You look like a drummer."

"I do?"

She pointed at his forearms. "You got muscle there."

He glanced at his arms and grinned.

Ellie went back to strumming her guitar.

Stephen noticed the paper on the grass in front of her. "May I?" he asked before picking it up.

"It's not finished." Ellie placed her Hummingbird face up in her lap and watched him read it.

"You're writing a song?"

She could tell he was impressed. "It's not very good."

"It's not good. It's great." Stephen handed the paper back to her.

"Did you just get home from school?" Ellie laid the paper before her once more.

"About a half hour ago."

"You don't play football?"

"No." Stephen plucked a strand of grass and stuck it in his mouth.

"Why not? Every boy in Tennessee plays football."

"Shawn quarterbacks."

"He doesn't throw the ball to his brothers?"

"I'm not a receiver."

She was starting to understand Stephen. "You're a quarter-back." She smiled at him. Right off she could see Stephen was a guy who needed a girl's smile. And she was preggo. No chance of Stephen falling for her, so she didn't worry about being too nice to him as she had with other guys in the past.

"The game we lost against you, I could have held that game," Stephen said.

"The Sutterville-Mountain View game?"

"When Shawn got hurt. I know I could have won that game. Even with that UT defensive end. Number 33." Stephen spit out his grass.

"Jamie isn't at UT yet."

"You know him?" Stephen sat straight up, his blue eyes bright with interest.

"He's a friend." Ellie felt the weight of the lie. She thought about the baby and realized it wasn't a lie now. She couldn't go back to Jamie.

"That guy can sure play football. What's he like?"

"He's nice." Ellie placed her guitar on the grass beside her. Song writing today was over. Stephen, full of questions, wasn't going anywhere anytime soon.

Chapter 11

When Jenny heard the beep on her brother's answering machine, she left this message: "Hi, Joe and Ava. Just calling to check on you. Have you had any contractions yet? I'm not talking to you, Joe. I'm asking you, Ava." Jenny hoped her voice sounded light and happy. "Please call us when your labor starts. Ken and I want to try and make it out to Tennessee for the birth."

Jenny hung up the phone and slipped out of the chair onto the rug. On her knees, she prayed God would give her the strength to hold Joe and Ava's baby when the time came. She hadn't touched a baby since Matthew.

Damn.

In the beginning, she thought cussing might make her feel better. It didn't so she was now trying to give it up for Ken's sake. As if thinking about him made him appear, he came into the room and crouched down beside her.

He put his arm around her shoulders, helping her to her feet. "Did you get a hold of your brother?"

"They weren't home." Jenny's brows knitted together. That frown between her eyebrows was becoming a permanent thing. "Do you think they are at the hospital already?"

Ken put his hands on her cheeks, pulling her worried face to his for a kiss. "He'll call you before they head to the hospital," he assured her.

"But what if it happens so fast he doesn't have time to call?"

"Joe will make time to call."

Jenny walked over to the window. The days were growing shorter. Soon winter would arrive. In a few more months, the holidays would be upon them. Then New Year's Eve. Her whole life revolved around that day. The quest to escape the pain of that day. It had been nearly two years, but it still felt like yesterday.

Ken came up behind her, wrapping his arms around her waist and leaning his head down on hers. The stubble of his goatee scratched her temple. "We don't have to go for the birth," he said. "We could wait a while, get pictures of the baby, and see how that goes."

"The baby might look like Matthew," Jenny said. "First cousins often look alike."

Ken held her tighter. "You've got to quit doing this, Jen."

"I can't."

"Yes, you can." He turned her around in his arms.

Tears pooled in Jenny's eyes. "I'm not you, Ken. I just can't go on with my life the way you have."

"It wasn't your fault. The guy was drunk. He crossed into our lane."

"If you'd been driving, you would have avoided the accident. You're a better driver than me." Tears trickled down Jenny's face.

Ken dropped his arms to his sides, letting go of her. "You still blame me." He shook his head, turning away from her. "I'm tired of this. Our home is like a cemetery. I want to hear your laughter again. I want to be happy with you, but you're drowning us in grief."

"I'm sorry. I don't blame you." Jenny's voice thickened. "I blame myself."

"How can you blame yourself? We've been over this a thousand times. We were hit by a drunk driver. It wasn't our fault. It just happened. Tragedies like this happen to people, Jen," he said in frustration. "Can we look into adoption? Just please, let's do this."

Something in the way he asked it made Jenny realize he might not bring adoption up again. Had Ken finally given up on wanting a family with her?

She turned away from him, unsure whether relief or regret rioted through her. "Adoption's too expensive," she said over her shoulder. "We're still paying the medical bills. We'll be paying on those for the rest of our lives."

"No, we won't." Ken's sharp tone spun her around. Usually, he was soft-spoken and endlessly patient with her grief, a dream husband. "I won't join your pity party, Jen. I'm going to live again, with or without you." He grabbed his sweatshirt off the back of the couch. "I'm going out for a while." He limped to the door and then stood there for a moment with his hand on the knob, his head bowed as if in prayer.

Jenny knew that's what he was doing. Praying. At first, Ken's dogged faith had comforted her. Now it frustrated her. "God doesn't hear your prayers." The bitterness rose up, and she let it spew out like vomit. She'd always been such a sweet person. Everyone said she was sweet. Their shattered lives had drained all that sweetness away. She felt like an empty husk harvested by pain.

Ken made one last attempt. "Come with me, Jen," he invited hoarsely. "The sun is shining. We'll drive to up to Pike's Peak. See the trees blazing their colors. Hold hands and take a long walk, like we did when we were dating. Stop at a diner on the way home and eat pancakes for dinner."

"You go. I'm going to rest in Matthew's room."

"Matthew's not there!" Ken exploded. "He's never been in that room! We never brought him home from the hospital!" Ken furiously limped passed her down the hall to the baby's nursery, where he ripped the pale blue Pottery Barn curtains off the window in one violent yank.

"Ken, stop it!" Jenny screamed.

He didn't stop. After throwing the curtains on the carpet, he grabbed the cherry wood changing table and flipped it end over end.

"What are you doing? Ken, stop!"

Piglet flew past her head. Ken wasn't throwing the stuffed animal at her. He seemed to have forgotten she was there. In a blind rage, he threw baskets and baby clothes all over the place. Then he violently shook the matching cherry wood crib, trying his best to rip the bed apart with his bare hands.

Jenny sat down in the rocking chair in the corner of the room and waited for Ken to come to his senses. He began to sob as he shook the crib.

"Ken," she called.

He leaned into the crib, lifting out Winnie-the-Pooh. Jenny thought he would throw the toy as he had the others, but instead he held Pooh to his chest, sobbing harder.

"Ken," she said gently. "Come here."

He turned to her, the stuffed bear in his arms. She hardly recognized her husband. Ken, the eternal optimist, always smiling. Mr. Outdoorsman, handicapped now with one leg shorter than the other from the accident. He owned special shoes to help with that, but he hated wearing them. Today he had on his favorite worn-out hiking boots that made his limp more pronounced.

"Please come here." She leaned forward in the rocking chair. Tears splashed down her cheeks. Jenny hardly noticed them. For the first time in two years, she surfaced from her own grief long enough to realize Ken was broken too. As broken inside as she was; he just hid it so much better.

He crossed the room with Pooh, dropping to his knees in front of her, burying his head in her jean-covered thighs. She plowed her fingers into his hair, kissing the top of his head.

Holding on to Pooh Bear, Ken wept in her lap.

"We'll adopt," she said as she stroked his hair.

Ken kept crying, but Jenny smiled through her tears. They'd had their breakthrough. And she felt God there. In the warmth. In the peace. In the promise of healing, God was there.

Chapter 12

Carrying a white leather duffel bag, Ellie headed for the driveway where the Klein family was packing their SUV for a camping trip. Just a few days ago, Miss Patsy had taken her shopping, buying her the white leather bag along with two pairs of jeans, several T-shirts and sweaters, and new bras with panties that matched. Ellie had never owned matching bras and panties. Didn't even know those lacy, pretty things that came together existed.

"We'll start small," Miss Patsy had said. "Your body will be changing, so we don't want to buy too many clothes in this tiny size." Miss Patsy had held up the jeans, turning them this way and that as if they should grow in her hands and become a size she approved of. Ellie was surprised that she wore a size two now. It must be the pregnancy. She usually wore size zero.

Never had Ellie seen such extravagance on a shopping trip. This wasn't starting small. This was buying the whole store. Spending more money than it cost to stock the diner's walk-in freezer for a month. After shopping, Miss Patsy had treated her to lunch in a little bistro, where they ordered entrées that came with edible flowers. Ellie didn't know people ate flowers.

"That's going to get dirty," Shawn said when he saw the white duffel bag she lugged along while thinking about edible flowers.

"It will be fine," Miss Patsy said. "Give Shawn your bag, and he'll put it in the back of the Suburban for you, honey."

Ellie liked how Miss Patsy called her "honey" all the time. It sounded so mom-ish. The same way she talked to her sons. Ellie handed Shawn the duffel, and he stared at it for a moment as if ready to protest, holding the luggage up in one strong arm.

"Put it in the back, Shawn," Pastor Sam commanded in his good-natured way.

Ellie didn't call Miss Patsy's husband Samuel. Only Miss Patsy called him that. She was starting to think of him as "Pastor Sam" because it seemed everyone outside of his family knew him that way. The Kleins were so different from any family Ellie had ever been around. Their manners were perfect, always treating each other so kindly, and she had yet to hear a cuss word come out of any of their mouths.

All the boys Ellie knew cussed. Sutterville girls swore all the time too. The only thing that kept her from slipping with a bad word was that she tended not to say much. When she was nervous, she didn't talk at all. She still felt nervous with the Kleins. All of them except Stephen. They had hung out every afternoon in the backyard since she'd arrived. He'd become a friend.

Without further comment, Shawn obeyed his father, placing her duffel on top of the other bags. Shawn hadn't been home when his parents carried her garbage sacks through the door, so Ellie cut him some slack. He didn't know she owned no other bags.

"Why don't you ride with Shawn in his truck," Miss Patsy suggested, surprising everyone standing there.

"I'm riding with Shawn." Seth held a dog leash and stepped in Shawn's direction.

"Not this time." Miss Patsy ruffled Seth's hair. "With football going on, Shawn hasn't been home long enough to get to know Ellie. This drive will do them good."

"Ellie's going to listen to my iPod with me in the 'Burb." Stephen held up his iPod. Everyone could see Stephen didn't like his mom's idea.

"Ellie's riding with Shawn." Miss Patsy stood firm.

Stephen jammed his earbuds in his ears and climbed into the Suburban. Shawn raised his eyebrows in Stephen's direction as if to say, *What's wrong with him?*

"Ignore your brother." Miss Patsy pushed Shawn and Ellie toward the truck together. The truck bed was loaded with four ice chests, a large tent folded up in a giant canvas bag, and a ton of random camping supplies.

Shawn glanced at Ellie. She could see he was uncomfortable with this arrangement. Pastor Sam was over at the Suburban looking concerned as well. Seth, having clipped the leash to Duncan's collar, was now coaxing the retriever into the SUV's backseat. Putting her head down, Ellie did as Miss Patsy said and climbed into the truck.

It took an hour and a half to drive to the lake where the Kleins always camped. Miss Patsy and Pastor Sam were celebrating their twentieth wedding anniversary. Why they decided to take four teenage kids along, Ellie couldn't fathom. She suspected it had to do with her being there. Maybe they felt they couldn't leave her home alone with their boys.

Whatever the case, they all left on Sunday afternoon after church. Saturday had been spent preparing for the trip, so on Sunday all they had to do was load their bags into the car. She and Miss Patsy had done the grocery shopping and Pastor Sam and the boys had gathered the camping gear from the garage, cleaning it up and packing it into Shawn's truck on Saturday afternoon.

Ellie had feigned sickness so she didn't have to attend church with the Kleins that morning. Past three months' pregnant, she'd didn't feel nauseated anymore but still used it as an excuse to hide in her room as often as possible. Mountain View Academy was still mulling over allowing her entry to the school. A board meeting was scheduled for tomorrow night, and on Monday a vote would be taken. When they returned home from the camping trip on Wednesday they would know whether or not she would be the first pregnant girl ever to walk the famed halls of MVA.

Shawn plugged his iPod into the power outlet and played songs on the radio Ellie had never heard before. She liked his music even after she realized most of it was Christian.

"You're seventeen," Shawn said to her. "So you're a junior, like Stephen?"

"I'm a senior." Ellie didn't look at him.

"A senior?" He turned down his music so they could talk better. "When's your birthday?"

"May." She didn't offer more information.

"May what?"

"May 20."

"So you'll be eighteen in May." He slowed the truck as they came upon a hairpin curve going up the mountain. This wasn't the road to Sutterville. They were driving in a different direction, much to Ellie's relief.

"So you like strawberry ice cream." Shawn smiled at her, coaxing her to warm up to him.

She didn't smile back. She wished he had the guts to flat out ask her about the pregnancy. So far only Miss Patsy talked about her condition and never in front of the family. Even Stephen wouldn't broach the subject, and Stephen could talk your ear off. They all just pretended like she wasn't pregnant.

"You're pretty quiet." Shawn turned up the radio and gave up talking to her for a while.

They drove just listening to the music for most of the trip. Ellie stared out the passenger window. Being in the truck with him made her think of things she didn't want to think about, like Jamie calling Shawn "Sunshine" before the football game. Shawn probably had no idea that's how he was known in Sutterville, and most of the guys hated him there simply because he was from a rich school in the valley and could really play football. She was watching the woods fly by thinking about this when Shawn hit the brakes.

The seat belt jerked tight across her shoulders and locked over her middle. The impact of something hitting the truck shocked Ellie.

They pulled off to the side of the road. Shawn sat there for a moment, as shaken as she was. "Are you okay?" he asked. "I hit a deer."

She hadn't seen the deer. "It's hurt?"

He leaned over, grabbing her seat belt, trying to pull it off her belly. "The baby?" He sounded so alarmed.

"A baby deer?" She looked at him and then tried to see out of the front of the truck.

"No. Your baby. Is it hurt?" He unbuckled her seat belt, putting his hand on her stomach. He had scooted so close she could smell the shampoo he used. The same shampoo she now used. Ellie found it hard to breathe with Shawn so near.

He was staring into her eyes. Never had she seen such concern in someone's face. And never had she been so breathless with anyone. "I think it's okay," she managed to say.

"Are you sure? My seat belt winded me."

"Winded you?" Her thoughts were all a jumble.

"Knocked the air out of me." He leaned over her lap, looking out her window. "Oh, man," he said. "That poor deer."

He was practically on top of her. Usually, she didn't want a guy getting this close, but something about Shawn seemed so safe and good. He sat up, grabbing her hand, scooting to his side of the truck and pulling her across the seat with him. "Are you sure you and E.J. are okay?"

"Who's E.J.?"

"Ellie Junior." He grinned, though he still looked scared. "Your baby."

Something cold and hard began to melt inside of her. She liked Shawn more than she ever expected to like anyone from Mountain View. "That pregnancy book your mom gave me says the baby is the size of a golf ball right now and is protected by my hip bones. I think it's all right."

Opening the truck door, he stepped out onto the road. "You don't want to see the deer. It's . . . dead."

Ellie swung her legs under the steering wheel and onto the truck's running board to get out of the cab. Shawn moved over, blocking her with his body. He put one hand on the steering wheel and the other hand on the driver's headrest to keep her between his arms. "Really, you don't want to see the deer. It's messed up bad."

She looked into his eyes and felt his warmth and compassion. He had beautiful eyes, blue and honest and so sweet. His voice was gentle and kind, like his dad's. "I want to help," Ellie told him.

"I don't know what to do with the deer," he admitted.

"We can drag it off the road." She leaned toward him to get out of the truck. Shawn didn't move, which put them nose to nose with each other.

"Please don't get out." His breath fanned her lips. She smelled spearmint gum. He put his hands on her shoulders, pressing her gently against his truck seat. "You just sit here and take care of E.J. I'll take care of the deer. Okay?"

The tender way he said E.J. went straight to her heart. In that moment, the baby became real to Ellie. She put a hand below her belly button. No bump yet, but E.J. grew there. She wondered if E.J. was a boy or a girl.

Shawn walked around to the front of the truck and stood looking down at the dead animal. Most people would have been staring sadly at their vehicle, Ellie could see he was sad over the deer. It didn't appear to cross Shawn's mind that his truck might be damaged. Jamie had hit a fawn with his truck last spring and didn't care a bit about the little deer. All he cared about was the dent in his old truck. She wondered how bad Shawn's new truck looked as he dragged the animal off the road by its hind legs. Apparently, Shawn wondered this too as he came back to the pickup and spent some time studying the front end. Ellie stayed behind the wheel. Pretty soon he walked over to her. "There really isn't much damage to my front end," he said, sounding surprised. "Are you sure you're all right?"

"We're fine." Ellie patted her flat stomach, searching his eyes for the approval she'd received earlier from him about the baby.

"Good," he said and then shocked her with a warm hug.

She returned his embrace and afterward scooted over to her spot so he could climb in.

"I've never hit anything before." He started the truck. Turning off his music, he carefully pulled back onto the narrow road. "This is the first thing I've ever killed."

"It wasn't your fault." Ellie smiled at him. By now, his parents were far ahead of them. She hoped Miss Patsy and Pastor Sam wouldn't worry too much when they arrived at the lake without them. "There aren't any other cars up here. Where is everyone?"

"It's late in the season for camping. And it's Sunday. Everyone's getting ready for work and school tomorrow." Shawn smiled back at her.

"Do you feel bad about missing school?" Ellie cared about her grades, and obviously Shawn did too.

"I've got an anatomy test I wish I wasn't missing." He looked at her a moment longer and then returned his gaze to the road. Things felt different between them now. Hitting the deer and talking about the baby had created a bond between them.

Ellie wished the lake was ten hours away instead of ten minutes. She wanted to get to know him better. "Anatomy, is that a hard class?"

"Sometimes."

"Are you taking it for college?"

"I'm probably going to medical school." Shawn kept his eyes on the road, glancing along the edges, watching for deer, no doubt.

"Do you want to be a doctor?"

He took a deep breath, releasing it wearily. "I used to. I don't know anymore. The closer college gets, the less I know where I want to go or what I want to do with my life."

"You don't have to know yet. You've got time to figure it out." She understood what he meant. Not about not knowing what to do because all her life she'd known exactly what she wanted to do with her future. Be a songwriter. But she understood that scary feeling of being a senior in high school and not knowing how your life would turn out after graduation. Especially when people expected your life to turn out just right and you knew it wouldn't. "You get straight As, don't you?"

Shawn laughed. "Do I look like a straight-A geek?"

She laughed too. "No. You look like a jock. But you're a straight-A geek, I can tell."

"How can you tell?"

She studied him, not answering his question.

"You get straight As," he said, figuring her out. "All your teachers, your friends, your family, they expect you to make something special of yourself, don't they?"

"Just my teachers." Ellie shrugged as if she didn't care about friends or family. Shawn took his eyes off the road to look at her. In that instant, she knew he saw right through her attempt to pretend she didn't care what others thought of her.

Returning his attention to driving, he turned serious. "So a straight-A student getting pregnant probably upset everyone pretty bad." His voice was soft now.

That tender tone made Ellie's throat tighten. She wrinkled her nose, fighting the sensation of tears. "When it happens, people give up on you." She didn't tell him nobody in Sutterville but Clive knew she was pregnant; the one who really felt like giving up was her.

"I won't give up on you." He didn't look at her again, but she believed him.

Sunshine.

She could almost hear the sarcastic way Jamie said that about Shawn. Could almost imagine what Jamie would do if he knew she was in Shawn's truck right now, her heart pounding out of her chest because she knew with everything inside her this was meant to happen. Maybe all of it, the good and the bad, was meant to happen. It felt like déjà vu. *You are my sunshine, my only sunshine . . .* The song swirled through her mind. Then she stopped it from swirling. A guy like Shawn would never see her as anything more than a poor, pregnant Sutterville girl. "Do you think I'll have a boy or a girl?" She brought up the baby because it was exactly the reason why nothing could ever happen with him.

"E.J.'s a girl," he said with such certainty Ellie laughed. She didn't feel like laughing—crying was more like it—but she made herself laugh instead like she really didn't care.

"We'll know if it's a boy or girl at twenty weeks. Your mom took me to see Dr. Hammons. He does all his ultrasounds at twenty weeks unless there is a problem before that."

"Did Mom tell you Dr. Hammons's wife was one of her best friends? Mrs. Hammons died last April from cancer."

Ellie's mind spun with the name Hammons. "Was Mrs. Hammons a teacher in Sutterville?"

"An English teacher. Did you ever have her?"

"I loved Mrs. Hammons. She was my favorite teacher. I was so sad when she died."

"That's why my mom took over A Woman's Hope up there. Mrs. Hammons asked her to keep the center open. Mrs. Hammons said Sutterville needed that place of hope."

Ellie remembered sitting in English class after Jana's abortion. "Is there anything I can do to help you, Ellie?" Mrs. Hammons had stopped by her desk to whisper to her during a test.

"I'm just feeling a little sad right now," Ellie had admitted because it was Mrs. Hammons. "I'll be all right." But she was never all right after Jana had her abortion and then left Sutterville, and Mrs. Hammons seemed to know she wasn't all right.

Jana's abortion was the beginning of the end of believing all her sister's talk about them getting out of Sutterville together and seeking stardom, like their mom. Their mom had never been a star, even if Jana said she was. A short stint in Nashville maybe, a special song that hit the radio like lightning, but one song didn't make a person a star, and their mom didn't even sing that song. She just wrote it. Someone else sang it.

Johnny Jones and some other woman.

"My mom changed after Mrs. Hammons died," Shawn said. "She became driven by that pregnancy crisis center up there in Sutterville. You moving in with us has been really good for Mom. She's happy again being at home."

They turned off the main road, and an amazing lake came into view. The setting sun shone on the crystal water, playing like light on a chandelier. Sparkling all over the place. Ellie had never been camping in her life, though living in a trailer was a lot like camping, she supposed. The kids from Sutterville went to the lake to party all the time. Sometimes Ellie went too, but it wasn't a lake like this one. Right away she could see this lake was a special place.

She looked over at Shawn. He pulled the truck off the dirt road beside the water. "Where's your family?" she asked.

"Right over there." He pointed to a campground in the distance at the water's edge. They couldn't see the Suburban through the trees, but a trail of smoke rose out of the grove of pines. "Dad's built his fire. Mom's probably all upset worrying where we are, so we better get over there real soon."

"Why did you pull off here, then?"

He stared at her for a moment, and her stomach did a little flip-flop at the way he was looking at her.

"I just wanted to see the sunset from here with you," he said and then smiled at her.

Chapter 13

Miss Patsy invited Ellie into the tent before the brothers, handing her a neatly folded set of blue flannel pajamas with white snowflakes on them. Ellie could tell the jammies were new, though they'd been washed. Miss Patsy donned pink flannel pajamas covered in polka dots. Hers appeared new too.

The boys entered the tent wearing gym shorts and T-shirts, Pastor Sam in shorts and T-shirt as well. The boys rushed to their sleeping bags, thrashing their legs around to heat their beds up. Pastor Sam said sleeping so close together would keep them warm. He prayed over his family, including Ellie in his blessing before they closed their eyes.

They were crowded into the tent like a litter of pups, sleeping practically on top of each other. Ellie's sleeping bag lay against the side of the tent. Miss Patsy slept beside her. Alongside Miss Patsy slept Pastor Sam and then Seth. Shawn and Stephen fit their sleeping bags at the ends of the four other bags, which put Stephen at Ellie's feet and Shawn near her head. Duncan slept with Stephen.

Ellie lay there adjusting to this strange experience, acutely aware of Shawn's pillow two feet away. Stephen and Seth talked softly for a while, planning tomorrow's activities: fishing, hiking, swimming, and fishing some more.

Using a flashlight, Shawn quietly read his Bible.

Miss Patsy and Pastor Sam kissed each other, then everyone said good night like *The Waltons*. She'd loved reruns of that show when she was younger. The workings of a real family fascinated Ellie. She had always wondered how people lived in a family. Husbands with wives. Parents with children. Kindergarten was about the time she realized her life with Clive and Jana was not normal. Other kids talked about families that sounded so different from hers. Now she was here with the Kleins, and the desire for a real family nearly overwhelmed her. She closed her eyes, half dreaming she belonged to these people. Had always belonged with the Klein family. Pregnancy made her so tired. She drifted off to sleep with Stephen and Seth's stories of their previous camping trips echoing in her ears.

Waking in the morning, she found herself alone in the tent. Dressing quickly, she stepped outside and found the Kleins preparing breakfast together using an open fire and their camp stove. They all called greetings to her and then cheerfully went about their chores. She found the campground restroom on her own: a latrine with no sink and no mirrors. When she'd asked Miss Patsy last night about a mirror, Miss Patsy informed her they camped without mirrors. "I just wash my face and go natural," she'd explained. Then Miss Patsy had done exactly that, scrubbing off her makeup in a bowl of warm water. Ellie had decided to sleep in her makeup. This morning she realized she might as well remove her makeup too. Walking back to camp, she asked Miss Patsy if she could wash her face in the bowl.

"I've already heated your water. Let me get the pan for you." Miss Patsy handed her soap and a washcloth and poured steaming water into the pot. Ellie could tell Miss Patsy was pleased she was going to wash her makeup off.

When she sat down for breakfast ten minutes later, no makeup remained on her face. She was self-conscious considering she hadn't left the trailer without her war paint since junior high. That's what Clive called make up. War paint. If anyone noticed her naked face, they didn't mention it. Stephen sat down beside her to eat his food. He had a bandana tied around his forehead. She could tell he really liked this camping thing.

"Do you know how to fish?" he asked.

"No. I've never fished."

"Have you ever camped?" Stephen shoveled eggs, potatoes, and sausage all scrambled together into his mouth.

"Never," Ellie admitted.

"What did you think of sleeping in a tent last night?"

"It was nice." She nibbled at her potatoes.

"Do you want to hike with us after breakfast?" Shawn asked, sitting down beside Seth across from her. With his gaze upon her, Ellie felt exposed without her makeup. He seemed to sense her anxiety and gave her a happy smile.

She turned to her food, dodging Shawn's attention. "Maybe," she quietly answered.

"Samuel and I are going to stay right here," Miss Patsy announced. "You can stay in camp with us if you want to, Ellie."

"Come on, go with us," Stephen beseeched. "We'll have a lot more fun than this camp."

"We'll hike slow," Shawn promised.

"Hike slow?" Stephen challenged him.

"My knee's not a hundred percent. And Ellie has E.J. to consider." Shawn grinned again at Ellie, sending butterflies to her stomach.

"E.J.?" Stephen had no idea what Shawn was talking about. Ellie's face reddened. Her ears burned, and her cheeks felt hot. She concentrated on finishing her breakfast, her stomach a swirling mess now.

"Ellie Junior, the baby." Shawn shoveled food in his mouth as if this was a normal conversation. Ellie loved how easy he was about her pregnancy, as if her having a baby was no problem at all.

Stephen was speechless. Pastor Sam cleared his throat. "Which hike are you planning on taking today, boys?"

"We're going to the top of that mountain." Seth pointed to a nearby peak.

Stephen spoke to Ellie, "We don't have to go all the way to the top," he assured her.

"What?" Seth cried. "We always go to the top. It's tradition."

Pastor Sam tossed his empty plate onto the fire. The flames came alive, gobbling up the thin cardboard. "Not this year. I'm staying put with your mom."

"Why?" Seth asked.

"It's our anniversary." Pastor Sam looked at Miss Patsy, and Miss Patsy smiled like a schoolgirl. At that moment, Ellie knew she had to do the hike with the boys. She couldn't stay in camp with anniversary people.

"You look really nice today," Shawn said as soon as Seth and Stephen continued up the trail without them. Ellie didn't believe him, though not believing Shawn was an impossible thing. He seemed so honest and sincere. She didn't respond to his compliment.

"You always wear your hair in a ponytail." It was a statement rather than a question.

They walked along the narrow path winding up the mountain. Ferns edged both sides of the trail, and tall trees kept them in the shade. Shawn was so nice. Continuing to let him carry the conversation all by himself now that his talkative brothers had raced ahead didn't seem fair.

"I've waitressed a long time. I guess I'm used to wearing my hair this way," she said.

"How long have you waitressed?"

"Five years." Ellie had to think about it because it seemed she'd waitressed forever.

"Five years?" He stopped walking, staring at her with widened eyes.

"My dad owns a diner." Ellie noticed how blue Shawn's eyes were this morning. He hadn't combed his hair. He looked like an adorable little boy.

"So you were twelve when you started working for your dad?" Shawn sat down on a log beside the trail, stretching out his knee as if it hurt him.

"Summer going into seventh grade I started waitressing." She didn't see anywhere else to sit except on the log beside Shawn. There wasn't much room there, so, even though she was tired, she decided to keep standing in the middle of the trail.

"Don't you want to rest? He patted the log. "I don't bite."

She wondered if he had any idea how he made her feel, all warm and confused and crazy inside.

"Come on, E.J. needs to sit down." He grinned so invitingly.

Slowly, she came to him. "I think you made your family uncomfortable this morning talking about the baby." For some reason, she needed to be honest with him. Never had she felt this way with anyone before, like he could already see inside her soul, so why hide it?

Shawn moved his leg out of the way for her settle down on the log beside him. "The sooner we talk about the baby, the better off we'll be." The intensity of his gaze unsettled her.

"In Sutterville, nobody knows I'm pregnant except Clive." She looked into the woods; they were so dark, very little sunlight penetrating the canopy of dense pines.

"What about the baby's father?" His question pierced her heart.

She tried to answer, wanting more than anything to tell Shawn the truth, but the words lodged in her throat.

He put his hand on her back, rubbing up and down the way Miss Patsy had done that day at the crisis center. His attempt to comfort her felt nothing like his mother's touch. "You don't have to tell me about the dad," he said, continuing to stroke her. She wore a T-shirt and could feel his warmth upon her skin through the thin fabric. They had begun the hike wearing sweatshirts, but within a half hour in the sun, they'd tied their sweatshirts around their waists as they walked. Ellie shivered under his caress.

"It's cool here in the shade, isn't it?" he asked.

"You think I've been with a lot of guys, don't you?" She looked at him, and their eyes locked and held. He removed his hand from her back.

"I'm not coming on to you." He scooted away from her as far as he could without abandoning the log.

"Do you have a girlfriend?" She found herself unable to breathe waiting for his answer.

He broke eye contact with her. "I do," he admitted.

"Of course you do." She set her eyes on a little yellow flower growing amongst the large ferns near the log. The spindly blossom, a tiny daisy, looked as if it would be smothered by the ferns any minute.

"My mom said to treat you like our sister. If I had a sister, I would take care of her. I want to take care of you, Ellie. That's all."

She laughed as if none of it mattered, but inside she hurt so badly.

He leaned his elbows on his knees, resting his chin in his hands, looking at the ground. "What's your middle name?"

"Rose."

"That fits." He looked back up at her, and that easy smile returned to his face.

"What's your middle name?" She tried to lighten up too. "Wait, let me guess."

Shawn's smile widened. "Go ahead, give it a guess."

"Walter."

"Walter?"

"You're not a Walter?"

His eyebrows knitted together, increasing his little-boy appeal. "Walter?" he echoed.

"You could be a Walter."

"Keep guessing." He straddled the log to face her now.

"Elwood?"

"What!"

"Elwood," she insisted with a laugh.

"I am not an Elwood."

Ellie laughed harder, loving this teasing play. Jamie never teased with her, and neither had anyone else. She didn't feel cautious with Shawn as she always had with Jamie about getting close to him. She felt young and free. "Elwood!" she yelled, surprising herself.

"Elwood!" he hollered back and then tickled her. She could tell he was being gentle. He was a big guy, not as large as Jamie, but tall and muscular and strong. Strapping, she decided. She laughed so hard she couldn't breathe under his hands as they fell off the log together into the ferns.

"Say I'm not an Elwood," he demanded, tickling her some more.

"You're not an Elwood," she gasped.

He stopped tickling her. Their eyes met, his so clear and guileless, so blue and beautiful. A slow grin spread over his lips. He reached for her knees.

"You're Elmer. Elmer Fudd!" She screamed when he tickled her knees.

Chapter 14

Shawn untangled himself from Ellie when Stephen came crashing through the trees. "What is going on?" Stephen demanded between breaths. Apparently, he'd sprinted down the mountain because of Ellie's screams. His brother stopped and stood there holding his sides, staring down at them in the ferns together in disbelief.

Ellie hopped to her feet. "Shawn was just tickling me." She smoothed down her hair, looking embarrassed.

Shawn rose to his feet more slowly to stand beside her, wondering what on earth had gotten into Stephen. Ellie's screams were only in fun. Didn't Stephen know that?

"Why was he tickling you?" When Ellie didn't answer, Stephen got right in Shawn's face. "Why were you tickling her?"

"She called me Elwood." He gave Stephen a shove to back him off.

"I was trying to guess his middle name," Ellie explained. "Nothing was going on with us," she assured Stephen.

"His middle name is Sherwood," Seth announced from behind Stephen. Seth was breathing hard too. He hopped up on the big log beside them. "Shawn Sherwood Klein." Seth opened his arms wide, appealing to the forest. "Like Sherwood forest in Robin Hood." Both Seth and Stephen dripped with sweat. Stephen wasn't happy, but Seth was laughing, which was normal for Seth.

"Sherwood?" Ellie laughed too. She jumped up on the log beside Seth. "Is Sherwood really his middle name?"

"Yeah," Seth answered. "Can you believe it?"

"It's a family name," Shawn defended himself. "Our mom's maiden name is Sherwood."

Ellie stepped off the log onto the other side to greet Duncan as he stumbled in among them. Shawn found it hard to believe Ellie was pregnant. She didn't look pregnant. Didn't act pregnant either. He really liked how she looked without makeup. Plopping down beside the log, Duncan panted like crazy while Ellie petted him.

"He could use a drink of water," Ellie said.

"We'll have to go back to the lake," Shawn told her.

Ellie coaxed Duncan to his feet. "Come on, boy. Let's go get you some water."

Stephen cut in front of Shawn to cross the log first. Shawn stepped out of his way, surprised at how Stephen was acting today. "What's your problem?" Shawn whispered for only Stephen to hear. Stephen ignored him.

"Did you make it to the top of the mountain?" Shawn asked Seth as Stephen jogged up alongside Ellie and Duncan.

"No, thanks to you, we didn't make it." Seth and Shawn caught up to Stephen and Ellie.

"Are you going to swim with us today?" Stephen asked Ellie.

"Is the lake cold?"

"Maybe a little, but it's refreshing," he assured her.

"Are you guys going swimming?" She turned around to Shawn and Seth.

"I always swim in the lake," said Seth.

Leaving the dark woods, they walked into the sunshine of a bright meadow. Small birds flew out of the grass. As they moved along, butterflies fluttered up around them.

"I might swim," Ellie said.

"You have to catch salamanders with us." Seth grinned. He was such a good-natured kid. The exact opposite of Stephen. Shawn wasn't sure what Stephen's problem was, but he didn't like the thoughts he was having about it as Stephen matched his steps to Ellie's.

"Salamanders?" Ellie did not look eager to see salamanders.

"They won't hurt you," Stephen assured her. "We always have a salamander contest. Who can catch the most each year."

"What do you do with the salamanders?" Ellie asked.

"We eat them," Stephen said.

Ellie's eyes rounded. "Really?"

Seth joined in the teasing, "Mom boils them in a pot over the fire."

"Alive," Stephen added. "You've got to cook salamanders alive like lobsters."

"Oh my gosh." Ellie covered her mouth.

"When the water boils, they jump right out of the pot like frogs." Seth couldn't hide his smile.

"No, they don't," Shawn interrupted, not liking the game his brothers were playing with Ellie.

"Yes, they do." Stephen glanced back over his shoulder, giving Shawn a chastising glance.

"We don't eat them," Shawn told Ellie. "My brothers are messing with you." Ellie had such pretty eyes and perfect skin touched by the sun, not crazy tanned like Jill's. Ellie looked back at him over her shoulder, and they exchanged a smile.

"We do too eat them," Stephen insisted, not willing to give up his salamander game yet.

"We dip them in butter," Seth said, helping Stephen out. "They taste like calamari."

"Calamari?" Ellie obviously had never heard of calamari.

"Squid," Stephen explained.

"You eat squid?" Ellie slowed down, and the guys lagged with her. Duncan's panting sounded like a chugging train.

"Shawn loves squid," Seth said.

"Calamari." Shawn clarified, bending down to inspect Duncan. "Only a little bit farther and we'll be at the lake," he told the dog, concerned about him. Duncan was getting old and too fat for his own good.

"You eat squid?" Ellie asked Shawn.

"Deep fried, it's really delicious," Shawn said.

"He likes escargot too," said Stephen.

"What's escargot?" Ellie looked at Shawn.

"You're a waitress and you haven't heard of escargot?" Shawn stopped petting Duncan for a moment.

"Snail," Stephen explained. "You're a waitress? Where did you used to work?"

"At my dad's diner." Ellie eyed Duncan. "Is he going to be okay?"

"He'll be fine." Shawn reached down and picked the retriever up in his arms. "Duncan, you've put on weight." He hefted the large dog more securely in his grasp. "You're obese now, boy."

Stephen leaned close to Ellie. "You have a leaf in your hair." Stephen pulled the leaf loose, showing it to Ellie before dropping it on the trail.

"Thanks," she said.

"You're welcome." Stephen grinned, and Shawn knew in that moment his brother was taken with Ellie. And he realized he kind of was too. The thought alarmed him.

Stephen had never really fallen for anyone before. He liked a girl here and there, but never anything remotely serious. Plenty of girls flirted with Stephen. He'd flirt back sometimes but had yet to take up a girlfriend. This morning when Ellie joined them by the fire at breakfast after washing her face, Stephen couldn't stop staring at her. She was even prettier without all that black eye makeup, but how could his brother be seriously interested in Ellie knowing she was pregnant?

Shawn wondered again who'd fathered Ellie's baby. Was it a boyfriend or a one-night stand? He found it hard to fathom she'd had sex with a guy. He'd heard his whole life he must save himself for marriage. A girl must do the same. Apparently, the guy Ellie had in Sutterville didn't care enough about her to keep her pure or see her through this pregnancy. What a jerk. If the baby had been his, Shawn would have married her. Maybe finish high school first and then marry her, but certainly he would marry her.

Carrying Duncan, he headed for the lake. Everybody followed him. Arriving at the water, he walked right in with his shorts and hiking boots on, placing Duncan down in the shallows. Stephen, Seth, and Ellie waited on the shore. After lapping up part of the lake, Duncan bounced around in the water. Shawn left him there and walked back up and stood with the others.

Stephen seemed eager to smooth things over. “Hey, Shawn, did Ellie tell you she knows Number 33?”

“The UT kid?” Shawn asked in surprise.

“Yeah. The guy who busted your knee.”

“So how do you know Number 33?” Shawn asked Ellie.

“Jamie’s older brother, Jenner, was my sister’s boyfriend.” Ellie swung her gaze back to the water. Shawn knew her well enough now to see she didn’t want to have this conversation.

“Do you and Number 33 still talk?” Stephen pressed.

“Where’s your sister now?” Shawn interrupted, trying to protect Ellie.

“Jana moved to LA to pursue acting.”

“Wow,” said Stephen. “Does she look like you?”

“No. Jana’s really beautiful.”

“You’re beautiful!”

Shawn considered throwing Stephen in the lake. He gave his brother a warning glare.

Stephen ignored him. “So your sister’s older than you?”

“She’s twenty.” Ellie wouldn’t look anywhere but the lake now. Shawn could tell she was really uncomfortable.

“Does she sing like you? Because you sing like a real singer. You could be famous someday.”

Shawn had had enough of Stephen. “Why don’t you and Seth go back to camp and get your swimsuits on, then you can catch Ellie a salamander,” he suggested.

“Do you want to go get your swimsuit on with us?” Stephen asked Ellie, all but pretending Shawn wasn’t part of the conversation.

“No thanks.” Ellie walked over to the edge of the water, off by herself.

"Go get your swimsuits," Shawn urged his brothers. The three of them shared a silent conference with their eyes. They could all see Ellie was upset. Shawn wanted to give her some space.

"I think number 33 is the father of her baby," Seth whispered.

Stephen looked ready to punch Seth.

"I'll talk to her," said Shawn. "Go on, get your swimsuits. Bring mine back too."

"Let me talk to her," said Stephen. "We've been hanging out after school. We're cool with each other."

"You better let Shawn talk to her," said Seth, eyeing Ellie as she bent down, running her fingers through the water. Hopefully out of earshot of this little powwow they were having.

Shawn stared at Stephen until his brother backed down. "Okay, you talk to her." Stephen turned and headed toward camp with Seth falling in behind him on the trail.

Chapter 15

After Stephen and Seth disappeared, Shawn walked over to Ellie. She sat on a rock now, staring at the lake. Duncan chased birds on the water, swimming all over the place but accomplishing very little. The birds weren't about to let Duncan get close to them.

"He's not that smart." Shawn tried to keep things light. He was talking about Duncan but thinking about Stephen.

"I can see that." Ellie didn't look up at him. She kept her gaze on Duncan out in the water.

"Rose," he said tentatively, "we don't have to talk about your past. You don't have to tell us anything about your life before we met you."

"Are you going to call me Rose, Sherwood?" She stared at the lake a moment longer before settling her wounded gaze on him. He wanted to give her a hug, wanted to make her feel better, but he didn't know how he should go about doing that.

"Do you like being called Rose?"

"Nobody has ever called me that. Rose was my mom's name."

"Really? Where is your mom now?"

"Dead and buried." Ellie shrugged as if she didn't care.

Shawn knew better. Reaching out, he tucked a lock of her hair behind her ear that had slipped free from her ponytail. "I'm really sorry your mom's gone."

"It's okay. I don't remember her. I was only two when she overdosed."

"That sucks." Shawn knelt down beside her and hugged Ellie. For an awkward second, she stiffened in his arms, but then she pressed into him like she really wanted to be held. He cradled her against his chest, liking having her in his arms. She just seemed to need this, someone to hold her. They stayed there for a while, him holding her as a breeze arose and rustled the pines along the edge of the water. Duncan swam after a loon. There was no way the dog could catch that bird, but that didn't mean Duncan wouldn't swim himself to death trying. "I guess I'm going to have to go in after him," Shawn said, resting his chin on the top of Ellie's head. Her silky hair caressed his neck.

She moved out of his arms, wiping her eyes. "You better go call him out of the water," she said.

Shawn pretended not to notice Ellie was crying. She didn't seem the type of girl who wanted his sympathy. He began to untie his wet boots. If they sat in the sun for a while, they would dry out. He stripped off his soaked socks and then shrugged out of his worn blue T-shirt.

Ellie no longer looked across the lake. Shawn caught her staring at his bare chest. An emotion hit him he wasn't about to explore. Instead, he handed her his shirt. "Do you mind holding this while I go get Duncan?"

She glanced at Duncan way out in the water and then back at Shawn. "He's practically across the lake."

"I know. He'll drown before giving up on that bird." He tried handing her his shirt again.

She accepted it this time and then took a deep breath as if to speak. Twisting the shirt in her hands, she ended up saying nothing.

"I need to rescue Duncan before he drowns." Shawn headed for the water, understanding why Stephen was falling for Ellie. There was something so appealing about her. Something he felt drawn to in a powerful way as well.

He swam hard, cutting across the lake in record time. Two summers ago, he'd been a lifeguard. And he'd grown up on a swim team. The lake posed no problem.

Duncan paddled along slowly now. The loon floated thirty feet away. "Come here, boy. You'll never catch that loon, you loony dog."

Duncan wouldn't give up. Shawn swam up to him, capturing his collar. Instead of dragging him all the way back across the lake, he hauled the dog to the opposite shore.

He gave Ellie, a slight figure on the other side of the lake, a wave before bringing Duncan around the water on dry ground. The day had grown even warmer. By the time he reached the spot where he'd left Ellie, she was no longer there. Seth and Stephen plowed into the water as he walked up.

"Where's Ellie?"

"I think she went to get her bathing suit on," Seth called to Shawn. He splashed Stephen, and Stephen splashed him back. Shawn's brothers began to dunk each other.

Shawn sat down on the shore, watching them roughhouse. Duncan plopped in the dirt beside him, immediately going to sleep. His thoughts spun back to Ellie. He'd enjoyed the hike with her so much. And the drive yesterday too, even though the deer died and his truck's grill was a little messed up. Ellie was nothing like Jill. Maybe that was why he enjoyed her company. Jill drove him crazy these days.

They'd gone out on Saturday to a movie and afterward to Jill's house to hang out. Jill hadn't told him Dr. and Mrs. Larson weren't home and that Lily was spending the night with a friend. As soon as they walked in the door, Jill had taken his hand and led him to the living room sofa. She'd tugged off his shirt and begun kissing him. Feeling like a fool, Shawn sprang off the couch and told her to stop it.

"Why can't you be hot for me," she'd said, pulling off her top to reveal a lacy black bra. The sight of the dark lingerie had left Shawn cold.

"Put your shirt back on," he'd demanded.

She'd risen from the couch, a seductive smile on her face. "No."

"I'm not playing, Jill. Get dressed."

"I know you want this as much as I do," she'd purred.

Shawn hadn't been about to tell her the only thing he wanted was out of that house.

She'd walked over to the giant flat-screen television and flipped it on. Within a moment of channel surfing, Jill had found what she searched for. Moving back to his side, she'd motioned to the big screen. It had taken Shawn a moment to figure out what was playing there. "That's porn, Jill." His voice had sounded raspy and scared even to himself. He'd hated the fear licking through him along with the heat.

Jill had grabbed his arm in an attempt to lead him back to the sofa.

He'd jerked away from her. Grabbing up his shirt, he'd headed for the door, forcing himself to walk, though he wanted to run.

"Don't leave," she'd begged. "There, I turned it off. Come back! We'll just talk tonight."

Shawn had ignored her. The night air had been cool against his burning face. His heart had pumped as he climbed into his truck. His pulse hadn't slowed down until he was on the road halfway home. With his windows rolled down, the wind rushing into the cab, Shawn had cranked on some worship music. Third Day eased his nerves but hadn't erased his anger at Jill.

The next morning at church, she'd acted as if nothing had happened. He'd played the piano, and she sang several songs with Stephen on the drums and Seth playing guitar. Then he and Jill had sung a duet about the love of Jesus. He'd refused to look at her the entire song, focusing instead on the overflowing church audience.

He was grateful now for this camping trip. He wouldn't have to deal with Jill for several days. Duncan looked past him, thumping his tail in greeting. Shawn turned to see Ellie. She wore a blue tankini bathing suit and looked anything but pregnant.

She smiled, and right away he could tell she was nervous.

"I like your bathing suit." He stood up to welcome her but turned around when Seth yelled something at him he didn't quite catch. Confused, he turned back to Ellie.

"I've got something on my shorts, don't I?" He asked, noting the direction of her wide-eyed gaze, realizing Seth had said something about his shorts.

She nodded an affirmative.

"Did I sit in loon poop?" Shawn tried to see his shorts but couldn't get a good view of his backside. Embarrassment washed over him.

"I think it's just dirt sticking to your wet pants," Ellie assured him.

"It's bear scat!" Seth yelled from the water.

Shawn grinned at Ellie. "I'll show that boy bear scat." He spun around and barreled into the water. In seconds, he was dunking Seth over and over again. Stephen sprang into the fight, and all three brothers about drowned each other in the lake.

Chapter 16

After dinner, the Klein boys pulled out their guitars, and Ellie reached for her Hummingbird. The sun had gone down, and the mountain air felt cold on her cheeks. Everyone wore sweatshirts, snuggling close to the fire. A million stars twinkled overhead. The fire popped and crackled, spreading warmth and smelling so good. She could smell the pines too and autumn in the air.

"Do Jeremy Camp," Seth told Shawn. "He sounds just like Camp, especially when he sings 'My Desire.'"

Ellie had no idea who Jeremy Camp was and had never heard 'My Desire.'

Shawn began to play. Picking up the tune, Ellie strummed backup for him. The Kleins all looked at her strangely, so she stopped strumming.

"Don't stop." Shawn interrupted his playing for her. "I love it. Keep strumming with me." He smiled, and her stomach did that flip-flop she was coming to expect with him. She looked out into the darkness, letting the song they strummed together engulf her. By the end of the ballad, she felt closer to Shawn than she'd ever felt to anyone in her life. That wasn't saying much, for she'd never allowed herself to really get attached to anyone but Jamie. And never had she played music with someone before. It felt so right.

"You knew that song," Shawn said when it was over.

Ellie could tell he was pleased with her. "No. I've never heard that song before." She looked around at everyone else staring at her, then back at Shawn.

"How could you play along if you didn't know the song?" Seth asked.

"I don't know." Ellie shrugged her shoulders.

"Let's do another one together." Shawn grinned and strummed once more on his guitar.

He began to sing, and Ellie backed him up. Music was as natural as breathing to her. Again, she stared into the darkness, feeling everyone's eyes on her. She imagined she could see the lake and remembered this afternoon, playing in the water with the Klein boys. How Shawn protected her from Stephen and Seth's splashing. How Miss Patsy and Pastor Sam eventually joined them in the lake and they all ended up chicken fighting. Miss Patsy on Pastor Sam's shoulders, Seth on Stephen's, and Ellie on Shawn's. She and Shawn lost to Seth and Stephen, but how fun it was to roughhouse with them.

"Do you sing too?" Shawn asked when the song ended.

Ellie nodded.

"Will you sing for us?" Stephen asked. He'd seemed bent out of shape this afternoon when Miss Patsy assigned Ellie to Shawn for chicken fighting. Stephen should have been happy considering he and Seth had won every round. She knew Stephen liked her, but Ellie wasn't too concerned. When her belly grew, his interest would fade. "What do you want me to sing?" she asked.

"How about 'The Rose'?" Shawn suggested.

"I can't do that song justice with a guitar. We need a piano."

"Songs don't get justice out here," Pastor Sam said. "They get slaughtered, especially when I sing them."

"Do you play music, Pastor Sam?" Ellie adjusted a string on her guitar.

"I golf." He smiled, looking like an older version of Shawn. "The boys provide the music for Patsy and me when it's our turn to sing."

"Neither one of us can play an instrument," Miss Patsy admitted.

"Sing 'The Rose,'" Stephen pressed, tuning his guitar as well.

"Okay." Ellie closed her eyes, listening to the fire crackle for a moment. Softly, she began to strum. She then sang the whole song with her eyes closed. Never had the words meant so much to her. As she sang, her mind played a video of the time she'd spent with the Kleins. This beautiful family. The day they picked her up at the trailer, carrying her garbage bags to the car. That first dinner when Shawn tripped over Duncan. Sitting by Miss Patsy's prayer garden writing songs. Riding in Shawn's truck up here. Hitting the deer. Him leaning over her to unbuckle her seat belt. Shawn's hair smelling so good as he pressed near her in the cab of the truck. Him not allowing her to see the dead deer. Shawn tickling her. Watching him swim across the lake to rescue Duncan. The look on his face when he saw her in the blue bathing suit Miss Patsy had given her. Chicken fighting on his shoulders. And best of all, making music with him now by the fire. Such a perfect day. An unbelievably perfect day.

She opened her eyes after ending the song. Nobody said a word. They all stared at her as if she'd grown two heads.

"I know. I told you it needs more than a guitar."

"Honey," Miss Patsy interrupted. "We're speechless. Really, we are. Wow."

"God has gifted you," Pastor Sam said. "You already have your heavenly voice. Most of us don't get that till we enter the pearly gates."

More than anything, Ellie wanted to look at Shawn. She'd sung the song for him but didn't want to admit it. Even to herself.

Both Seth and Stephen jumped in, telling her how great she could sing. "You have to join our worship band." Stephen sounded so excited. "Jill's out of business," he said with glee.

"Stephen," Miss Patsy chastised him.

"You could sing 'The Rose' at church on Sunday. It's a song about love. God is love, right, Dad?" Seth asked.

"God is love, but he's also our judge. Though God loves people, whoever doesn't accept his Son will spend eternity without him."

Ellie felt like Pastor Sam was talking to her. She stared down at her guitar, wishing she hadn't opened herself up by singing for them. Shawn remained silent, which bummed her out even more.

"Do you mind if I go to bed?" she quietly asked Miss Patsy. She refused to make eye contact with anyone else. Miss Patsy felt safe. Miss Patsy really cared about her.

"Of course you can, honey." Miss Patsy stood up.

"Sing another song," Stephen begged.

"I'm really tired. I'm sorry," she said.

"Go to bed, sweetheart. We'll join you in a little while," Miss Patsy said.

As she walked toward the tent, Ellie heard Miss Patsy whispering, "She's going to have a baby. She needs lots of rest, boys."

Hot tears filled Ellie's eyes. She hadn't looked at Shawn at all after singing "The Rose" for him. Outside the tent, over at the fire, the Kleins no longer played music. They talked softly. Probably about her. Ellie hoped she'd fall asleep before they came to bed.

And she did.

She awoke the next morning, opening her eyes to find Shawn staring at her. Their pillows were so close together. Nobody else stirred in the tent. It was early, dawn perhaps.

Shawn smiled at her.

Half-asleep, she smiled back at him.

"I loved 'The Rose,'" he said so softly she mostly just read his lips. He looked intently at her a moment longer before rolling over to face the opposite direction.

How long had he been watching her sleep? Had he just woken up, or was he lying there for a while looking at her? The whole sleeping together in the tent felt awkward, but she wouldn't have missed it for the world with Shawn telling her he had loved "The Rose."

Pastor Sam snored quietly, and she could hear Miss Patsy breathing evenly in sleep beside her. Seth and Stephen lay buried in their bags. Duncan slept at Stephen's feet near the tent flap that remained zipped closed against the cold.

Ellie wondered if Shawn was awake or if he'd gone back to sleep. She stared at the side of the tent, thinking about him until she finally dozed off again.

Chapter 17

Allen Larson headed Mountain View Academy's school board, another reason Jill was proud of her father. She attended the school board meeting Monday night with him, and it didn't go as Daddy had planned.

Daddy was pretty peeved over it.

Mr. Hartman had surprised everyone. The "punk" principal, Daddy called Mr. Hartman because he was young and challenged Daddy every chance he got. Especially when Daddy put him on the spot in front of the board saying, "Real Christians walk the walk by helping the poor and needy. Ellie Ryan is poor and needy. Not to mention pregnant. She deserves a desk at Mountain View Academy."

Mr. Hartman, sweat beading his bald head, disagreed. It wasn't even warm outside or in the building. Mr. Hartman must be sweating because he was nervous standing up to Daddy. Allen Larson did that to other men, made them sweat. Jill loved it.

"How is Miss Ryan going to sit in one of our desks?" Mr. Hartman asked, wiping his perspiring brow. "Our desks are not made for pregnant students. MVA's school policy does not allow students to be sexually active, let alone pregnant. Each student signs a contract promising to remain pure while attending our school. Expulsion is the result of sexual immorality. How can we let a pregnant girl into our school under these conditions?"

"Would you stop the Virgin Mary from attending MVA?" Daddy asked him with the school board members, a bunch of narrow-minded old geezers, listening intently.

"Ellie Ryan is not the Virgin Mary. She's a girl whose immoral behavior has resulted in pregnancy. I know she's living with Pastor Sam's family now, and I would love to let her come to our school along with the Klein boys, but I just can't do it. I won't do it!" Mr. Hartman exclaimed, surprising everyone with his passion.

"Well, it's not up to you," Daddy practically growled. "The same board who hired you, Josh, will vote on this tonight, and then we'll see if Pastor Sam's girl gets in or not."

To Daddy's and Jill's utter astonishment, the board voted in Mr. Hartman's favor. Ellie Ryan would not be attending Mountain View Academy.

"And I'm so glad," Jill said when they got home from the meeting and Daddy told her mom and Lily how the meeting unfolded. "I don't want to look at some pregnant girl walking around our school all day anyway." Jill wrinkled her nose in disgust.

"When did you get so high and mighty, young lady?" Daddy asked.

"I'm not high and mighty, Daddy. I'm a Christian, and I don't want that girl's sin flaunted in my face."

"As Christians, aren't we suppose to love and accept everyone? Even pregnant girls?" Lily asked, her eyes all big and innocent and full of stupidity. Jill hated when Lily did this to her.

"Of course we are," Daddy replied.

"Your dad's good at that," Beth said. It went right over Lily's head, but Jill immediately sensed her mom's sarcasm.

"Josh is an idiot. He's young and idealistic. I should have never recommended him for principal." Daddy loosened his tie in frustration.

"You like them young and idealistic, don't you, Allen?"

Daddy gave Beth a sharp look, then turned to Lily and Jill. "It's late, you girls have school tomorrow. Go to bed."

Lily kissed him sweetly on the cheek and did as she was told. Jill wasn't about to be treated like a child. Not at seventeen years old, going on eighteen soon.

"I'm not ready for bed. I haven't looked at my social media yet." Jill headed for the study, where the family shared a computer. She hated that she wasn't allowed an iPhone like all her friends. Daddy made her carry his old flip phone. She felt like she lived in the dark ages. He'd decided a few years back that keeping just one family computer was the best way to monitor everyone's online activity. He had his own computer at the office, so he only used the computer in the den after everyone went to bed. Every night Daddy got on the computer. Jill wondered if he was really working like he said he was or if he was doing something else. Something she didn't want to think about considering she'd found a way to access porn on their TV and computer.

"I wasn't making a suggestion, Jill. I gave you an order to go to bed."

Jill spun around. "I'm three years older than Lily. I should get to stay up later than my sister."

"I don't care if you're three years older than Noah when he built his ark. I told you to go to bed, young lady."

Jill made a nasty face before turning toward the stairs.

"She *is* older than Lily. I think Jill should get to stay up," her mother argued for her.

Daddy turned on his wife. *His second wife.*

Just the other day in an argument, Jill had overheard Daddy say he should have kept his first wife. "At least Trudy said what was on her mind. You just stew about things, Beth," Daddy had said. Tonight he growled, "Let's have it out, Beth. I'm tired of your insinuations. Tell me what you're really thinking."

She crossed her arms, that frozen look on her face, refusing to answer him.

"You're mad that I'm going to Rio de Janeiro without you? It's a doctor's conference, for heaven's sake. You'd be bored out of your mind. Besides, you're working for Sam now." Daddy tried not to show how he felt about Beth being Pastor Sam's personal secretary, but Jill knew Daddy didn't like it one bit.

"Come to the study with me," Beth said.

Daddy's radar went up. Jill could tell by the look on his face. He'd grown cautious, but he followed her mom to the den.

Jill tagged after them. They'd been arguing in her presence for several years now. She became invisible when they went after each other this way. Beth hardly knew how to turn on a computer, let alone track someone's net activities, so Jill was really curious about what would happen in the den. And, of course, she wanted to get on the computer herself when her parents left the room.

Jill hung back out of the line of fire but moved in close enough to see the computer screen. It was a tower computer with a really large screen, so she didn't have to move very far into the room, which was dark except for the screen, bright and glowing in wallpaper mode with a picture of a beach in Jamaica.

Jill's Instagram page popped up as soon as her mom hit the mouse. Daddy did a double take upon seeing the photo of her in a nude-colored bikini, which made Jill look naked on the screen, twisted around another blond girl in a hot pink string bikini. The photo oozed sexuality. Who was stupid enough to post a picture like that for everyone to see?

It had to have been Miss Hot Pink Bikini's idiot boyfriend snapping photos back in August with his iPhone. Jill's parents didn't know about her nude-colored bikini. Or the trip to the lake with Maddy, the other doctor's daughter wearing the hot pink bikini. Beth gave Daddy an accusing glare before exiting out of the Instagram site. "She must take after you, and Maddy must take after your Rio de Janeiro buddy, Roger. Maddy certainly doesn't take after her buttoned-up mother. I think I'll call Marcy and tell her about it."

"About Jill and Maddy?" Daddy asked like an idiot.

"About you and Roger," Beth said with a sweetness that soured Jill's stomach. Nothing about her mother was sweet, except her perfume. Beth was classy, fantastic, and fit, but she wasn't sweet.

"What's that supposed to mean?" Daddy asked, plopping down in the high-backed leather chair, leaving Beth standing there with her hand on the mouse.

Swirling the mouse around, she clicked into the computer's history. She must have learned to do this at church while working for Pastor Sam.

Daddy gripped the chair's padded arms like he was hanging on for dear life on a scary ride at Disney World, where they'd gone as a family last year.

"I know why you stay up late on this computer," Beth said.

"I work," said Daddy, all puffed up like the truth was on his side.

"How long are you going to lie to me?" She found what she searched for, pulling porn up on the screen.

Daddy leaned back in his chair like he was really shocked. And then really tired and ready to confess everything. "What do you expect from me, Beth? You hold out like a groundhog coming out once a year. You see my shadow in the bedroom and you pretend you're asleep. A man needs relief, and if I can't get relief from my wife, I'm going to get it somewhere else."

"You call this relief?" Her mother ripped the mouse from the computer, shocking Jill with the intensity of her wrath. Usually, she was the queen of no reaction. "I want a divorce."

"You want a divorce over porn?" Daddy sat upright in his chair.

Beth threw the mouse across the room. "Yes." She didn't yell. Her mom never yelled, but her voice bled venom.

"We can't get a divorce. We're Christians. God hates divorce," said Daddy.

Beth laughed. "You've already gotten one divorce. What's wrong with two, Allen?"

"Think about Jill and Lily," Daddy beseeched.

"I am thinking about the girls. Look what Jill's doing on the Internet. At the lake with Roger and Marcy's daughter. Do you think she gets that trashy behavior from me?"

Daddy rose from his chair. "Of course she doesn't get trashy behavior from you. You're perfect. Ice perfect, honey."

"Don't accuse me of being icy. I know what you do at your doctors' conferences."

"What do I do at my doctors' conferences?"

"Porn and I'm sure more." She didn't elaborate further.

Daddy walked over to the bookshelf, pulling down a Bible Grandpa had given him years ago. He weighed the big Bible in his hand, then faced her mother and palmed the Bible for her to see. "This is too heavy for me. I can't measure up to what's in here, honey."

"Don't be that way with me. I know you too well, Allen." When she stepped past him to leave the study, Daddy handed her the Bible.

"God wants us to work through this. Read the Good Book; that will help you."

Beth clutched the Bible to her chest. "God doesn't want you looking at porn, Allen." Then she bolted from the room, Jill sliding back into the darkness so her mom didn't notice her when she passed by before rushing up the stairs.

Daddy returned to his chair. He moved as if very tired. Jill's grandparents had become Christians when Daddy was twelve years old. Life changed drastically after that, Daddy once told them. Grandpa still practiced medicine, but they sold their big house in DC and moved out to the farm in Tennessee.

Her grandparents still lived on that modest farm built a hundred and fifty years ago. Grandpa was retired now and spent most of his time teaching Bible classes at Holy Mountain Church. Grandma taught Bible classes there too. They often told Daddy they prayed for him to be saved. For her whole family to be saved, which made Jill really mad. Everyone had accepted Jesus as their Savior in her family. They'd all been baptized as well. What more did Grandpa and Grandma Larson want? Should they become missionaries and die in Africa or some other god-awful country to prove they were saved?

"You don't know God's Son," Grandpa said to Daddy a few months back at a family dinner. "If you knew Jesus, you wouldn't be trying to run his universe, Allen."

"I'm not trying to run the universe," Daddy had argued.

Grandpa had smiled in that way of his. Grandpa was the most humble man Jill knew, even though he was always after everyone about Jesus. "Yes, you are, Allen," Grandpa had said. "You use your doctor's reputation and your big bank account to control folks. When will you see you wouldn't be able to put on your own shoes if Christ didn't allow it?"

Daddy reached for the computer mouse but then seemed to remember her mother had thrown it across the room. He was leaving for Rio on Friday. Was there really a doctors' conference there, or were he and Maddy's daddy sneaking off for a vacation without their wives?

Taking a deep breath, Daddy leaned down and shut off the computer. Then he picked up his phone on the desk beside the computer and dialed. When someone answered, they began to talk. Jill knew it was her grandpa just by the way Daddy spoke into the phone. Now Daddy would be sitting there on the phone for who knew how long with Grandpa, and she'd never get to use the computer.

At least she could text Maddy to warn her about the bikini Instagram post. And she prayed Shawn wouldn't see the picture on Instagram either. A picture like that would really upset Shawn.

Chapter 18

Football practice ended early, giving Shawn enough time to drive out to the Larson's farm. Since both of Shawn's real grandfathers had passed away, Grandpa Larson was even more important to him. Shawn had only seen his grandfathers once a year when they were alive, and he'd never been close to either of them. Grandpa Larson was a different story. From the moment they moved to Mountain View, Grandpa Larson had adopted Shawn and his brothers as his own grandsons. He was a retired heart surgeon; the man knew the human heart better than anyone Shawn had ever known, not just the physical human heart—though he surely knew that too—but the spiritual human heart. He was Jill's grandfather, but Jill rarely made time for her grandparents. "They're always bugging me about Jesus," she said. "I don't want to talk about Jesus all the time, like my grandparents do."

Shawn didn't mind talking about Jesus with Grandpa Larson. He loved being with the old man, and Grandma Larson made the best blackberry pie in Tennessee.

Their farm was about twenty minutes from Mountain View. Shawn rolled down his window, enjoying smelling the fields of hay he passed along the way. Tomorrow he had a home football game, and he wanted to invite Grandpa to come. He also wanted Grandpa Larson to pray with him about his future. When Grandpa prayed, God listened. There was nobody closer to the Lord than his grandpa.

Shawn found Grandpa out in the barn, forking hay to his horses. He gave the old man a big hug and then took the pitchfork and finished feeding the animals as Grandpa stood by nodding and smiling.

"You didn't have football practice today?" Grandpa leaned against the fence.

"Thursday practices are usually short. Coach doesn't want to wear us out before a game. Can you and Grandma come tomorrow night? We're playing at home. I'll have Dad and Mom save you a seat in the bleachers with them."

"I'll be there, but I don't think Mary will make it. She's been feeling poorly."

Shawn stopped forking the hay for a moment. "Is Grandma all right?" He couldn't hide the alarm in his voice.

"She's fine. Just old, like me."

Studying Grandpa, Shawn decided he hoped to look so good at that age. Grandpa hadn't changed in the ten years Shawn had known him. Sweeping up another load of hay, he pitched it to a shy gelding standing off by himself, patiently waiting for his supper.

"What's on your mind today, Shawny?" Grandpa had called him Shawny since he was eight years old.

All the horses were fed now. Shawn leaned on the wooden handle of the pitchfork. "I don't know what I want to do with my life anymore."

Grandpa grinned. "You better decide before your birthday arrives."

Shawn's birthday loomed but a week away. "At eighteen, I should know for sure what I want to do, right?"

"For sure." Grandpa grinned wider, proud he could talk like a teenager, Shawn supposed. He took the pitchfork from Shawn's hand and hung it back on the side of the barn. "Knowing your Grandma, she's got some sweets ready for you by now."

Slowly, they walked to the house. Shawn did the talking, and Grandpa just listened. It was often this way. Once they reached the porch, Grandpa told Shawn to have a seat on the veranda. He returned a moment later with Grandma Larson, carrying two slices of blackberry pie with a scoop of vanilla ice cream on top of each one.

Shawn jumped up and hugged the little white-haired woman and then sat back down at the patio table and let Grandma serve him and Grandpa. Grandma went back into the house, and after saying a blessing, Grandpa dug into his pie.

"If you hadn't come, I wouldn't have gotten the ice cream today. Your grandma monitors my sugar the way she used to monitor my patients."

Grandma had been Grandpa's nurse over fifty years ago. It was how they met. As soon as they married, Grandma gave up nursing to raise a family, but Grandpa never stopped referring to her as his best nurse. Shawn thought their marriage the ideal of what a couple should be. He'd once hoped he and Jill could grow old together that way, but now Jill had become like everything else in his life—uncertain.

As if reading his mind, Grandpa chose the moment to ask about her. "How's my granddaughter doing?"

Shawn shifted uncomfortably in his chair. He took another bite of pie before answering, giving himself a moment to figure out how to respond. He decided to keep it simple. "Jill's fine."

"Fine as in 'fine,' like you kids say, or fine as in 'fine,' as we old folks say it?"

Shawn smiled. "Kids don't say 'fine' these days, Grandpa. They say hot."

"Hot." Grandpa moved the pie around in his mouth, mulling over the term. "Hot, huh?"

"If you get on social media, you'll learn all that stuff."

"I can hardly figure out a phone book these days, let alone that Facebook people use now."

Shawn knew better. Grandpa could still use a phone book just fine and would have no problem on the Internet as well. He was a brilliant man. One of Washington DC's top heart surgeons before moving his practice to Tennessee. Soon after that, he gave up surgery altogether, retiring to his farm, where he now invited people to come for spiritual healing. One day Shawn had asked Grandpa why he'd stopped being a doctor when he was so good at it and had healed so many people in the past. "The only real heart surgeon is Jesus. I've found I can do more good doctoring spiritual hearts than physical ones in my old age," he'd replied.

"So you and Jill are on the outs, huh?"

"We're still together," Shawn assured him, not wanting to talk about Jill.

"But something's wrong." Grandpa pushed his empty pie plate away.

"I don't know. I guess so."

"The real question is: Do you and Jill know Jesus? Does your relationship include our Lord and Savior's plans for your lives?"

"Why would you say that, Grandpa? Of course we know Jesus! We sing in the worship band." Shawn pushed his plate away too.

Grandpa rested his elbows on the table, studying Shawn intently. "A lot of folks think they know Jesus, Shawny. And they do. They say their prayers. They go to church. They may even teach Sunday school or sing worship, but they don't love our Lord Jesus. They love themselves, plain and simple."

That was a perfect description of Jill. She loved herself.

Shawn leaned his elbows on the table like Grandpa, resting his head in his hands. When Grandpa looked at you, it was as if he could see right into your heart. Shawn didn't want Grandpa seeing into his heart. He feared what was there.

Grandpa put his hand on top of Shawn's head. Shawn knew Grandpa prayed for him. After praying silently for a while, Grandpa began to pray out loud. He blessed Shawn's future and lifted up Jill and Shawn's relationship to the Lord. Then he prayed for their salvation. Again, Shawn was taken aback by his grandpa doubting his salvation.

"You don't think I'm saved?" Shawn couldn't hide his hurt.

"Salvation belongs to the Lord, Shawny." Grandpa smiled. "I told you I'm not the heart surgeon. Jesus is." Grandpa's gaze pierced Shawn. "Have you fought for your faith yet, Shawny? Have you wrestled with God, like Jacob? Sat in prison, like Joseph? Have you, like Timothy, worked out your salvation with fear and trembling?"

"Gosh, Grandpa. That's deep Bible stuff."

"That's truth, my boy. The truth will set you free. Search for the Lord's truth in your life."

Shawn rested his head against the back of the patio chair, letting Grandpa's words sink in. The sun cast a golden glow over the meadow where the Larsons' farm bordered a rushing creek. Grandpa leaned his head against the back of his seat too, looking out at the meadow the way Shawn did. A slight breeze swayed the nearby pines, and Shawn could smell something delicious besides the pie wafting from Grandma's kitchen.

"How's the pregnant girl doing at your house?" Grandpa asked after a quiet spell.

"She's something."

Grandpa's weathered cheeks lifted with a grin. He kept staring at the meadow. "I said that about your grandma the first time I saw her too."

Shawn sat straight up in his chair, alarmed Grandpa had misinterpreted him. "I didn't mean it that way."

"I know you, Shawny. I know what you meant." The old man gave him a sly grin.

Shawn stood up. He picked up the two empty plates. "She sings like you can't imagine, Grandpa," he attempted to explain.

"So when is she going to sing in your worship band?"

"Sunday morning."

"I'll make sure not to miss church this week."

"You never miss church." Shawn laughed, feeling nervous now that Grandpa knew how he was feeling about Ellie.

"Two years ago, I missed church. One of my mares got a foal caught up in her, and I had to go the OBGYN route. That OBGYN stuff is not for me. Too messy." Grandpa shook his head.

"Isn't surgery messy?"

"Of course not." Grandpa rose from his seat and stepped over to open the screen door for Shawn. "A good heart surgeon does clean work, just like the Lord.

Chapter 19

"Isn't this like being halfway to heaven?" Pastor Sam asked Ellie as the two drove up a steep hill to Holy Mountain Church that morning after Miss Patsy left for work. Pulling into the vast, empty parking lot, Pastor Sam cruised around the immaculate church grounds that occupied the entire hilltop overlooking the city of Mountain View. Blue sky stretched in all directions as far as the eye could see. A massive brick sanctuary dominated the location. On the backside of the sprawling church, Pastor Sam parked next to an old Chevy truck with its hood open. Underneath the hood was a guy up to his elbows in grease. Pastor Sam got out of the car and came around to open the passenger door for Ellie. She climbed out, and the two of them walked over to the guy working on the truck.

The guy stuck out his greasy hand to Pastor Sam for a handshake.

"No thanks," said a laughing Pastor Sam. He then introduced Ellie to the greasy-handed Pastor Joe Mullens. The guy was probably in his thirties, but he appeared younger. When he smiled, big dimples split his cheeks. His large brown eyes shone with kindness. Ellie liked him right off.

"I'm happy to meet you, Ellie," said Pastor Joe.

Ellie held out her hand to him.

He raised his eyebrows, his big brown eyes looking even bigger. "You don't mind getting your hand greasy, young lady?"

"I don't mind a bit," said Ellie.

Pastor Joe grabbed a towel draped over the radiator. He did his best to wipe the grease off before shaking her hand. "Unlike Sam, you're much too pretty to wipe grease on," he said.

Ellie smiled.

After shaking her hand, Pastor Joe closed the Chevy's hood. Pastor Sam led them into the church, making small talk about the weather, how rain was expected on Sunday, and he sure hoped it wasn't a downpour that'd keep folks from attending the service because Ellie was going to sing.

"It will only take me a minute to wash up," Pastor Joe said. "I'll meet you and Ellie in your office, Sam."

While Pastor Joe headed down one hall, Pastor Sam led Ellie down another to a secretary's office, where a second door stood behind the secretary's gleaming wooden desk.

"Sam," the secretary scolded with a beaming smile. "You missed your nine o'clock this morning. I took care of it for you. You're rescheduled for tomorrow at nine now." The attractive secretary didn't address him as "pastor" and appeared very fond of him. Too fond of him.

"Beth, this is our sweet little Ellie," said Pastor Sam.

The blond secretary extended a hand with long, lacquered finger nails. "Hello, sweet, little Ellie."

"Hi," Ellie murmured. Though she acted really nice, Ellie sensed the secretary didn't like her. The secretary's eyes lingered on Ellie's midsection for a moment; apparently, someone had informed her already about the pregnancy.

"So you're living with all those Klein boys. How's that going?" The secretary tidied papers on her desk before rising from her chair to open a door that led into a larger office behind hers.

"Just fine. They're really nice," Ellie said as she followed Pastor Sam, trailing the secretary with her hips swaying in a fitted skirt, into a room that reeked of wealth just like the rest of this church. Nice paintings, expensive woodwork, a large sheepskin rug spread in front of a dark leather couch.

Pastor Sam took a seat in a leather chair behind the biggest desk Ellie had ever seen. It gleamed like the secretary's smaller desk, both made of mahogany wood. Two walls of mahogany bookcases matched the massive desk. Ellie knew it was mahogany because Clive always pointed out wood: pine, oak, cherry, and mahogany. Jana used to make fun of Clive about it behind his back, but Ellie liked knowing all kinds of wood. Clive had made furniture for a living before he opened the diner. He was one of those guys who could do about anything, fix anything, build anything, Clive was smart that way.

The secretary turned around and did her hip-swaying walk out of Pastor Sam's office, the smile she tossed over her shoulder eating Pastor Sam up before she left. To Ellie's relief, Pastor Sam seemed oblivious to the secretary, sitting there at his big desk shuffling through a stack of phone messages with a wrinkled brow.

Thankful for the secretary's departure, Ellie glanced around, noticing the beautiful family portrait on Pastor Sam's wall. The Kleins all wore white button-up shirts and blue jeans. Ellie studied Shawn, tall and smiling and so very handsome, standing between Pastor Sam and Stephen, who stood beside Seth, leaning against their mother with a forest of trees in the background, all leafed out in autumn glory. Such an amazing family. It hurt Ellie just to look at them. This was how she'd envisioned the perfect family would be, and now she lived with them. Unbelievable. Just like she still found it unbelievable that she was really pregnant.

Pastor Sam said they'd come here today to talk about the baby. Its adoption, he'd specified. "Let's not tell Patsy about this meeting until everything gets ironed out," he'd said as they drove to the church. "I don't want Patsy stirred up when there's no need for it yet."

Ellie didn't ask any questions. She was taking life with the Kleins the way she took everything—quietly, cautiously, and temporarily. The Kleins were a means to an end, she reminded herself, though the life she was living with them was all she'd ever dreamed of. A real family in a real house with a real retriever to take on long walks. Duncan even slept on the floor beside her bed now. It helped with her nightmares. She still had them, but when she awoke, Duncan's nose pressed against her hand like he knew the awful dream she'd wandered into and was trying to wake her up from it.

Her thoughts returned to her pregnancy when Pastor Joe walked into the office, closing the door behind him. Pastor Sam said Pastor Joe had a sister who wanted to adopt a baby. Pastor Joe wore fancy slacks and a clean light blue dress shirt now, having changed out of his greasy clothes. "So, Sam," he said, "have you told Ellie about Jenny yet?" Ellie noted the grease under the pastor's fingernails and smiled because, aside from the grease, he looked like a guy who would never work on an engine, or drive an old Chevy truck for that matter.

"I thought I'd let you tell Ellie about Jenny," said Pastor Sam.

Joe cleared his throat. His brown eyes were so expressive for a grown man; he looked about to cry. Ellie wasn't used to a man crying.

"Ellie, why don't you and Joe take a seat in those two seats in front of my desk? I'll just sit back here and listen." Pastor Sam made himself comfortable in his big leather chair.

Joe waited until Ellie chose a chair before sitting down in the other one. "I'm sorry to get a little emotional," he said. "Jen's my little sister, and I've always taken care of her."

"There's nothing wrong with tears on a man's cheeks," said Pastor Sam. "Jesus wept."

Pastor Joe nodded, pressing his fingers to his eyes for a moment to stop the flow.

Ellie stared at him with her eyes stinging as well. And then, within ten minutes of him talking about his sister, her heart ached badly too. He told her how he and Jenny grew up in a Kentucky hollow, how their birth mom died when Jenny was two years old, just like Ellie's mom. Joe and Jenny had been born into poverty, with strip mines eroding the hillsides above their run-down cabin and an alcoholic father eroding their hopes until the day a bright-faced lawyer named William Mullens came to the mountains to stop the strip mining.

The Mullens eventually adopted Joe and Jenny, saving them from a bleak future in the hollow. "For years after that, we had it so good," he continued. "Jenny and I became Christians. We went to college, met people we loved, and married them. I moved here, and Jenny and Ken settled in Colorado, Ken's home state. Then, when Jenny was nine months pregnant, the accident occurred. The crash ruptured Jenny's uterus. Baby Matthew lived only a few weeks. Now Jenny can no longer have children." Pastor Joe had tears on his cheeks again. "My sister hasn't been the same since the accident. She'll never bear her own children, and I don't understand it because God created Jenny to be a mother. And Ken wants little ones nearly as bad as Jen. Can I ask when your baby's due, Ellie?"

"I'm three months along." Ellie could no longer meet Pastor Joe's eyes. Talking about the pregnancy filled her with shame.

"Is the father willing to put the baby up for adoption?" Pastor Joe gently probed.

Ellie stared at the sheepskin rug. It must have been a bunch of sheep sewn together because it was a lot bigger than just one sheep. It looked real soft. On the leather couch rested matching red throw pillows. One said "Faith." The other pillow said "Hope."

"It's important, Ellie, that you tell us how the father of the baby feels about adoption," said Pastor Sam. Like Pastor Joe, his voice was all gentle coaxing.

Ellie bit her lip, staring at the red pillows. Red like blood. If Jamie found out about this baby there would be blood. She closed her eyes, agonizing over what to say.

"The father will have to sign some papers to put your baby up for adoption. Do you think he might want to keep his child?" asked Pastor Joe.

"Nobody wants this child," Ellie said softly, even though everything inside her was screaming wildly. Both pastors waited. The silence in the room was crushing. "Things are different up in Sutterville," she explained. "This baby wasn't meant to be. A lot of babies up there aren't meant to be."

"Every baby is meant to be," said Pastor Sam. "God is the author of life, Ellie."

"Well, God wasn't a part of this life," said Ellie, trembling in her chair, ready to come undone.

Pastor Joe put his hand on her arm. He didn't say anything, just looked at her with those soft brown eyes, seeing into her soul, she supposed. Hot tears scalded her cheeks.

"Let's all say a prayer together," said Pastor Sam. While he prayed, tears she couldn't stop streaked Ellie's face. Pastor Joe held on to her arm, his head bowed close to hers. When it was over, Pastor Sam said, "Do you want to name the baby's father for us now?"

Ellie shook her head, feeling sick inside.

"We don't have to work this out today," said Pastor Joe. "If you don't name the father of your baby, the state will put an ad in the newspaper when the child's born, notifying your hometown of the birth. Then we wait for the father to come forward. If he doesn't come forward, the adoption will proceed without him." Pastor Joe smiled at her. She saw no judgment on his face, only compassion.

"Speaking of babies, how is your baby girl doing?" Pastor Sam asked Pastor Joe.

"She's doing fine. Keeping us up at night." Pastor Joe turned to Ellie. "My wife gave birth a few days ago. Jenny and Ken are coming to meet our baby this weekend. I was hoping they could meet you, too. And that you would consider having them adopt your baby, Ellie."

Chapter 20

The baby's heartbeat sounded like hummingbird wings. Dr. Hammons assured Ellie and Miss Patsy all was well with the fetus's development. "On your next visit, we'll schedule the ultrasound," the doctor said. He was a tall, soft-spoken, stoop-shouldered man with bifocal glasses perched on the bridge of his nose.

"Ellie was one of Kathy's students," Miss Patsy told Dr. Hammons there in the exam room. While the two adults talked, Ellie stared at a black-and-white picture on the wall of a pregnant woman with her hands lovingly holding her enormous belly. The woman looked so peaceful and beautiful, but the photo filled Ellie with something akin to horror. Would her belly grow that big before she gave birth?

"Really?" Dr. Hammons smiled, but behind his glasses his eyes appeared grieved. "Did you take any of my wife's creative writing classes? That was her favorite subject to teach. She loved writing and was published in lots of magazines."

"Mrs. Hammons was amazing," said Ellie. "She encouraged me to keep writing my own songs in her creative writing class. She really believed in me."

Dr. Hammons eyes widened, and he took off his glasses. "You're the little girl who sings so pretty. My wife told me about you. She said you're a very gifted young lady." Dr. Hammons rubbed the bridge of his nose and then put his glasses back on. "Where is the boy who put you in this predicament?"

"He doesn't want the baby." Ellie looked to Miss Patsy for help.

"Ellie has chosen adoption for her baby," said Miss Patsy. "Isn't that wonderful, Dennis?"

"Life is a precious gift. As a doctor, I've always known that, but Kathy's passing has made me realize it all the more."

Miss Patsy put her hand on Dr. Hammons shoulder. "How are your girls doing?"

"They're adjusting. Everything is a new normal now. I'm glad they're both away at college. The house is so empty without Kathy."

"Why don't you come over for dinner? Samuel would love to see you."

"How is Sam?"

"He's fine. We just got back from a camping trip. Samuel completely enjoyed himself. The quiet of the mountains was so good for him."

"I could use that quiet myself. A trip up to the lake for some fishing sounds fantastic."

"By all means, you should go. And please come to dinner when you can."

A nurse peeked her head into the room, informing Dr. Hammons his next patient waited in room three. "I will certainly make good on that dinner invitation. Thank you, Patsy," he said before leaving.

"Thank you, Dennis. I know you weren't taking any new patients. Samuel and I really appreciate you seeing Ellie."

"I wouldn't miss delivering Ellie's baby for anything." Dr. Hammons said good-bye and exited the exam room.

"Are you ready for some lunch?" Miss Patsy asked with a big smile.

"Sure." Ellie hopped down from the exam table. She couldn't wait to get out of that clinic. It was a nice place, elegant furniture in the waiting room, classy black and white framed photos of pregnant women and newborn babies on the walls, really nice nurses, but it felt like a boulder was on her chest, and her legs trembled as they walked across the parking lot to the black Suburban being warmed by the sun.

They drove a few blocks over to Ruthie's Café, both ordering the Friday special: clam chowder soup and the house salad. While they ate, Pastor Sam and his secretary in her tight-fitting skirt arrived at the café. Pastor Sam came right to their table, but the secretary acted uncomfortable and, instead of walking over with Pastor Sam, went to the takeout counter, turning her back on them.

"How did it go with the doctor?" Pastor Sam asked with a smile on his face. Pastor Sam always smiled.

"We heard the baby's heartbeat," Miss Patsy said, looking past him at the secretary.

"That's great." Pastor Sam sat down in the booth beside Miss Patsy.

"What's wrong with Beth?" A funny look was on Miss Patsy's face.

Pastor Sam glanced over at the secretary. "She needs the Italian special," he answered with a laugh that sounded forced.

He then turned to Ellie. "I talked with Pastor Joe this morning. His sister has her heart set on meeting you this weekend."

Ellie stopped eating her soup.

Pastor Sam reassured her with a smile. "Pastor Joe says they're very interested in adopting your baby."

"No!" Patsy gasped.

Pastor Sam and Ellie looked at Miss Pasty in surprise.

"Ellie's baby can't go to strangers," Miss Patsy said, all flustered.

"Joe isn't a stranger. I've worked with him for three years. He's like a brother to me," said Pastor Sam.

"But we don't know his sister at all." Miss Patsy shoved her soup away. Ellie had never seen Miss Patsy upset like this. She felt awkward sitting there with the tension building between husband and wife.

"I'm sure Joe's sister loves the Lord just like he does," said Pastor Sam. "I think we should meet with them and let them get to know Ellie. They're here visiting from Colorado Springs."

"Colorado Springs? That's so far away." Miss Patsy folded her hands on the table as if in prayer. Ellie could see her knuckles whitening as she squeezed her fingers together. "Do they have other children?"

"No. They were in an automobile accident a few years back. Pastor Joe's sister was pregnant at the time. Their baby died after the crash, and his sister can no longer bear children."

"That's awful, but it doesn't mean they should have Ellie's child." Miss Pasty's voice wobbled with emotion.

"Patsy," Pastor Sam warned in a tone that surprised Ellie. He was usually so good-natured and kind with his wife.

The secretary chose that very moment to interrupt them. "Our Italian specials are ready, Sam. Hello, Patsy . . . Ellie," she added as if in afterthought.

Miss Patsy stared hard at the secretary and then turned to Pastor Sam. "You don't eat salami."

"Yes, I do."

"Since when?"

"Since Beth hooked me on the Italian special."

"Really?" Miss Patsy's eyes widened in surprise and then narrowed on the secretary.

"I didn't hook Sam on anything," said the secretary. "The only thing Sam is hooked on is golf with Allen on Saturdays. You know that, Patsy." The secretary laughed, but it sounded fake, like Pastor Sam's forced laugh.

Miss Patsy didn't laugh. She appeared on the verge of tears.

The secretary suddenly grew concerned. "You're really upset, aren't you? What's wrong, Patsy?" Obviously these women were friends. Close friends, Ellie decided when the secretary crouched down at the table to speak confidentially with Miss Patsy.

"Joe Mullen's sister wants Ellie's baby," Miss Pasty whispered to her.

"Really?" the secretary raised her perfectly groomed eyebrows at Pastor Sam.

"I'm not sure we should be discussing this here," Pastor Sam said quietly.

"Why not?" Miss Patsy raised her voice.

"Well, you're upset, and Beth works for me. You and I need to talk this over at home, Patsy. We don't want folks going on about their pastors' private lives," Pastor Sam stuck to his quiet tone.

"Sam, I'm smarter than that," the secretary said with another laugh that grated on Ellie's nerves. Like everyone else Ellie had met in Mountain View, this woman's teeth shone bone white and straight as piano keys. Perfect teeth. Something you didn't see in Sutterville very often. Nobody got braces up there. "I won't mention this to another soul," the smiling secretary promised.

Ellie didn't believe her one bit. She seemed like one of those women who pretended to be your friend and then stabbed you in the back when you least expected it. Miss Patsy needed to watch herself.

Pastor Sam appeared trapped between the two women. He looked at his silver wristwatch. "I've got to get back to the office. I have a one o'clock appointment."

The secretary stood up and stepped out of his way as he exited the booth. "Call me later," she mouthed to Miss Patsy behind Pastor Sam's back as they left.

Chapter 21

Jenny held Joe and Ava's newborn, Claire, up to her face, smelling that precious baby smell that flooded her with memories of Matthew. A jolt of raw emotion ripped through her. Would she ever get past this pain? Losing her baby and the ability to have more babies in one dark swoop of someone else's sin. A drunk driver now sitting in prison for manslaughter, his life a wreckage too after his third DUI arrest. She'd written that twenty-eight-year-old man a letter.

Dear Ronald Shirley: I forgive you for taking Matthew's life . . .

Her grief counselor had suggested it. "Forgiveness is something we do with our will. It's not about how we feel. In time, the heart will come around to accepting the decision the will makes to forgive," the counselor had said. Maybe her heart was coming around because she didn't feel angry anymore. After her breakdown, it was as if that wound had been lanced, the infection of rage over the accident burned out of her. The breakdown left her feeling tired and fragile, but free from all that fury she'd hidden behind a quiet Christian demeanor after the accident.

Since then, she'd given up working at the church in the children's ministry and let go of leading ladies' Bible studies and helping out with the teens on Wednesday nights. Even attending Sunday services with Ken proved unbearable for a while after she'd lost it at the New Year's Eve party last year. Facing all those people at church who knew about her breakdown felt like walking out of her house without clothes on. Being naked wasn't pretty. Even attractive people looked vulnerable, kind of like plucked chickens, when they were naked. And there were all kinds of ways a person could be naked. You could be socially naked. Emotionally naked. Spiritually naked. You could be naked with your feelings and naked with your love. Grief could make you naked. Grief could strip you bare right in front of people. Jenny knew the nakedness of unbearable pain every day of her life now.

And she also knew what it was like to be clothed by God's grace. To be given the time to come back together after breaking apart. To get up in the morning with a whole day ahead of you. A whole life ahead of you. And to feel hope again. The kind of hope that paints a house and plants a garden. She loved how their house turned out after she'd spent all that time painting it herself. Every brush stroke somehow stroking the pain out of her hurting heart. Helping bring beauty to her life again. Helping her hope again.

She'd always wanted to grow her own vegetables and flowers but had never had the time between work and all her church commitments to do that. She'd convinced Ken to stop paying for yard service and buy a John Deere lawn mower for her. They lived on several acres and Jenny began to mow it herself on that little green tractor. She planted more trees, mostly pines, and flowers everywhere she could find a spot for them.

Especially daffodil bulbs when fall came. Sticking bulbs in the ground before winter helped her prepare for the coming snow.

Swirling snow reminded her of the accident. It was really about all she could remember of that night. Snow coming down out of the sky like frozen tears settling on the windshield before they crashed. And then those uncertain days in the hospital with their precious Matthew fighting a losing battle for life and it snowed the whole time. With the possibility of Ken never walking again. Along with her being stripped of the ability to bear more children. It all seemed so cruel. As if God had pulled back his hand and let them fall into a very deep, dark winter. An endless storm that buried them in frozen snow.

She still didn't understand why the accident had happened, but acceptance had blossomed after her breakdown. And later, hope as she painted the house, and rode her John Deere mower around the yard, seeing the grounds of their lovely home so differently once it came under her care. Once she had to do the work to keep it lovely. She'd always taken their beautiful yard for granted, hardly ever noticing the hard-working crew of Mexican immigrants that quietly came and went, caring for their grass and planters and vast backyard, which Jenny transformed after her breakdown by adding trees, and flowers, and the garden. Now she knew all the effort it took to grow a yard. To grow a garden. To grow life. If she couldn't grow babies, she'd grow other living things. Letting go of all the church work and a future law career proved easy. She wasn't that driven career woman anymore. But letting go of God was an entirely different matter. Jenny had found that God wasn't about to let go of her, even when she wanted to let go of him.

Joe had told her that all along. Flying out to be at her bedside at the hospital. Dedicating Matthew for them before he died. Filling Ken with the faith to set his sights on walking again. Joe and Ava had settled into Jenny and Ken's Colorado home and took care of it until she and Ken finally returned there two months after the accident. By then, she and Ken were broken in every possible way, Joe and Ava doing everything they could to help them adjust to their new, shattered lives.

Now here she and Ken were settled into Joe and Ava's spare bedroom in Tennessee more than two years later. Joe at work. Ava out getting her hair done. Ken had taken a hike somewhere in the nearby mountains. Jenny wondered how he was doing with his new hiking boots, custom-made to compensate for his shorter leg.

When Joe walked through the door an hour after lunch, it surprised her. She didn't think he would be home till later that afternoon.

"You're here early," she said, settling the baby on her lap.

"How's Claire?" Joe came over to where Jenny sat in the gliding rocker, crouching down beside the chair to examine his tiny daughter.

"She's wonderful. She hasn't made a peep since Ava left."

"How are you?" he asked with more concern than that question would normally warrant.

She smiled. "I'm all right."

It was hard to believe, but she was all right. Since the day Ken had torn apart the nursery, she'd steadily risen through the shadows of her own grief toward the light of God's unfailing love. Facing the birth of her brother's baby was difficult, but not as difficult as she'd thought it would be.

Joe smiled. "I have good news," he paused, his face cautious. "Ellie's willing to meet you and Ken this weekend."

Jenny's heart skipped a beat. Was it possible the girl would give them her baby?

"Sam just told me Ellie will be singing at church on Sunday. He says you and Ken could come to the service to hear her sing, and then if she doesn't change her mind, meet with her after church. He says her voice is incredible, and she writes her own songs." Joe stroked Claire's fuzz of blond hair.

"What if Ellie doesn't like us?" Jenny swallowed the lump in her throat. She held Claire more firmly, wishing she could spend the rest of her life with a baby in her arms.

Joe put his hand on her shoulder. "What's not to like about the two of you? You're incredible people. And God has good plans for you. Just wait and see."

The reference to Jeremiah 29:11 didn't upset Jenny anymore. In fact, she believed the promise now and grinned at Joe, her dimples matching his.

Chapter 22

Ellie's knees shook as she stepped onto the stage holding her Hummingbird across her body like a shield. Shawn encouraged her with a smile. He sat at the piano, ready to play for her as they had done in rehearsal. The bright stage lights blinded her, casting the audience in shadow. Pastor Sam had finished his sermon on the love of Christ. He'd compared that love to a rose.

Now it was Ellie's turn to sing "The Rose" for all these nice church people, and the only thing that kept her from fleeing was Shawn's expectant gaze holding her onstage.

The lyrics of the song were simple yet profound. Ellie knew the words so well she could sing them in her sleep. She didn't look out at the audience. Instead, she looked at Shawn. He gazed back at her so sweetly. Strangely, it felt like just the two of them were onstage. As if the room full of people melted away and only she and Shawn remained.

When he began to play the piano, ushering in the song, she closed her eyes, surprising herself with the heartfelt little prayer she said before singing. Her voice then swirled through the church without a hitch. Shawn was on her mind while she sang

"The Rose." She found herself thinking about him constantly since the camping trip and loved his beaming smile upon her now as she performed.

After thunderous applause, Pastor Sam stepped up onstage with them. "Thank you, Ellie, for that beautiful song. We are so happy to welcome you into our church family here at Holy Mountain." Pastor Sam then turned to the audience, repeating the words to the ending of the song. The words Pastor Sam read ran across a huge screen lowered onto the stage behind him. Ellie saw how the screen replaced the word "sun" in the song with "Son," referring to Jesus. A clever play on words.

"Love is not for the lucky and the strong," Pastor Sam continued. "Love is for the broken and the weak. His love is for those who accept what Jesus did for them on the cross. It's autumn outside today, folks, but it might be winter in your hearts. Some bitter snow might be falling on your life right now. If this is you and your heart is cold, I want to pray for you right now."

Ellie thought of her pregnancy. So unfair. How her heart felt frozen since the night it happened. She shouldn't have gone to that party at the lake. Shouldn't have drunk that beer. Shouldn't have climbed into that truck with Jamie so drunk and Jenner so strangely quiet behind the wheel.

"Remember that underneath that snow on your heart lies a seed; a seed that with the Son's love in the spring becomes the rose," Pastor Sam's words eased Ellie's bitter memories.

He prayed, "Dear Heavenly Father, we lift up all those hurting right now. You know these snow-covered people, and I ask that you melt away their pain. Bring your Holy Spirit right now to warm their hearts. To comfort them. To heal their wounds. In Jesus's name, amen."

Trembling, Ellie walked off the stage through a side door that led down a long hallway. That prayer did something to her. She wasn't sure what, but she felt all warm inside. And stronger. She couldn't explain it. Stopping in the hall, she leaned against the wall for a moment with her eyes closed. Just breathing in and out. In and out, feeling touched by the hand of God.

Her first realization was that she accepted this pregnancy now. Her future would be okay. Better than okay. She didn't know how she knew this, she just knew. Laughter bubbled up in her as tears spilled down her face. Relief overwhelmed her. Hope hit her too. Hope so big it covered all her fears. All her shame. Sensing she wasn't alone, she opened her eyes to find Shawn standing there with her.

"Are you all right?"

A laugh burst out of her mouth. Tears splashed down her cheeks. She couldn't answer him.

Stepping over to her, he took her in his arms. Her guitar was like a child crushed between them. Shawn leaned away, taking the Hummingbird from her. Then he drew her snugly against his chest.

"Shawn, what's going on?" demanded a woman striding down the hall toward them.

"Not now, Jill," Shawn answered her.

"Yes, now," the woman insisted shrilly. She was in front of them now.

"No," he said. "I'll meet you out in the lobby when I'm done."

"I'm not leaving," she said.

Raising her head from his chest, Ellie peeked at the woman. She had sounded like a mom but was actually a girl their age. A very pretty but very angry girl.

"Ellie, this is Jill."

Ellie stepped away from Shawn, bumping into the wall trying to escape. She didn't need to be told this was Shawn's girlfriend. Jill's possessive attitude screamed that.

Shawn still held her Hummingbird. Ellie reached for it, and for a moment he wouldn't let it go. With both of them grasping the guitar, Shawn's eyes apologized to her.

"Give her the guitar," Jill snapped.

Releasing the Hummingbird, Shawn turned his body to shield Ellie from Jill's wrath.

Pastor Sam was leading a couple down the hall. Jill was too incensed to notice the three adults headed their way.

"What were you doing with her?" Jill demanded.

Shawn looked past her to his father. "Hey, Dad. What's up?"

"Ellie, Shawn, Jill, this is Jenny and Ken McBride," said Pastor Sam.

Jill swung around in surprise. "Oh, hello, y'all." She used a completely different tone with the adults. Smiling, Jill stepped right over to shake the McBrides' hands.

"Jill, would you mind leaving us alone? The McBrides would like to speak with Ellie in private," Pastor Sam asked with a smile.

Jill looked at Shawn. He showed no sign of leaving. "Daddy wants you to come to the club with us for brunch," she said sweetly.

"I think my mom has something planned for my birthday," Shawn hedged.

"Be home by five o'clock," Pastor Sam told Shawn. "Your mother's plans are for this evening."

"You played the piano beautifully," Jenny McBride told Shawn. She seemed so sweet, all big brown eyes and dimples.

"Thanks, but Ellie was the amazing one." Shawn stepped aside, reaching his hand back to pull Ellie forward.

Ellie clutched her guitar to her body, shielding her stomach from view. She felt the bite of Jill's hostility, though it was veiled now. She also sensed the McBrides' kindness. And eagerness to know her.

"Ellie, this is Jenny, Pastor Joe's sister." Pastor Sam nodded his head at Shawn that it was time for him and Jill to go.

Regret in his gaze, Shawn headed down the hall with his girlfriend.

Jill grabbed Shawn's hand as they walked away. They appeared the perfect couple, both tall and crazy beautiful. Ellie's heart sank while watching them go.

"I've never heard 'The Rose' sung more beautifully, even by Bette Midler," Jenny said.

"Thank you." Ellie noted Jenny had Pastor Joe's sincere brown eyes. Right off, Ellie liked her.

"For a little thing, you have a mighty big voice," Jenny's husband, Ken, said.

Ellie turned to him, noting he too had sincere eyes, but they were greenish gold and sparkled with humor.

"You're from Colorado?" Ellie wondered if Colorado was far enough away. She wanted the baby to have a future well away from Sutterville.

"Yes," Jenny answered.

"Colorado Springs," Ken added.

Ellie liked how they spoke as a couple. Clearly, they were on the same team. Some couples you could tell right off were on opposing sides. The McBrides came across as united.

"You want to adopt my baby?" Ellie never could stomach small talk, especially in a tense situation. She needed to get to the point right away.

"Well," Ken said, "Jen and I haven't really talked it through yet."

"Why not?" Ellie looked at Jenny and watched tears flood her big brown eyes.

"We had a baby, Matthew," Jenny began.

Ken put his arm around his wife when she started crying. "I'm ready for a baby, but Jen might not be." He pulled his wife close, smiling at Ellie. "When I sing, the shower drain plugs its ears. It sure would be nice to have a son or daughter who can sing like you."

"I'm sorry," Jenny murmured. "I'm having a hard time letting go of our Matthew."

"No need to be sorry," Pastor Sam replied. "The Lord has good plans for you." He looked at Ellie. "All of you. Ellie, Jenny, Ken, please allow me to pray for you."

"Certainly," Ken said, bowing his head. Jenny rested her head against Ken's shoulder.

Ellie put her head down too, staring at her guitar. She wished Shawn still stood beside her, holding her by the shoulder the way Ken held Jenny.

"Lord, thank you for your good plans for your people, plans to prosper and not harm them, plans to give them a future and a hope. In Jesus's name. Amen."

The simple prayer gave the same impression Ellie had gotten in the hall leaning against the wall. A future and a hope. *Exactly.*

"May we take you to lunch?" Ken asked Ellie.

Ellie looked at Pastor Sam.

"Would you like to go with them?" he asked her.

A future and a hope. The McBrides were searching for that too. "Yes," Ellie answered, putting this couple's need before her own. What she really wanted to do was go home and wait for Shawn to get there. Miss Patsy was fixing him a birthday dinner tonight, though his birthday fell on Tuesday. He had football practice Tuesday, so Miss Patsy had chosen Sunday for the celebration.

"We'll drive you home after lunch," Ken said. "What's your favorite food?"

"Chinese," Ellie answered.

Ken whooped. "Chinese is our favorite food too."

"Really?" Ellie searched his eyes to see if he was lying.

"Really, we love Chinese," he assured her with an honest smile.

Chapter 23

The Larsons threw Shawn a lavish birthday party at the country club. It seemed half the congregation from church came, but Shawn's family didn't attend. The celebration took place on the club's sweeping lawn. A pumpkin hollowed out and filled with autumn flowers garnished each table. Jill, in a clingy white dress that hugged every curve of her lithe body, breathlessly sang him happy birthday over a microphone. Shawn wondered if she'd studied the Marilyn Monroe video of the actress singing happy birthday to President Kennedy. The spectacle of it embarrassed him immensely. The only redeeming aspect of the day was when Grandpa Larson presented him with a Bible. Not just any Bible, but a worn and tattered, endlessly underlined and highlighted Bible that had guided Grandpa for the past thirty years.

Dr. Larson gave Shawn a top-of-the-line set of golf clubs and said now that he was a man, he must regularly golf with them—them meaning Dr. Larson and his dad. Dr. Larson also paid for a full club membership for Shawn because, at eighteen, he could no longer ride on his parents' country club membership, which Dr. Larson paid for each year too.

Jill presented him with a Rolex watch. Other church and school friends—he really couldn't separate the two because almost all the families from his school attended his church as well—showered him with expensive gifts.

Shawn was shocked his family was not a part of this surprise party. Nobody said a word about the Kleins' absence. Shawn was too embarrassed to broach the subject. He heard whispers about Ellie singing during the service. The pregnant Sutterville girl sure could sing, but what was Pastor Sam thinking sharing the pulpit with the likes of her?

Shawn loved these church people, but he suddenly felt out of place among them. After Jill's brazen birthday song, he went and sat with Grandpa Larson, who seemed as uncomfortable with the lavish proceedings as Shawn was.

By four thirty that afternoon, Shawn was relieved to leave the party. Jill and Lily helped him load all the presents into his truck. Lily scampered off when Jill began to nag him.

"I'm really upset with your parents. Daddy said they chose to make their own birthday plans and refused to be a part of our party. They've changed since that pregnant Sutterville girl moved in with you."

Shawn didn't know how to answer Jill. He agreed that his parents acted differently these days. His mom hadn't been the same since Miss Kathy died, and his dad, well, Shawn didn't know what was going on there, and he told Jill so. After they talked, Jill planted a passionate kiss on his lips that made Shawn back against the door of his truck trying to escape her. He'd come to the conclusion she was bent on seducing him, and a war raged in him because of it. Part of him wanted to surrender to her. But another part of him despised Jill for turning their relationship into a battlefield. He'd made a vow to God to remain a virgin until marriage, and now it constantly felt like that vow was under assault.

"You shouldn't kiss me like that in public," he chastised her afterward.

Jill smiled seductively at him. "If you would let me kiss you like that in private, I wouldn't have to do it in public."

"What about the promise we made together at youth group two years ago?" Shawn opened his door, eager for the safety of his truck.

"What promise?" Jill edged her body against his, behind the truck door where nobody could see what she did with her hips, pressing her pelvis against him.

"The purity vow," Shawn rasped.

"The vow was to keep ourselves pure for each other. We've done that. God knows we're going to get married. This is no big deal, Shawn." She rubbed against him like a friendly cat.

Shawn untangled himself from her and climbed into the truck cab. She wouldn't allow him to close the door. "I've got to get home. My mom's fixing supper."

Jill pouted. "Your parents ruined our party. Just like your dad ruined church today by letting Ellie sing. Did you see how many people cried? Nobody wants to cry in church."

"I don't agree." Shawn reached past Jill and grabbed the door handle. He firmly nudged her out of the way as he closed the door.

She stood there glaring through the closed window as he started the engine and backed out of the parking space.

He drove home from the club in a foul mood. When he walked through the door of his house, everyone yelled, "Surprise!"

To his relief, he realized it was only his parents, brothers, and Ellie shouting, unlike the sea of people several hours ago hollering, "Surprise!"

His mom came forward to kiss his cheek. "How was your party at the club?"

"Why didn't you come?" He looked from his mom, to his dad, to Stephen and Seth, and then to Ellie. She wore the same pretty dress she'd had on at church that morning. It was modest but flattering on her petite frame. His mom had picked it out for her.

"Dad and I decided we didn't want to make a big deal out of your eighteenth birthday. Last year the Larsons bought you a truck. This year they insisted on a huge party at the club. We don't know what to do with them, Shawn."

Shawn looked at his brothers. "I didn't want to go anyway," Stephen said. "Most of those people are fakes."

"Grandpa and Grandma Larson were there." Shawn walked over to look at the cake his mom had made him. It was his favorite, strawberry. His old G.I. Joe soldier stood on the cake, up to his knees in frosting. As if rising from a fog, Shawn remembered how much he'd once wanted to be an army helicopter pilot. Out of nowhere, tears sprang to his eyes. He blinked hard, swallowing the tightness in his throat before turning to face his family.

"Why didn't you come, Seth? Your friends were there. Tommy's family gave me a hundred-dollar Amazon card."

Seth looked at their parents but didn't answer him.

Shawn could see Seth was disappointed to have missed the party.

"We felt it was time for our family to circle the wagons," Dad said, stepping over to Shawn. "Let's go for a walk, son."

Shawn's stomach tightened. When Dad called one of them "son," it usually meant something serious. He wasn't ready for a heart-to-heart with his dad. He didn't know what his heart was feeling these days.

"Samuel, can we eat first?" his mom asked. It wasn't like his mom to be tentative, which put Shawn on alert.

His dad sighed, hugged Shawn by the shoulder, then let go and headed for the dining room. Seth and Stephen followed. Ellie picked up a bowl of salad from the counter and looked at Shawn. He smiled at her. She sure looked pretty. It was the first time he'd ever seen her in a dress. She needed to wear those more often.

"You did a great job singing this morning," he told her.

"Thanks." She waited for him to go ahead of her into the dining room.

He wanted to ask her about meeting the McBrides but decided he would ask later. He also wanted to talk to her about how he'd found her in the hall at the church, laughing and crying. He knew it was a God thing and wanted to ask her about it. He couldn't remember the last time he'd felt God's presence. The thought saddened him.

"Are you ready for prime rib?" Mom gave him a big smile. Prime rib was the ultimate. His mom's homemade French fries, string beans, and corn on the cob drenched in butter and salt rounded out Shawn's favorite meal.

"Thanks, Mom." He walked over and gave her a hug and a kiss, taking the platter of prime rib from her hands so she wouldn't have to carry the large tray to the dining room herself.

"I'm sorry we missed your party," Mom said.

"This party is much better."

"Really?" She looked about to cry.

"Really." He kissed her on the cheek again and then followed Ellie to the dining room.

After dinner, his family presented him with presents. Nothing expensive. His mom's and Seth's were homemade gifts.

Mom had knit him a pretty cool sweater. It looked store bought and was black and soft.

Seth had carved him a little wooden car like the ones they used to race at church camp years ago. Those church camp races were serious competitions. The Klein boys often won with cars they made themselves.

Stephen presented him with a pocket knife, and Dad gave him a Bible. A men's devotional Bible. His dad also gave him a John Eldredge book. Shawn decided not to tell Dad about Grandpa Larson's Bible.

"I know you have a Bible, but this Bible addresses men's struggles," Dad explained.

"And John Eldredge. I must be a man now." Shawn held up the book with a grin. His dad had made him read *Wild at Heart* by Eldredge when he turned sixteen. Eldredge would be Dad's idol if Dad had an idol.

Ellie handed him an envelope. He could tell she was nervous about giving it to him. He opened it carefully, wondering what it might be. It took him a moment to realize she'd written him a song. The title of the song was "Come with Me."

"Are you going to sing this for us?" Shawn asked her.

"It's written for a guy to sing," she answered.

"You'll have to sing it for us, Shawn," his mom gushed.

"I'll have to practice it first." Shawn gave Ellie a great big smile.

They ended the evening with a fierce game of Yahtzee. Growing up, Shawn loved Yahtzee and usually won. When he didn't win, he would pout for the rest of the night.

"If you lose, no pouting," his mom warned.

"I'm eighteen, I don't pout anymore," Shawn assured her.

"I bet you pout if you lose," Seth said.

"I'll bet you ten dollars I don't pout and I don't lose," Shawn answered.

"Bet on," Seth eagerly agreed.

Shawn lost in Yahtzee.

Seth actually won the game, crowing like a rooster over the win, which made Shawn want to pound him. He paid Seth ten dollars and did his best to hide his pout from his family. "I'm ready for bed," he soon announced, stewing over his Yahtzee defeat.

After saying good night to everyone, Shawn brushed his teeth and took a shower. Once in bed, he lay there with his lamp on, reading Ellie's song. It was surprisingly spiritual, and he wasn't sure what he thought about it. Laying it aside, he picked up Grandpa Larson's Bible. Flipping it open, it landed on the book of Isaiah. He read for a while, and it reminded him of Ellie's song. He picked up her song and went over it again. She had to have read the Bible to have written these words. The song talked about a man and a woman coming to a mountain where God lived. About finding redemption at that mountain when everything else on earth failed them.

Again, Shawn put the song aside. He tucked Grandpa Larson's Bible away as well. He felt weary, especially remembering his coach had said this was a big week. The Vanderbilt scouts were coming. And they faced Sutterville again. Number 33 would be waiting. Shawn flexed his knee. It finally felt healed, but not strong like before the injury.

The G.I. Joe on his birthday cake crossed his mind. Jill would lose it if he even hinted he might be interested in joining the military. Reliving her birthday song to him this afternoon made him wince. What had gotten into her? He realized he was beginning to dread Jill's company and crave time with Ellie.

During the Yahtzee game, Ellie had thrown her head back and laughed. In that moment, it had hit him how amazing she was. Since the camping trip, she'd stopped wearing the dark eye makeup. Today at church she looked wholesome and sweet, and when she'd stepped out on the stage and her eyes had fastened on him in that way of hers, that you-are-my-lifeline way, he would have moved the Blue Ridge Mountains for her if he had to.

He flipped over on his stomach, burying his head in the pillow. *Sister,* he reminded himself. *She is nothing but a sister. A pregnant sister, you freak.*

Rolling onto his back again, he stared at the ceiling for another hour.

Finally, he got up and went downstairs for a glass of milk. He was opening the fridge when he heard something. Closing the refrigerator door, he listened. There it was again. A woman's whimper.

He strode out of the kitchen into the living room. For a few moments, all was still, and then it came again from down the hall.

Ellie.

He turned on the hall light and walked swiftly to her door. It was closed. All was quiet now. He was about to leave when he finally heard it again. Whimpering.

Turning the knob as quietly as possible, he stepped into Ellie's bedroom with his heart in his throat.

Chapter 24

Shawn walked to Ellie's side, overwhelmed with relief that she was alone in the room without the attacker he'd imagined there. "Ellie, wake up."

She cried out, startling him.

"Ellie, wake up," he said more urgently.

She began to howl.

He lifted her into his arms. "Ellie, you're having a nightmare. Wake up."

She grabbed him around the neck, holding on for dear life. When he sat down on the bed with her in his lap, she began to sob.

"Are you awake?" He stroked her hair, long and silky under his fingers.

She nodded, clinging to him.

"You scared the daylights out of me."

They sat that way for a while. Shawn was certain his parents and brothers would soon arrive, but no one came downstairs. He realized Ellie probably hadn't made enough noise for them to hear her, especially with the fans running upstairs. A warm spell was upon them. Everyone slept with a box fan in their window and would now until autumn changed the weather.

"What were you dreaming about?" he asked Ellie.

She shook her head, unwilling to answer.

"You don't want to talk about it?"

"No," she whispered.

"Okay." He tucked her against his chest. How long he held her that way, he didn't know. Resting his head on hers, he became aware of how soft her hair felt on his face and how sweet she smelled. She was smaller than Jill and fit perfectly in his lap. The need to protect her overwhelmed him.

"Do you have nightmares often?"

"Yes." Her voice came out soft and shaky.

"What do you do here alone after a nightmare?"

She took a deep, trembling breath. "I pray."

He smiled. "Does God help you?"

"I don't know." Ellie loosened her grip on his T-shirt.

Shawn didn't want to let her go. "The song you wrote for me, it's kind of spiritual."

"Is it?" She sat back on his lap to look in his eyes. The light from a full moon poured in the window, casting her in moonbeams. The sight of her took his breath away.

"Your song makes me think you believe I need to be saved."

She didn't break eye contact. "I think we all need to be saved."

"What kind of saving?"

"For you? Saving from your perfect life." Ellie scooted off his lap onto the bed beside him. "For me? Everything the opposite of your life."

Shawn would have liked to have held her longer. He lay back across the mattress, watching her. She looked fantastic there in the moonlight. "I'm sorry about the way Jill treated you today."

Ellie lay down too. She didn't respond to his apology. Her window was open, letting in the air and the night sounds. A whip-poor-will sang somewhere nearby. Shawn turned toward her, propping himself on an elbow to see her better. "What did you think of Jill?"

"She's beautiful."

"But you don't like her."

"I didn't say I didn't like her. I know girls like her. Head cheerleader, right?"

Shawn smiled and then grew serious again. "What's wrong with cheerleaders?"

"Nothing."

"Some cheerleaders are really nice."

"Some are."

He searched her face, drawn in by the delicateness of her features. Her hair covered one cheek, looking very dark without the sun highlighting it. "Do you feel pregnant yet?"

Ellie's eyes widened, and her mouth formed a little *O*. He couldn't tell if she was upset by his question or simply surprised by it. "Sometimes I feel pregnant."

"Do you have a belly at all? Because you still don't look pregnant to me."

Ellie rolled onto her back. Grabbing his hand, she placed it in the space between her hipbones, holding his palm there. "You tell me. Am I pregnant?"

For a moment, he was taken aback by the intimacy of touching her down there. Then the slight swell of her abdomen pushed all other thoughts from his mind. "Have you felt the baby move yet?"

"No." She stared at the ceiling.

"Do you miss the baby's dad?"

"No," she whispered adamantly.

His heart pounded hard and fast now. He removed his hand from her body. Relief poured through him upon learning she didn't miss the baby's father. He studied her face, trying to figure out what she was thinking. She still wouldn't look at him. When she took a sighing breath, a tear slipped out of the corner of her eye, rolling down her face onto the sheets.

"You think I'm easy." The accusation in her voice rocked him.

"No." He shook his head. "Now that I've gotten to know you, I don't think that at all."

"I've never made love to anyone."

He waited for her to explain, but she didn't.

"But you're pregnant?"

"I've never made love," she insisted.

"Okay." It was Shawn's turn to roll onto his back to stare at the ceiling. He knew she wasn't lying. Something was wrong. He leaned into the silence, into his confusion.

Ellie confused him. Jill confused him. His own life confused him.

Last year on his birthday, he'd been so certain of everything. This birthday he was certain of nothing. But he'd learned something: things weren't always what they seemed. Even though Ellie wasn't telling him everything, she was a lot more honest than Jill.

Together he and Ellie stared at the ceiling, not saying anything for a while, just thinking their own thoughts. The whip-poor-will outside sounded closer to the house now and more forlorn.

"I doubt you have any secrets." Ellie finally turned her head to look at him.

"I cheated on my anatomy test two weeks ago." Shawn's eyes connected with hers.

"Why?"

"I didn't have time to study, and Jill said the test was really hard. She gave me her cheat sheet. She took the test early because she had to miss class that day. Jill cheats all the time. I've never cheated before. I wish I hadn't two weeks ago. It would have been better to fail."

Ellie smiled.

"Have you ever cheated?"

"No."

"Really, not ever?"

"Not ever. I like studying."

"Have you ever lied?"

Her smile disappeared. "Yes."

"Often?"

"To certain people."

"Like who?"

"Like Clive."

"Who's Clive?"

"My dad."

"Who else?"

"Jamie."

"Jamie, your boyfriend?"

"Number 33," she admitted.

Emotion tore through Shawn. "The UT guy is your boyfriend?" He was stunned.

"Not anymore." Ellie turned her head to stare at the ceiling again.

Shawn sat up on the bed, running both hands through his hair. Somehow, he felt betrayed to find out Number 33 was her boyfriend. "I've got to get to bed; it's late." He knew his voice came out clipped, but he couldn't help it. All of a sudden, he was tangled up in knots.

Ellie didn't look at him. Wouldn't answer him.

At a loss for what to say now, Shawn got off the bed and walked out of the room. The whip-poor-will sounded like it was right outside the window now, singing its lonely song.

"I'll leave the hall light on for you," he told her from the door. Looking at her lying there on top of the covers, he realized she only wore a large T-shirt. Her hair lay tangled around her shoulders, and her bare legs stretched out slender and shapely on the bed. He remembered how soft her hair felt in his fingers. How good she smelled in his lap. How much he enjoyed being with her tonight. Had she looked like that for Number 33?

Number 33.

It cut him to the bone.

He stepped into the hall, closing his eyes for a moment against the ache he felt over Ellie with Number 33. The whip-poor-will continued its mournful song outside her window. Duncan, looking worried, slipped by him and padded into Ellie's room.

Heading for the kitchen, he finally got that glass of milk he'd been after, but his stomach hurt so bad he couldn't drink it. On the counter sat the remains of his birthday cake, G.I. Joe sprawled on his face on the plate.

Chapter 25

Jamie tied his cleats tight as he waited for the game against Mountain View to begin. The stadium at MVA looked like a college arena. It always galled Jamie to play down here in the valley at this rich school. This field might as well have been sodded with money instead of the fake turf that snagged his cleats when he least expected it, ruining a rush that guaranteed him the sack.

Back in Sutterville, the stadium doubled as the fairground's rodeo arena. In September, when you hit the ground in Sutterville, you might come up with horse or cow crap in your teeth, considering the fair ran through August and nobody bothered to clean up the manure after the rodeo.

In the past day, the weather had finally blown in cold. Jamie put his helmet on, and his freezing ears slowly warmed up. Quincy Bronson sat down beside him on the bench. He didn't particularly like Bronson, but Bronson was a solid teammate. The guy played hard and dirty. A pillar on the line because nobody got by Bloody Bronson. That's what everybody called him.

"I heard something real interesting," Bronson said.

Jamie didn't want to talk. He wondered why Bronson pursued this conversation, considering Bronson, like everybody else, knew Jamie didn't like to chat before games. Jamie ignored him, hoping he'd shut up.

"Ellie's here." Bronson stared at him. Clearly, he had more to say.

Jamie jumped out of his seat. "Where is she?"

"She's sitting with Number 7's mom and dad."

"Hudson's folks?"

"Not our Number 7. MVA's Number 7." Bronson pointed to the home stands.

Jamie took off his helmet. "Their pretty boy quarterback? Sunshine?"

"Yeah." Bronson clamped his teeth shut, making a clicking sound.

"Why would Ellie be sitting over there?" Jamie tried to see across the field into MVA's stands. It felt like Ellie had been gone forever. Nobody knew where she'd disappeared to except her old man, and he wasn't talking.

"Cooper knows a guy on the other team. He says everyone in Mountain View knows Ellie's knocked up."

"What are you talking about?" Jamie sat back down hard enough to rattle the bench. The whole defensive line listened to their conversation now.

"Ellie's pregnant. She's living with MVA's quarterback."

The announcer asked everyone to stand for the national anthem. Jamie tucked his helmet under his arm, laying his other hand across his heart. He could hardly breathe. His eyes scanned MVA's line across the field. They too were standing now with their helmets under their arms and their hands on their hearts. Jamie picked out the MVA pretty boy quarterback by his number. Seven. How could Ellie be living with him? It felt like he was having a nightmare, but he was wide awake and ready to slay someone.

Mountain View won the toss and received the kickoff. His mind reeling with Ellie, Jamie watched from the sidelines until special teams came off the field and his defensive team rushed on. He found his place on the field in a daze of thoughts. The play broke and MVA's quarterback, Sunshine, pulled his ghost move. Jamie ended up sprawled on his back, hit hard by an MVA offensive lineman as he went all out for the sack. He stared up into the bright lights of the stadium, wondering how on earth Ellie could do this to him. Didn't she know how much he loved her?

Bronson leaned over Jamie. "Hey, man, get up. Can you get up?" He grabbed Jamie's jersey with both hands, hefting him to his feet. "Get your head in the game. I told you about Ellie so you would take out Number 7. The Vanderbilt scouts are here tonight. Don't you want to bury Number 7 in front of those scouts?"

The shock was wearing off. A surge of fury unfurled in Jamie. Bronson smacked him hard on the back. "Let's do this thing!" Bronson shouted in his face.

With Bronson's spit on his cheeks, Jamie jogged back behind the line just in time for the next play. Again, Number 7 disappeared in the rush, throwing a long pass that ended in a touchdown for MVA. The crowd went wild. Two minutes into the game and Jamie felt like a complete and total loser. He jogged off the field wondering if he dreamed all this. It was an unbelievable nightmare tangling his thoughts and ability to play ball.

On the bench, while watching his offensive team take a beating, Jamie replayed the past summer over in his mind. How could Ellie have ended up with MVA's quarterback? It seemed impossible. Absolutely, out of this world impossible.

During the last game in Sutterville, when he put Number 7 in a pretzel that ripped Sunshine's knee, Jamie remembered the pretty boy's eyes. There was no anger in his gaze. And after the game, when Jamie went over to apologize for messing up his knee, Number 7 couldn't have been a nicer guy.

"Don't worry about it," Number 7 had said, smiling while icing his knee.

Jamie was going to kill him. Literally kill Number 7 tonight.

He didn't care if Sutterville won or lost this game. He didn't care if he missed every ball-carrying receiver that came his way. His one focus tonight was Number 7.

Death to Number 7.

Chapter 26

In the third quarter of the game, MVA pushed ahead with a touchdown. Shawn rolled out of the touchdown play marveling at how well the night was going. He reminded himself the Vanderbilt scouts sat in the stands. He should mess up to discourage them from recruiting him, but his competitive nature proved too strong. He'd always been like that, super competitive in everything. It was a curse as well as a blessing.

His passes connected like bullets tonight. He hadn't been sacked at all, even with Number 33 zeroed in on him like a heat-seeking missile. Shawn read each play before it unfolded, his instincts never more sure. Like the cold finally arriving in Tennessee, Shawn had bite. He passed to Brown, who took the ball into the end zone for the touchdown.

Turning to the sidelines after the touchdown, Shawn watched Jill do her tumbling routine. Three consecutive flips and a split, then Jill waving her pom-poms to him as she always did. As was his habit, he waved back at her. And then he looked above Jill to the sidelines, scanning the stands for his parents and Ellie.

He found Ellie standing beside his mom, looking small, wearing a coat that belonged to his mom. He wondered how she felt watching Sutterville losing this game. They hadn't really spoken since her nightmare. Since her confession about Number 33. And even though he ached over it, he missed her more than he wanted to admit. He sure was glad she had come to the game tonight. At least he could look up in the stands from time to time and see her there watching him. He hoped she watched him and not Number 33.

Ellie's baby daddy.

Shawn couldn't stop thinking about it. He jogged off the field and drank some water.

On the return kickoff, MVA knocked the ball loose from the Sutterville receiver. Shawn was back on the field before his breathing leveled out from the touchdown play. In the huddle, he called for a long pass. Brown, his fastest receiver, would accept the ball on the left side of the field. The play unfolded perfectly until Brown, for some unknown reason, ran to the right.

What's Brown doing?

Shawn scrambled for more time to complete the pass. Brown finally worked over to the left side. Shawn snapped the ball off to him with Sutterville's defenders hot on his heels. With the ball out of his hands, Shawn didn't expect the hit. He got plowed over like a freight train. His leg snapped. The sound of his thigh bone breaking exploded on the field like a gunshot. The pain stunned him.

Number 33 stood over him.

Shawn thrashed in agony on the ground.

"That was for Ellie," the Sutterville player said before he walked away.

Through a haze of pain, Shawn wondered if he had heard Number 33 correctly. What was for Ellie?

Referees swarmed Number 33, throwing yellow flags in his face.

Medics ran onto the field with the coaches. A moment later, Shawn's dad grabbed his hand.

"I'm here, son."

"My leg's broken," Shawn said on a burst of adrenaline.

"I know. We heard it in the stands," his dad said.

"You're in my hands, Shawny. I'll take care of you." Dr. Larson bent over him, nudging his dad out of the way.

Dad released his hand and stepped back to let Dr. Larson do his work.

After that, with Dr. Larson holding his leg, Shawn blacked out.

He came to in the ambulance when they stuck an IV in his arm but then blacked out again. At the hospital, they put Shawn completely under for surgery.

Dr. Larson operated.

A day later, Shawn was still in the hospital, his leg up in traction. When he awoke, Ellie was the first person he saw in his room. She stood there beside his mom. Seth sat in one chair and Stephen in another, playing cards at a little table near the window of his hospital room.

"Dr. Larson pulled some strings for this private suite," his mom explained with a smile.

The room didn't look like a suite to Shawn. "How bad's my leg?" he asked.

"The surgery went well," his mom answered.

Shawn looked at Ellie and could tell right away she hadn't slept. His mom appeared haggard too. Seth and Stephen looked fine. They didn't even stop their card game to greet him.

A moment later, his dad and Dr. Larson walked into the room. Both men carried a cup of coffee. Dad was in the same clothes he'd worn the night before at the football game. Dr. Larson wore dull green scrubs.

"Shawny, good to see you awake," Dr. Larson said.

"How are you feeling, son?" Dad put his arm around Mom.

"How bad is my leg?" Shawn asked Dr. Larson.

Dr. Larson smiled. "It should be good as new by January."

"January?" Shawn was taken aback.

"You're done with football for this year, but you'll be able to play for Vanderbilt next year," Dr. Larson said. "I do good work. I made sure of that."

"The scouts talked to your coaches after the game. They want you, Shawn. If your leg heals all right," Dad explained.

"It'll heal perfect." Dr. Larson sounded offended by his dad's use of the word "if."

"Do you mind, Allen?" his dad said.

"Mind what?" Dr. Larson pretended he didn't understand. Shawn knew better. He could sense the tension between the two men, once the best of friends, now at odds. What was going on?

"Do you mind letting us have some time alone with our son?"

"You're not alone with your son." Dr. Larson gave Ellie a pointed look.

"I'll leave." Ellie headed for the door.

"No, you won't," Mom said. "You're a part of this family, Ellie. You stay, honey. Dr. Larson is leaving."

Shawn could tell his parents had had it with Dr. Larson.

"I told Jill I would call her as soon as you were awake." Dr. Larson turned his back on his parents, giving his full attention to Shawn. "She has been very worried about you, Shawny."

"That's why she's here," Stephen said sarcastically, dropping a handful of cards onto the table.

"Jill went home to freshen up." Shawn could tell Dr. Larson was annoyed with Stephen. Actually, Dr. Larson seemed irritated with everyone in the room but him.

"Considering she's the only one who slept all night, Jill should be fresh as the morning dew." Stephen gathered up the cards and began to shuffle without looking at Dr. Larson.

"She needs to get some sleep." Dr. Larson nodded to Ellie. "You're a child carrying a child," he told her. "Go lay down somewhere, young lady."

Ellie paled under his attack.

"Allen, I will handle my family," Dad said with more resolve than Shawn had ever heard from him with Dr. Larson.

"Teenage pregnancies are risky . . ." Dr. Larson began.

Mom put her arm around Ellie. Dad stepped to Ellie's other side. "Dennis Hammons says Ellie and her baby are doing great," Mom responded, her voice clipped.

"Dennis is lost in a fog of grief. I wouldn't allow him to care for my pregnant cat right now," said Dr. Larson.

"Dennis is a more than competent doctor," Mom argued.

"Have you gained any weight?" Dr. Larson asked Ellie, ignoring Shawn's mom.

Ellie didn't answer him. She looked about to cry.

"She's fine." Dad seemed determined to get Dr. Larson to back down. He moved to Dr. Larson's side. "Let's go refill our coffees. I need to talk to you alone, Allen."

Dr. Larson leaned over Shawn's bed. "Jill's on her way over right now," he said, though he hadn't even called his daughter yet.

"Sure," Shawn answered, concerned mostly for Ellie.

Dr. Larson left the room with his dad.

"I've had it with that man!" said Mom. "Don't you let him upset you, honey. Your baby is perfect. Dennis said you will start putting on weight now that you are hitting your second trimester."

Ellie shrugged her shoulders, but tears swam in her eyes.

"Come over here. You're tired." Shawn patted the bed. His hospital bed was wide enough for two people, even with the contraption his leg hung in.

Mom loosened her arm, and Ellie moved toward him. She looked exhausted. And upset.

"Lie down with me." He scooted a little to make room for her. He felt fuzzy and kind of drunk from the pain meds, though he'd never been drunk in his life, and really didn't know what drunk felt like.

"Yes," Mom agreed. "We won't be leaving for a while. You need to rest, Ellie."

"Where are we going to lie down?" Stephen motioned to himself and Seth.

Mom walked to the door. "You can find a comfortable bench in the lobby, or you and Seth can come along with me. I'm going to get breakfast for us."

Seth jumped to his feet. "I'm starved. I'm going with you, Mom."

After sullenly glancing at Shawn and Ellie in the bed, Stephen followed them out the door.

Chapter 27

Shawn watched television with the volume down low, enjoying Ellie cuddled beside him on his hospital bed—until Jill arrived.

"This is ridiculous," Jill said from the doorway when she saw them lying there together.

Ellie stumbled off the bed, nearly falling on the floor in her haste to escape Jill's wrath.

"Lay back down, Rose," Shawn commanded, unable to do anything more with his leg in traction.

Ellie took one look at Jill and fled the room.

"Rose?" Jill stalked over to the bed. "I thought her name was Ellie."

"Ellie Rose," Shawn answered, angry at Jill, but doing his best to keep his cool.

"I won't tolerate that slut here. Your parents need to send her back to Gutterville."

"You mean Sutterville?"

"You heard me, Shawn. Gutterville."

"Your true colors are showing, Jill."

"My true colors? What are my true colors?" She plopped down in the chair beside his bed.

"It's all about you. You've always been that way."

"And you're not?" Jill laughed without humor.

"Not like you." Shawn stared at the TV. *The Today Show* hummed along.

Changing tactics, Jill made herself comfortable in the chair. "Don't you see what's happening?" Her tone turned consoling. "The devil wants to break us up, and he's using that pregnant skank to do it."

Shawn gave up pretending to watch Matt Lauer reporting from Brazil on the acai berry. "You've got to be kidding me?"

"Can't you see it, babe?"

"No," he said, frustrated beyond measure with Jill. "I can't see that at all."

"We haven't gotten along since she got here. Your parents have changed too. It's all Ellie's fault. She's a messed-up girl from a messed-up town. She came from a trailer park, Shawn."

He turned off the television, glaring at Jill. He wished he could jump out of the bed and shake some sense into her.

"It's true." Jill rose from the chair and sat down on his bedside. "After the game, Lauren told me Number 33 bragged about taking you out. He said he did it for Ellie. All these bad things are happening because of her."

Shawn rang the call bell on his bed, summoning the nurse. When the nurse arrived, he asked for more pain medication.

"We gave you pain medication a little while ago." The nurse checked the IV bandaged to his arm. Liquid dripped down the line from a bag of fluid the nurse adjusted.

"Okay. Sorry for bothering you." Shawn threw his head back on the pillow in frustration.

"I'll send the doctor in to talk to you about your pain level when he returns," the nurse said.

"No," Shawn told the nurse. "I don't want to see the doctor."

"You don't want to see Daddy?" Jill asked sweetly.

The nurse raised her eyebrows at the two of them.

"You can go," Jill informed the nurse.

The nurse looked at Shawn sympathetically before leaving.

"You're so rude." Shawn refused to look at Jill now. He stared out the window at the maples blazing red in the hospital courtyard.

"The painkillers are making you cranky." Jill smoothed the sheet on his bed.

"It's not the painkillers, it's you," he said.

"Look at me," she demanded.

Shawn kept his gaze on the maples.

Jill dug her nails into his arm. "We need to pray together."

Shawn laughed.

"Why are you laughing?"

"You never want to pray."

"That's not true!"

"Lower your voice. This is a hospital."

Jill jumped to her feet. "I don't care if this is a hospital! My daddy owns this hospital!"

"I want to break up." Shawn steeled himself, expecting her to really make a scene now.

"No way!" she screamed.

"I'm serious." Shawn lowered his voice as Jill raised hers.

"So am I! You are not breaking up with me, Shawn Klein!"

"You're screaming, Jill. The whole hospital can hear you freaking out."

The same nurse Jill had asked to leave returned.

"Get out of here! This is none of your business!" Jill screeched at the nurse when she walked through the door.

"I'm going to have to ask you to leave, young lady," the nurse replied.

"I am Dr. Allen Larson's daughter." Jill softened her voice. "I will have you fired for asking me to leave, Nurse Parker." Jill read the nurse's name off her badge.

The nurse did not respond to the threat.

"Stop, Jill. I can't take anymore," Shawn said.

Jill stared at Shawn for a fierce moment. The nurse stood her ground.

"I'm so done with this. You and your father have controlled me for years. I'm sick of it." Shawn kicked his good leg in frustration.

"Is he on morphine?" Jill asked the nurse.

The nurse refused to answer her.

"We'll finish this conversation later when you are in your right mind." Jill stalked from the room, glaring the nurse down as she left.

"Can you please give me more painkiller?" Shawn begged the nurse.

"It will put you back to sleep," the nurse said.

"Good. Give me a month's dose."

"Only a month?" the nurse teased.

Shawn was relieved the nurse didn't seem worried about losing her job. He was anxious she might. "Two months would be good. Better yet, make it eight months."

"Why eight months?" The nurse came over to check his IV again.

"I graduate high school in eight months."

"The nurse smiled. "You don't want to miss the rest of your senior year, do you?"

"We go to school together." Shawn nodded toward the door Jill had just flounced through.

The nurse took out a syringe and injected a shot of medicine into his IV line. "Good night, sweet prince."

"Dr. Larson will be mad at you." Shawn tried to focus on the nurse.

"Don't worry, Dr. Larson likes me." The nurse winked at him before Shawn surrendered to sleep.

Chapter 28

Upon returning home from the hospital, Shawn began home-schooling with Ellie.

Jill came by unexpectedly several weeks after his injury. “Shawn, where are you?” she called, letting herself in the front door as she always did, then breezing into the living room with a carton of strawberry ice cream in her hand.

Shawn lay on the couch. He and Ellie had just started eating strawberry ice cream. At the sound of Jill’s voice, Ellie set down her bowl and rushed out of the room. It was mid-morning. Shawn wondered why Jill wasn’t at school.

“Oh, you already have ice cream. Where’s Ellie?” Jill looked around with a smile on her face.

Seeing that smile, Shawn’s guard slid squarely into place. “Hiding from you.”

“Really?” Jill feigned surprise.

“What do you want with Ellie?”

“I brought the ice cream for you. I’m taking Ellie shopping in Knoxville with me today.”

"You're kidding." Shawn put his half-eaten ice cream beside Ellie's bowl on the end table. Ellie's ice cream was beginning to melt.

"I'm not kidding. Did she go upstairs?"

"She's probably in her room down the hall." Shawn sat upright on the couch, wrestling his broken leg into a comfortable position.

Jill headed down the hall in search of Ellie. She came back in a little while with Ellie in tow.

Ellie had her purse tucked under her arm. Her hair was pulled up into a ponytail, and she wore a sweatshirt with jeans and tennis shoes.

"You're going to Knoxville?" Staring at the two of them together, Shawn couldn't believe it.

"Of course we are," Jill answered.

Ellie didn't say a thing. Shawn couldn't read her face. She didn't look happy. She didn't look sad. She looked ready to leave the house.

"I'll have her back before your mom and dad get home." Jill knew Shawn's parents' schedule better than he did. She was like that, into everybody's business all the time.

"You didn't eat your ice cream," Shawn told Ellie, not wanting her to go.

"I'm taking her to lunch," Jill answered before Ellie could respond. Jill looped her arm through Ellie's. Ellie looked surprised but didn't protest.

Shawn wondered what Jill had said to Ellie to convince her to go shopping. A moment later, they disappeared out the door.

He considered hobbling over to the window to watch them drive away in Jill's white Mercedes but decided against it because his leg hurt. With Ellie there with him, he hadn't noticed how his leg throbbed, but now that she was gone with Jill, the pain pounded away at him.

He picked up the bottle of eight-hundred-milligram Motrin on the end table and tossed one pill in his mouth, drinking Ellie's melted ice cream straight out of the bowl to wash it down.

Seeing Jill helped him remember how hard Dr. Larson was taking their breakup. When he'd tried to return his truck a few days ago, Dr. Larson wouldn't hear of it. "You're the only son I have. Keep the truck. What would I do with a pickup? Go fishing? I don't fish. I golf. Can you see me driving your truck around the golf course?" Dr. Larson had continued to examine Shawn's leg, even though he was upset.

"What about your older daughter's husband?" Shawn had asked. "Maybe Phillip would like to have the truck."

"Phillip's an idiot. I'd rather dump the truck at the junkyard than give it to him." After that, Dr. Larson had assured Shawn his leg was healing just fine and sent him on his way with a sad smile.

Later that afternoon, Ellie returned from her trip to Knoxville with Jill. She entered the house by herself and went straight to her room. Shawn tried to talk to her as she passed through the living room, but she waved and kept walking. He could tell she had a lot on her mind.

That night at dinner, when she finally came out of her room, he noticed Ellie's nails were painted bright pink. Jill always got her nails done in Knoxville. Ellie had probably had her toes done too. This bothered him. Jill loved manicures and pedicures, but Shawn had decided since Ellie moved in that he much preferred a girl who painted her own fingers and toes. He'd watched Ellie do it herself several times and was fascinated by the act. Stephen and Seth also became open-mouthed spectators when Ellie painted her toenails. There was something utterly intriguing about the way Ellie rolled her jeans up her calves, her long hair draping her face as she painted each toe.

After dinner, Ellie and her pink nails quietly returned to her room. She'd said only "please" and a "thank you" at the table and wouldn't talk about anything with the rest of them. Shawn decided not to rat her out and tell his parents she's spent the day in Knoxville with Jill. Because of his broken leg, he now slept on the living room couch. He couldn't get up and down the stairs without a load of pain and trouble. Lying on the couch after everyone went to bed that night, Shawn watched *I Love Lucy* videos with the volume turned down. He longed for Ellie to have a nightmare so he could go to her, keeping his ear cocked for any sound from her room.

He must have drifted off to sleep for a while because when he finally heard Ellie, it felt like the middle of the night. He propped himself up on his crutches and went to her. Entering her room, he made his way over to the bed and lay down beside her. "Hey, Rose, I'm here," he said, reaching out to touch her.

She rolled right into his arms, cuddling up close. Now he could sleep for several hours. Because of his broken leg, he never slept more than a few hours at a stretch. It was easy to wake before his parents and brothers and get back to the couch without anyone the wiser.

He and Ellie never talked about this sleeping arrangement between them. In the night, he came to be with her when she had nightmares, and in the morning, both pretended it never happened. Imagining he hadn't held her for hours happened easily because it felt like a dream to him anyway. A dream he liked so much that on the nights Ellie didn't have a nightmare, he was downright disappointed not to sleep with her.

Most mornings, Ellie did not rise till everyone else left the house. When she came from her room the day after shopping with Jill, she was dressed in jeans and a sweatshirt with her hair in a neat ponytail, ready to go somewhere. The bright pink nail polish was no longer on her fingers.

"Hey," Shawn said to her as she passed the couch.

"Hey," she responded but kept walking.

"You going somewhere?"

"If I can use your truck." She had her purse draped over her shoulder.

Shawn had never asked if she had a driver's license. There had never been a need for Ellie to drive. He reached for his crutches. In sweatpants and a T-shirt, he figured he was good to go if Ellie ran upstairs and got him his tennis shoe. "So you can drive?" he asked her.

She shrugged her shoulders like driving was no big deal.

"Okay, let's go. Can you please go get my shoe for me? The left one. It's in my closet. I need socks too."

Ellie's face was unreadable, but he sensed she did not want him tagging along today. "Sorry," he said. "I can't let you take my truck without me. Mom and Dad would be upset."

"Do you think your mom and dad want you up walking around?" Ellie challenged him.

"Nope. But you look set on going someplace, so let's go."

"You can't go with me." She moved her purse to her other shoulder, avoiding looking into his eyes.

They'd grown close since he'd injured his leg. He knew she was anxious. "I know something's wrong. Did Jill upset you yesterday?"

"No. Jill was really nice to me."

He took a deep breath, frustrated that she wouldn't tell him the truth. "I need my shoe and some socks. Please get them for me."

Ellie dropped her purse on the couch and left. She returned a few minutes later with his shoe and two white ankle socks.

"You got the right socks. I can't wear a knee sock with this cast."

"Shawn . . ."

He was slipping on the socks when she said his name. "Yeah?"

"You can't go with me."

Before answering her, he put on his shoe. "Why not?"

"You just can't go."

Shawn used his crutch to get to his feet. With both crutches under his arms, he propelled himself over to the door. "You can't take my truck without me."

She scooped her purse off the couch. For a moment, she stared at him hard, and then said, "Come on."

The smell of new asphalt lingered from the neighborhood streets being repaved a week earlier. "I should get a sweatshirt," Shawn said as he stepped out of the warm house onto the front porch. It was a crystal-clear autumn morning. Color splashed the trees in gold, orange, and red splendor. A chill in the air made everything crisp and clear.

"I'll grab it." Ellie turned back at the door.

Shawn slowly made his way to the truck. Ellie came out with his MVA sweatshirt and locked the door behind her. He climbed in the passenger seat using mostly arm strength to situate himself in the pickup cab. "These are going to have to ride in the back," he told Ellie, motioning to the crutches he held out the door.

She came around and took them from him, placing the padded poles in the truck bed. Then she went to the driver's side and climbed behind the wheel. Scooting the seat up, she made herself comfortable. She looked cute behind the wheel. "Do you know how to drive?" he asked.

"Yes, but it's been a while." It took her a moment to figure out how to start the truck.

"A long while or a short while?"

She didn't answer him. Within five minutes, he knew she wasn't an experienced driver. He kept his mouth shut about it. When he was learning to drive, he hated how his mom offered endless advice from the passenger seat.

"Is where we're going a surprise?"

Ellie didn't respond. She chewed her bottom lip, concentrating on the road.

They cruised through Mountain View, postcard perfect today with her maples and oaks ablaze. When they reached the highway, Shawn realized they were headed for Knoxville. "Are we going shopping again?"

"No. I have an appointment." Ellie didn't take her eyes off the road. She drove like a little old lady, which made him grin.

"Where is your appointment? Are you going to have them put a different color on your nails?" Jill had done that before. Not liking her nail polish, she'd returned to the salon to have them repainted the next day.

"We're going to Volunteer Women's Medical Clinic," Ellie admitted.

"I thought Dr. Hammons was taking care of you."

Merging onto the highway, Ellie nearly sideswiped an eighteen-wheeler. Shawn squealed like a little kid. His scream caused Ellie to swerve back into the right lane. The truck boiled past, blaring its horn.

Ellie cursed.

Shawn had never heard her use foul language before. The four-letter word surprised him more than almost getting wiped off the road by a semi.

"Take the next exit," he commanded. He could see her hands shaking on the wheel. The exit happened to be the same one they took for the lake where they'd camped. "Just pull over when the shoulder opens up after we're off the freeway."

She didn't pull over after exiting the freeway.

"You can ease off the road right up here. There. Right there." Shawn pointed to a turnout shaded by red-leafed trees. Woods ablaze in autumn glory lined the turnout, casting deep shadows.

Ellie kept driving.

"Are you going to pull over?"

Without looking at him, she shook her head. Tears slipped out of her eyes, falling down her cheeks.

"Are we going to the lake now?" Shawn didn't know what to make of Ellie's behavior, but he realized they had all day to figure it out.

"Can we head for the lake?" she asked with a sniffle.

"Sure. Mom and Dad won't be home till tonight. We just need to be back by this afternoon."

They drove nearly all the way to the lake without speaking. Now that the highway was behind them, Ellie drove better. "Watch for deer," Shawn warned as the woods along the road thickened. She no longer cried, but she didn't talk either as they drove into the mountains.

When the lake came into view, Shawn smiled. "I wish we'd brought Duncan."

Ellie didn't look at him until she parked the truck in the place where they'd watched the sunset together upon their last visit here.

The woods around the lake appeared painted by a master craftsman. Shawn knew only God could make a landscape so beautiful. The smell of wood smoke wafted in the air, though they saw no fires. Campgrounds dotted the lake. Perhaps someone had a fire going. It was cold up here.

They sat in the truck, watching the lake. Two loons swam out in the water, diving now and then in search of a meal. Not a person in sight. Being at the lake reminded Shawn of all the good times he had camping here while growing up. And in this very spot, he first realized what a special girl Ellie was. That being with her made him happy. His leg hurt right now, but he didn't care. He wouldn't have missed this trip to the lake with her for anything.

"Duncan would be swimming after those loons had we brought him. I wouldn't be able to rescue him right now. It's better he didn't come." Shawn smiled at Ellie, and she finally smiled back, but her eyes shone with sadness.

A bad feeling crept over him. Like insect legs crawling up his spine. Something was wrong. He could feel it. He could see it on Ellie's face. "So why were you going to that women's clinic?"

She returned her attention to the lake. "This place is so pretty. I feel God here. Don't you feel Him here?"

"Do they do abortions at that clinic?"

Ellie looked surprised by his question.

"Did Jill talk you into getting an abortion?" he pressed.

Gripping the steering wheel, she took a deep breath. "I don't know why, but Jill wants to help me. She took me to the clinic yesterday. The woman I spoke with there really cared about me. All the women there cared."

"Jill doesn't want to help you. She wants to get you away from me." Shawn scooted toward Ellie. It took some real effort with his broken leg to get closer to her on the truck seat. "If you have an abortion, you'll be done with us. You'll go back to Sutterville, just like Jill wants."

Ellie closed her eyes, bent her head to rest it on the steering wheel, as if she was so very tired.

Shawn could feel her despair. It was like a cold black cloud in the truck. He reached out and placed his hand on her back. Under her ponytail. The silkiness of her hair brushed the back of his fingers. With the sun pouring through the truck's windows, he noticed the red in her tresses. Ellie's hair was brown, definitely brown, but under the sun, some red appeared. A red that surprised him. Usually, he forgot Ellie was pregnant. She didn't look pregnant. Didn't act pregnant either. But today he knew she was pregnant. Like the red in her hair you only saw in the sunshine, a baby was inside her. Growing. Developing. A real baby.

"Come here," he said, motioning her to slide over to him. He could scoot no farther because of his broken leg.

Finally, she came to him. Crying, but making no sound. Shawn had never seen someone weep silently that way before.

He pulled her into his arms, up against his chest nice and tight.

She trembled, grief shaking her the way earthquakes tremble the ground.

"Don't listen to Jill," he whispered in her ear. "She only knows how to live selfishly. You are doing what's best for the baby. That's sacrifice, and sacrifice is a beautiful thing. I love that you are sacrificing your life right now to give your baby a life."

Ellie looked up at him, her eyes flooded with tears. "Please don't lie to me."

"I'm not lying. I mean it." It hit him that he wanted to kiss her. Right then he wanted to kiss her.

"You don't really know me," she said, tears spilling down her cheeks.

"How can you say that? I've never held a girl in my arms as much as I've held you. I love holding you, Ellie. It makes me happy that you have nightmares. Not because of the nightmares, but because I get to hold you during the night." He smiled, but he was scared to death of telling her how he truly felt. Tears came to his eyes too. He wanted her to know how much he cared about her. That together they would see this pregnancy through. Perhaps together they could raise the baby.

She looked at him for an intense moment, tears streaking her face, like she might tell him something he needed to know. He could see she wanted to confess something. But then she closed her eyes, took a shaky breath, and opened her eyes to look at him again. "Do you mind if I go for a walk around the lake?"

Disappointment tore through him. He hadn't expected her to walk away. Loosening his arms, he allowed her to slide away from him on the seat.

"Shawn . . ." She reached out and grabbed his hand, weaving her fingers through his for a second. "Thanks for being my friend."

"Sure." His throat ached with emotion.

She let go of his hand and then opened the truck door and got out. Cold mountain air poured into the truck. "I won't be long," she assured him.

He watched her walk toward the water and then skirt the lake. A lone figure growing smaller. Maybe if he had kissed her, she would have told him that important thing. He could see she longed to say something he probably needed to know. *Thanks for being my friend.* Is that all he was to her? Just a friend?

She was a speck now in the distance. He could see the loons on the water better than he could see Ellie. The birds had split up and hunted on their own now. Miles of lake stretched between the two birds.

Leave it to Jill to take Ellie to get an abortion. How tempting for a girl to get rid of a pregnancy and just go on with her life. No baby to worry about. Ellie could go back to high school in Sutterville. Probably go back to Number 33.

Shawn remembered the look on Number 33's face when he said, "That was for Ellie," after the late hit. He leaned his head on the seat and closed his eyes. The sun was like a warm blanket on his face, though the truck cab felt cold. His leg throbbed, and he wished he'd brought his pain pills along. The pills fuzzed out his brain, making everything okay even when it wasn't.

Chapter 29

Tomorrow marked the halfway point of Ellie's pregnancy. She was going for her ultrasound. Shawn wanted to go too. That night, he talked to his mom about it.

"I don't know if it's appropriate that you are in the room during the ultrasound," his mom said.

"I'm Ellie's family too," Shawn argued.

"I'll think about it." Mom helped him get comfortable in bed, propping pillows around his leg. "Isn't Jill upset over you and Ellie being such good friends?" His mom never was good at fishing for information. She usually just laid things out there.

"Jill and I are taking a break." Shawn grabbed Grandpa Larson's Bible off his nightstand. He'd been reading it faithfully since he quit taking the pain medication.

"Stephen and Seth are really upset that Jill has taken over as worship leader."

"What does Dad say?"

"Your dad is upset too. Jill won't sing any of the songs he requests, and she won't let anyone else sing either."

"What about the choir twice a month? Don't they still sing?"

"Jill doesn't have any say over the choir, but Paul leads the choir, and he's also refusing to do your dad's songs these days."

Shawn hadn't been to church since breaking his leg. At first it was hard to go anywhere. Ellie had volunteered to stay home with him on Sundays. Now they'd just fallen into that habit. All of a sudden, he missed church. Especially missed leading worship.

"Tell Stephen to take over. Stephen knows how to lead worship."

"Your dad is waiting for you. He said when you come back to church things will smooth out." His mom smiled at the Bible in his hands. "Your dad and I have noticed you getting serious about God."

Shawn smiled. "Grandpa Larson's Bible is pretty serious."

"Seriously used." His mom gently took the old book.

"God knew I would have a lot of time to read. He made sure all the good stuff was underlined for me."

His mom flipped through the pages. Dates and commentary were scrawled on nearly every page. "I've never seen a Bible so devoured." His mom placed the Bible back in his hands. "I guess it won't hurt for you to come with us tomorrow to the ultrasound. I've noticed Ellie relies on you. You're good company for her. I still can't believe MVA wouldn't let her in. She's a great student. I see how hard she works on her home studies."

"You know MVA's policy about pregnancy." Shawn turned on his bedside lamp so he could still read his Bible when his mom turned off the overhead light on her way out.

"Jesus didn't make policies. He gave people second chances." His mom still sounded bent out of shape over MVA not letting Ellie in.

"Ellie's better off here at home. At school, she would have to deal with girls like Jill."

"Are you and Jill really over?" His mom placed an extra quilt at his feet because snow was forecast during the night.

"I don't miss her. I'm glad it's over."

"Me too," Mom said, kissing his forehead.

Shawn didn't want to talk about Jill. "What time are we leaving for the ultrasound in the morning?"

"Eight."

"That early?"

"That's what time you've always left for school. You're going to have to get used to getting up early again to go back to your classes one of these days."

"I like homeschooling."

"Don't you want to graduate with your friends?"

Not anymore, but he didn't say that out loud. His mom would have a fit if he told her he didn't want to return to MVA at all.

"Football season is about over. This Friday is the last game. You should come and watch your team." Mom now had a smile on her face.

"I'm going to stay home with Ellie. She needs me."

His mom took a deep breath. "Ellie needs Jesus."

Shawn had heard that line about someone needing Jesus many times. Hearing it about Ellie frustrated him. "Ellie is more squared away than most people I know." Shawn tried to keep the defensiveness from his voice.

"We all need Jesus, honey." His mom headed for the light switch. She flicked it off, bathing the room in the glow of the bedside lamp. "Get some sleep. Tomorrow's a big day."

Shawn realized his mom meant it was a big day not just for Ellie, but for him too because he'd be leaving the house to go somewhere. His mom didn't know about the trip to the lake. All she knew was that he hadn't left the house except for doctors' appointments since he'd broken his leg. Physical therapists came to the house thanks to Dr. Larson.

Realizing Ellie's pregnancy was more than halfway over, Shawn wondered what life would bring once the baby arrived. The thought of Ellie leaving depressed him. She had become his best friend. Just yesterday they'd taken turns watching their favorite movies together. Shawn was kind of embarrassed to admit the Disney movie *Aladdin* remained his favorite. He'd even ended up singing "A Whole New World" along with the characters for Ellie during the show. She'd laughed her head off at his silly performance.

Ellie's favorite movie was *Titanic*. They watched it after watching *Aladdin*.

Who would he watch old movies with when Ellie left? Who would cook his bacon extra crispy and spread his toast with mayo instead of butter like she did every morning now? Who would test snippets of their songs on him? Throw popcorn at him when he teased her because she got teary-eyed over sad shows? Who would make him strawberry milkshakes and then drink them unashamedly with him in the afternoon?

He couldn't imagine life after Ellie had the baby, and yet beyond the baby, a whole new world awaited her. She'd told him yesterday that after she put the baby up for adoption, she was going to Nashville to become a singer/songwriter like her mom.

Normally, he would have told her she couldn't do that, she must finish high school first, but life wasn't normal anymore.

Jill was right about one thing. Everything was different now because of Ellie.

The ultrasound was the coolest thing Shawn had ever seen. The baby turned all the way around during the procedure. He knew Ellie was really nervous and did his best to assure her that the baby looked perfect.

"So you want to know the baby's sex?" the technician asked.

The technician ran the ultrasound down to the top of Ellie's panties, then circled the device around. Shawn averted his gaze from Ellie's pink underwear, studying the computer screen, trying to figure out the baby's sex before the technician announced it.

"Anyone want to guess?" Now that the technician had finished the serious part of the exam, she smiled a lot.

Shawn was pretty sure of what he saw on the screen. "E.J. is a girl," he said triumphantly.

"Dad's right," answered the pleased technician.

Patsy clapped her hands in delight, and then turned on the technician. "My son is not the baby's father!"

"Then why is he here?" The technician no longer smiled.

"He's family," said Mom.

"A brother?" The technician draped the long cord around her neck and tapped the computer screen, freezing the baby's image on the screen.

"Not quite," Mom admitted.

"You're going to have to leave," the technician told Shawn.

"Sure." He grinned at Ellie before exiting the room.

A half hour later, Ellie and his mom entered the waiting room, where Shawn sat flipping through a *Ladies' Home Journal* magazine. He picked up his crutches and hobbled onto his feet. Ellie looked relieved. His mom seemed super happy.

"I knew E.J. was a girl all along," Shawn said proudly.

"I'm just glad she's healthy," Ellie said.

His mom held up a black-and-white picture. Clearly, the photo revealed a baby cradled in its mother's womb. "She's beautiful," Mom said.

"Just like Ellie," Shawn announced without thinking about it.

His mom snapped out of her giddy state. "How's your leg, Shawn? Do we need to get you off your feet?"

"My leg's good. I'm fine."

"Good enough to grab some lunch?"

"Definitely." Shawn fell into step beside his mom on their way out of the ultrasound office. Ellie trailed behind them.

"I need to pick up our turkey for Thanksgiving," Mom said.

"Let's get the biggest one in the store." Shawn was starving.

"We'll grab some lunch before we get the bird," Mom said.

Shawn turned around and winked at Ellie.

She smiled back at him. Now that she'd made it a habit of wearing hardly any makeup, she looked so sweet and pretty. And still didn't appear pregnant in her clothes, though with her belly bare during the ultrasound, her baby bump was certainly growing.

"E.J.'s hungry too." Shawn caught the door with his crutch as a lady going out ahead of them released it. His mom hurried to hold the door open and then helped Shawn into the Suburban. Ellie held his crutches as he used his arm strength to lift himself into the passenger seat. Ellie climbed in the backseat, laying the crutches beside her.

Today the sun shone, melting last night's snowfall. Mountain View looked postcard perfect for the wintry moment, all those old brick buildings with snowy roofs. Shawn wondered if Ellie appreciated the town's beauty. He looked forward to the holidays with her here. Already he had decided to buy Ellie an iPod for Christmas. She'd never had one and loved listening to his and Stephen's iPods.

Now that Stephen was practicing with the football team, he didn't spend much time with Ellie. Shawn was happy about that. Since he'd broken his leg and broken things off with Jill, the pressure of his life had gone way down. There was no football team or worship crew to lead these days. No honors classes to prep for. No Larsons to impress—except for Grandpa Larson. Shawn studied the old man's Bible, hoping the next time he saw Grandpa, he'd be able to share the stuff he'd read. Most of all, he enjoyed being with Ellie all day, every day. He turned around and smiled at her in the backseat.

She returned his smile.

"After lunch and grocery shopping, can we drive out and show Ellie where Grandpa and Grandma Larson live?" Shawn asked his mom.

"If you are feeling up to it," Mom answered. She gave him a funny look and then turned her attention back to the road.

He wondered for a moment what that look meant but then got to thinking about what he wanted for lunch. A roast beef sandwich sounded delicious, and he told his mom so.

"Roast beef it is. Ellie, do you like roast beef sandwiches?" Mom asked.

"Whatever Shawn likes is fine with me," Ellie said from the backseat.

Again, his mom gave him that funny look. Shawn winked at her, and his mom smiled, appearing to relax back into her driving. He wondered what his mom was thinking, but honestly, he didn't really want to know.

Chapter 30

Ellie walked Duncan out of their quiet neighborhood and down the road to town. It was a long walk, but she felt full of energy today, restless as the snow melted on a warmer than normal November day. At least it felt that way to Ellie. Shawn kept talking about the baby, how she was a girl, just like he'd said. How the baby was going to look like her. Maybe even have a little dimple under her eye when she smiled. Shawn liked to tease her about that dimple. "I can tell when you're honestly happy because when you really smile, that little dimple comes out on your cheek under your eye," he'd said this morning. He kept wanting to touch her stomach to see if he could feel the baby moving. Did he have any idea what that did to her?

She had to get out of the house today. Shawn had grown too attached to the baby. And after the ultrasound yesterday, she wasn't sure how she felt. Seeing the baby on the black-and-white screen made it all the more real. All the more inescapable. She realized that's what she'd being doing lately, trying to escape the reality of the pregnancy as she hung out with Shawn and grew attached to him. He was such a great guy. Incredible, really. She needed to walk. To think. To escape.

Duncan was all for it. The retriever had a spring in his step too. This warmer weather must have felt good on his old bones. His fluffy golden tail never quit swishing with happiness as they strolled down the sidewalk. Ellie had grown so fond of him. She liked to pretend he was her dog. And he slept in her room every night now. Right beside her bed, as if protecting her was his job.

The massive old maple trees that lined the road had shed their autumn leaves. They now resembled naked statues with bare branches stretched into the sky. The trees reminded Ellie of bony old women filled with the wisdom of the ages. What stories they would tell if they could talk, watching people stroll past for more than a century.

Duncan seemed to know they were headed for the city park downtown. Ellie had only been there once before with Miss Patsy, but it was such a pretty place; she wanted to see it again. It too was filled with massive old maple trees and a large playground for children. Just a month ago, it had been ablaze with autumn glory, but now all the colorful leaves were gone.

The park was beautiful, just as she remembered. There were no laughing children playing on the playground today, but it was still a special place. She walked Duncan around the whole thing. They even stopped and rested a while on a park bench, watching some industrious little birds searching for food as the snow melted.

She heard the 300ZX before she saw it. What was Pastor Sam doing here? He pulled up and parked between some other cars. For a moment, she thought he and Miss Patsy were having lunch together. But that didn't make sense because Miss Patsy was up in Sutterville today. So who was the blond lady in Pastor Sam's car with him?

They weren't looking her way, which relieved Ellie to no end. The blond woman threw her head back and laughed, and Ellie could see Pastor Sam was laughing too. Pretty soon they were eating sandwiches together. People in other cars were parked there too, having lunch. It was a pretty lunch spot, but what was Pastor Sam doing with that woman?

His hot secretary in her tight skirts.

Jill's mother.

Miss Patsy's best friend.

Ellie felt sick to her stomach as she stroked Duncan's soft back, watching them. A part of her wished Pastor Sam would look over and see her there sitting on the cold bench, staring at the car, but the other part of her just wanted to escape.

How stupid could he be?

How stupid could *she* be?

Thinking Pastor Sam was the perfect man. A loving father. An amazing husband to Miss Patsy. A pastor everyone adored. That obviously wasn't the case. At least as far as it came to being an amazing husband to Miss Patsy.

An amazing husband would never have lunch with that woman. Jill's mother kept throwing her head back and laughing all seductively, at least that was how Ellie imagined it; she couldn't hear her laughing, just saw it from a distance through the car window. Ellie wanted to scoop up what was left of the melting snow and throw it in the woman's face.

Instead, she stood up and told Duncan they were going home. He looked at her with his soulful eyes, and she knelt down and scratched his jaw the way he liked it. "You're such a good dog. You would never do that, would you? You're loyal. Dogs are loyal." Ellie leaned her head against Duncan and squeezed her eyes hard to stop the tears.

Men weren't loyal. Ellie knew that. She'd known that all her life, so why was she so surprised and felt like she was going to either throw up or cry?

She had hoped that Christian men were different. She so wanted to believe that Shawn's family was the perfect church family, just as they appeared to be. That faith in God was real. And it could make people different. She'd thought Pastor Sam was different than Clive. Different than the other Sutterville men she knew. Duncan licked her face, and she opened her eyes. "We better get home. Shawn's probably wondering where we went."

Duncan's brown eyes were full of understanding. He licked her again and nudged her hand with his head, wanting more petting. "At least God made dogs faithful," she said. "Maybe it's not what I think. What do you think, Duncan?"

Duncan looked toward the 300ZX and then back at her. She was convinced he understood what she was saying. "Maybe they're just eating lunch together. Discussing business. Maybe Pastor Sam is counseling her.

Duncan stood up, swishing his tail. He whined a little.

"You're ready to go home. I can tell." Ellie petted him again as she stared at Pastor Sam's car. The windows were fogging up. They wouldn't see her now, that was for sure. "I just can't believe he'd choose that woman over Miss Patsy. And in plain daylight. Stone-cold sober." She was sure Pastor Sam didn't drink. But until about fifteen minutes ago, she'd been sure he was a faithful husband. Now she wasn't sure of anything. Least of all her life here with Shawn's family. "I guess you're the only thing I'm sure of," she told Duncan. "Jana says men are dogs, but they're not. Dogs are so much better than men."

Duncan all but dragged her home to Shawn, as if knowing that's where she needed to be.

When they walked through the door, Shawn was up on his crutches, waiting for her in the foyer. "Where did you go? You've been gone for hours. I was getting worried."

"We had a good long walk." Ellie avoided Shawn's searching gaze. The last thing she wanted to tell him was that she'd seen his dad with Mrs. Larson.

"Did you walk to China?"

"No, we walked to the park."

"Which park?"

"The downtown one."

"Did you meet someone there?"

"No, why would I meet someone there?"

"I don't know. That's a long walk, Ellie. Duncan's old. You're pregnant. Why would you walk all the way downtown?"

Duncan collapsed on the floor between them, already falling asleep.

"It wasn't as far as our hike in the mountains," Ellie said defensively. And she wanted to stay well away from the conversation of seeing someone she knew at the park.

She didn't want to think about what Pastor Sam was doing, much less talk about it with Shawn. "I'm tired. I'm going to lay down for a while." Stepping past him without meeting his worried eyes, she hurried down the hall to her bedroom.

Chapter 31

On a Saturday in December, the first time driving his truck since breaking his leg, Shawn took Ellie out to meet Grandma and Grandpa Larson. When they'd gone out to the farm in November on the day of the ultrasound, the Larsons hadn't been home.

Ellie loved the farm with the barns and horses and meadow and rushing stream. They stopped along the way where the stream crossed under the road and used Shawn's iPhone to take goofy pictures of themselves together on the bridge. Shawn pulled Ellie to him and stuck his tongue out at the camera, encouraging Ellie to do the same.

"I'm not good at making funny faces," Ellie told him.

"Come on, just do this." Shawn crossed his eyes.

"You're a nut." She laughed.

"A nut? What does that make you? A squirrel?"

"You're crazy." Ellie gave him a little push.

Shawn pulled her back into his arms. "Stick out your tongue."

"No."

"Like this." He put his tongue to her cheek and licked her.

She reared back in his arms, laughing.

He tucked her up close again.

"You're too strong." She looked into his eyes, the smile easing off her face.

He raised the camera and snapped a picture of them. "Come on. Just once stick out your tongue for me."

She finally did.

Shawn wasn't quick enough and missed the picture. "Do it again."

"No."

"Yes." He held the camera ready, his other arm anchoring her against his chest.

"What if a car comes?" Ellie looked down the road.

"If a car comes, we'll have the driver pull over and take our picture."

"This doesn't embarrass you at all?"

He stared into her eyes for a moment, wanting so much to feel her relax in his embrace. How he enjoyed holding her in his arms with the water rushing beneath them under the bridge. The sun blazed on her hair, highlighting the red strands. He wrinkled his nose at her. "Nope. Doesn't embarrass me a bit. Sorry it embarrasses you." He raised the camera and took another photo.

"You don't know how big and strong you are," she told him. "Nobody's ever forced you to do something you didn't want to do." Something in her eyes warned him. He eased his grip, letting her go, hoping she wouldn't step too far away.

"I would never hurt a girl." The change in her confused him.

"I know." She tried to smile, but it didn't ease things. He could feel the tenseness in her. Deep in the night, she wasn't like this with him. Not when he held her after a nightmare and she snuggled up against him so trustingly and went right back to sleep. Awake, Ellie was cautious. Always cautious of being touched. Always cautious of being loved.

"Has a guy hurt you, Ellie?"

Her eyes widened. She shook her head.

He didn't believe her. He took her face in his hands. "I would pound someone for hurting you." He searched her eyes. What he felt surprised him. All he wanted to do was keep her safe. Keep her close.

Leaning down, he kissed her forehead.

"You didn't take a picture of that." She tried teasing him.

"Or that," he said, kissing the tip of her nose.

She took a halting breath. "Shawn—"

He raised the camera, pressed his lips lightly to hers, and took a picture.

"What do you think of that?" He showed her the photo of the kiss.

"You should get a job for *National Geographic*. We look like monkeys." But a smile spread across her face.

"*National Geographic*? We do not look like monkeys."

"You're quick with that camera."

"You think so?"

"I do." She stepped out of his arms. "A car's coming."

"I'll race you to the truck." With his bum leg, Shawn knew he wouldn't win. He was just being playful.

Ellie took off so fast he blinked.

"Dang," he said at the truck. "I didn't know you could run that fast."

They drove to the farm just listening to the radio. He so wanted Ellie to meet the Larsons, but he worried about their reaction to her, considering he no longer dated their granddaughter.

He needn't have worried. The Larsons welcomed Ellie into their home like she was family. And they didn't mention Jill in front of Ellie.

A fire blazed in the wood-burning stove in the Larsons' living room. Grandma Larson, in her apron, was in the middle of canning blackberry jam with berries she'd picked during the summer. "I freeze them to can on a winter day like today," she explained to Shawn and Ellie.

"Ellie can come to the kitchen to help me while you and Grandpa play a game of chess." Grandma suggested.

"Is that okay with you?" Shawn asked Ellie. He could tell Ellie was nervous but eager for Grandma to like her.

"Sure," she responded.

Before going to the kitchen, Grandma draped an apron like the one she wore over Ellie's head, tying a bow at the back of Ellie's waist. Ellie looked so cute in the apron. Shawn imagined Grandma looked that way in an apron when she had been a teenager too. Grandma was petite like Ellie. She still wore her wavy white hair in a forties-style bob with bobby pins clipping up the sides. Her blue eyes snapped with life and humor.

"Good thing your hair's already in a ponytail," Grandma told Ellie. "You kids probably don't even know what a hairnet is. You'd have to wear one in my kitchen with that long hair of yours if you didn't have it in a rubber band already."

"My dad owns a diner," Ellie answered. "I've seen hairnets."

"I use my hairnets now to keep the squirrels out of the henhouse." Grandma grinned. "My hair used to be long and pretty like yours, but when I turned seventy, I decided it was time to cut my hair."

"I told your grandma not to cut it," Grandpa joined the conversation. "But she's always been a bit on the rebellious side. Your grandma ordered this new magazine for us. *Senior Moments*. Something like that. She read this silly article about how mature women shouldn't have long hair because it ages their faces." Grandpa laughed.

"Your grandpa still thinks I'm forty," Grandma intervened. "A week ago, your grandpa asked me to go dancing the day after I had a corn removed from my big toe. How am I supposed to dance with a tender toe?"

"What's a little corn removal?" Grandpa said. "Back when we were a team, Mary and I used to remove heart valves together and then sew in new ones. Just like that. And that was like walking on the moon in those days. Your grandma always looked so pretty in the operating room."

"I can barely remember those days," Grandma said. "Stop boring these young folks with our old memories."

"I'm not bored," Shawn said.

"Me neither." Ellie smiled one of her big, happy smiles. Shawn loved that her teeth weren't perfectly straight. It made her smile all the more endearing.

After Ellie disappeared with Grandma to can blackberries, Shawn settled down at the chess table near the fire. Grandpa took his chess games very seriously. He even had one of those permanent tables with the chessboard ingrained in the wood. They were halfway through a game before they finally spoke to each other.

"You been reading that Bible I gave you for your birthday?" Grandpa asked as he concentrated on moving his knight away from Shawn's queen.

"Yeah. I've had lots of time to read." Shawn motioned to his broken leg.

"How's that leg doing?"

"Fine. Dr. Larson says I'm ahead of schedule. It's healing great."

"Is my son a good doctor?" Grandpa moved his knight to trap Shawn's rook.

"He's the best doctor." Shawn studied the board, trying to figure out a way to get Grandpa's knight off the table.

"Is he giving you any trouble for breaking up with Jill?"

"I wondered when you would ask me about that." Shawn worried Grandpa might be upset they were no longer a couple.

"The Lord has a lot of work to do on my granddaughter. I'm sad to say I understand why you called it off with her."

"I'm sorry. I wish I could be a real part of your family, but I don't think Jill and I are meant for each other."

Grandpa lifted his head from studying the chess board. His warm brown eyes shone brightly. "You are a real part of our family, Shawny. Don't you ever doubt that. Do you know what the Bible says about family?"

"I haven't read that far in your Bible yet," Shawn admitted.

"The Bible says, 'If anyone comes to me and does not hate his father and mother, his wife and children, his brothers and sisters—yes, even his own life—he cannot be my disciple.' Read it for yourself in Luke, chapter fourteen."

"That makes no sense to me, Grandpa. It's words like this in the Bible that confuse me."

Grandpa straightened the reading glasses that had slipped down his nose. He didn't take his eyes off the chess board. "You see the game we're playing here." He pointed to the chess pieces. "There is a war going on between you and me. Let's say this war is not between you and me. Let's say this war is actually between good and evil. You ready to make your move with good and evil in mind?"

"Sure." Shawn used his queen to rescue his rook, killing off Grandpa's knight with her. He was sure happy to get rid of Grandpa's mighty knight.

"I know you don't want to lose any men in this chess game, even a rook, but you're missing the big picture, Shawny." Grandpa moved a rook on the far side of the board to take Shawn's queen.

Shawn hadn't seen that coming and threw his hands in the air. "My queen! Grandpa!"

"You didn't see the move that cost you your queen because you focused on saving your rook. You're losing the war because you're unwilling to sacrifice, Shawn. That's what Luke, chapter fourteen talks about. Sacrificing your friends, your family, even your own life if the Lord calls on you to do that for Him." Grandpa finally took a break from studying the board, leaning back in his chair to give Shawn his full attention.

"I was taught in Sunday school that Jesus loves everybody. Families are supposed to love each other, not sacrifice each other in some war I don't see."

Grandpa smiled. "Just because you don't see the war doesn't mean it isn't there. It's a spiritual war, and we can't see it unless the Lord opens our eyes to it. Once your eyes are open, you'll understand love and hate. Love died on a cross, and hate does everything it can to hide that from people. That's the war. The real war. A war for folks' souls."

"You're talking in circles, Grandpa."

Grandpa sighed. "All right, I'll keep it simple. What really makes people family, Shawny, is a love for Jesus. And a love for Jesus places you smack dab in the middle of the war. My granddaughter thinks the war is at the mall. Until the Lord changes Jill's heart, she's not for you. Let's talk about that little pregnant girl in there with Grandma. She might be the girl for you."

"Gosh, Grandpa, I'm not sure what to say about that."

"Just tell me the truth, that's all you gotta do. How do you feel about Ellie?"

Chapter 32

The holidays passed in a pleasant whirl for Ellie. Being with a family celebrating Thanksgiving, Christmas, and New Year's proved as sweet and satisfying as she'd always dreamed it would be, but after Shawn went back to school in January, she really missed him.

During the day, all she had was Duncan, and sensing her need, the golden retriever wouldn't leave her side. His big brown eyes, as sweet as hot cocoa, kept watch over her constantly, that feathery golden tail always swishing in eager friendship. They spent February taking walks together, the retriever's faithfulness a great comfort. It was true, life with a dog couldn't compare to life without one. Duncan loved her unconditionally. She wished people could love that way. Every day she and Duncan strolled down to the pond at the end of the neighborhood, where Duncan harassed the ducks while she stood on the snowy bank watching him. She was seven months pregnant now and could no longer hide her belly. Shawn didn't seem to mind. When he was home, he constantly had his hand on her midsection, waiting for E.J. to kick.

"She's going to be a soccer player," Shawn predicted. He was off his crutches now and once again leading worship at church. Ellie now accompanied the Kleins to services and had grown to love it there—except for Jill and Dr. Larson. Ellie did her best to avoid them both. Shawn had been after her to attend youth group with him on Wednesday nights. Tonight she'd finally agreed to go. After taking Duncan on his walk that afternoon, she spent extra time fixing her hair and dressing as nice as possible, which included doing everything she could to disguise her pregnancy. She'd pretty much given up on wearing makeup except for some mascara and lip gloss. Shawn preferred the natural look.

Several hours later, she sat beside him in the church pew, waiting for the speaker to come onstage. "I don't know this pastor," Shawn whispered in her ear. "Sorry, Pastor Joe's out of town. Dr. Larson brought this youth group guy here from some other church. Jill says the guy's amazing." Shawn made a silly face.

Ellie knew Shawn was as diligent as she was about avoiding Jill and her father these days.

The speaker introduced himself as Pastor Jerrod. He was a large, good-looking guy holding a long-stemmed red rose in his hand. "I want you kids to pass this rose around while I talk," he said. "Handle the rose all you want. Stroke its petals. Consume its fragrance. Twist its stem. The rose is yours to trash tonight."

Pastor Jerrod then went on to talk about purity. About how important it was to wait until marriage to have sex. He explained all the sexually transmitted diseases and how teen pregnancy destroyed lives. Both Shawn and Ellie squirmed in their seats. Shawn soon reached out and grabbed Ellie's hand, threading his fingers through hers. That was the only thing that kept Ellie from fleeing the church. When the rose was passed to her, Shawn grabbed the flower and quickly passed it on, his eyes glued to Pastor Jerrod.

"We all want true love," Pastor Jerrod was saying. He motioned to the front row. Jill stood up with the rose that had been passed throughout the audience. Triumphantly, she carried it to the stage, handing the broken rose along with another beautiful new rose to Pastor Jerrod.

The pastor held up both flowers. The rose that had been passed around hung limply in his hand. Crushed rose petals fell like drops of blood to the floor at the pastor's feet. The other rose stood tall and lovely in his grip.

"If you were going to choose the rose you wanted to spend the rest of your life with, wouldn't you choose this one?" Pastor Jerrod held up the unmarred flower. He smiled at Jill and handed the beautiful rose back to her, keeping the crushed rose in his hand.

Jill left the stage with her prized rose as Pastor Jerrod carried on. "This rose is used." He held up the flower everyone had fondled. "Who wants a used rose? Nobody in their right mind would choose this broken rose."

Ellie couldn't take anymore. She jerked her hand away from Shawn's. Swallowing the sob clawing up her throat, she pushed her way down the aisle of teenagers and rushed for the door.

Out in the cold, tears stung her cheeks. She despised herself for crying and hated Shawn for putting her through this awful night. Let him keep his stupid church with all those stupid, judgmental Christians.

She began walking toward the mountains with tears freezing on her face.

Shawn soon pulled up beside her in his truck. "Rose, get in."

"Don't call me that." Ellie could hardly speak.

"Please, Ellie, get in the truck," he pleaded.

Other cars passed by. Drivers and passengers staring out their windows at them. Ellie knew most were teenagers from the youth group, driving down the hill to the town of Mountain View. Humiliation forced her into Shawn's truck.

The crushed rose lay on the seat beside him.

"Why do you have that?" A fresh sob hit her.

"I want this rose," he said.

At the bottom of the hill, before they entered Mountain View, Shawn turned onto a road Ellie had never been on before.

A few minutes later, he parked the truck beside a snow-covered meadow. Moonlight streamed down onto the snow, bathing the field in a white shimmer that stretched to the edge of the dark mountains. Silence filled the truck. Finally, Shawn said more adamantly, "I want this rose." He tenderly picked the broken flower off the seat.

Ellie put her face in her hands and sobbed.

Shawn pulled her into his arms, holding her. "I'm sorry. That wasn't a normal youth group. I know that was terrible for you. I'm so sorry, Ellie."

He raised her chin with his fingers so he could look into her eyes. "I love you." He lowered his lips and kissed her softly, then passionately until Ellie pulled away from him. "You don't know what you're doing."

"I know what I'm doing," he insisted.

"No, you don't. You don't really know me." She wiped her wet face with her shirt sleeves.

He laughed, but in the laugh, Ellie heard his uncertainty. "I've talked more to you than any girl ever. You know everything about me. I know everything about you," Shawn said.

"No, you don't."

"What don't I know about you?" He searched her face.

"You see this rose?" She grabbed it off the seat and opened the door, throwing it out into the snow. "It's dirty, Shawn."

"Dirtier than Number 33?" he rasped.

Ellie closed her eyes.

"God knows what you have done, and He still loves you," Shawn said.

"God doesn't love me. If He loved me, I wouldn't be pregnant!" Ellie punched herself in the belly.

"Don't do that!" Shawn grabbed both her wrists. "You'll hurt E.J. You'll hurt yourself, Ellie."

"I don't care!" she screamed in his face. "Let me go!"

"I care! I'm not letting you go!" he hollered back. Then he kissed her again. "I love you," he insisted after kissing her. "I don't care what you've done. Jesus wants you, Rose, and so do I." Tears ran down Shawn's cheeks too.

Seeing his tears, Ellie cried harder.

Shawn gathered her into his arms. "We'll keep E.J. We'll get married and move to Nashville together. It will be great. You'll see."

"No!" Ellie cried.

"Why not?" he demanded.

"I've made up my mind. The baby belongs to the McBrides."

Shawn brushed the hair back from her tear-drenched face. "But what if E.J. looks like you?"

"What if she looks like her father?" Ellie couldn't hide how crushed she felt.

"Number 33 is a good-looking guy," Shawn offered.

Ellie bit her bottom lip so hard she tasted blood. "I'm not keeping the baby."

"Okay." He tucked her hair behind her ears and then stroked her wet cheeks with his thumbs. "We'll still get married. I'll do ROTC at Vanderbilt. We'll live in Nashville. If I have to, I'll play football there. That will pay for my schooling if they won't give me an ROTC scholarship."

"How long have you been thinking about this?" Ellie couldn't believe it.

"E.J. will be here in two months. Then she'll be gone, and you'll be gone with her. I'm not letting you go. I've been making plans for us."

"What will your parents say?"

"I don't care what they say." Shawn smiled. "My mind's made up."

"You can't be serious?"

"I am serious."

Ellie looked at the breathtaking moonlit meadow of snow under a night sky endless with stars as sharp as diamonds and, against all odds, believed it was possible. A life with Shawn was possible. Just like this snow on the ground. Usually, snow this deep didn't happen in Tennessee, but an unusually cold winter had turned Tennessee into a wonderland.

She remembered hearing in church that all things were possible with God. Hope welled up in her. "Have you ever made a snow angel?" she asked Shawn.

"Not at night in this meadow." He took her hand and opened the truck door.

Together they walked out into the snow to make angels together.

Chapter 33

As if her life couldn't get worse, Jill's car wouldn't start in the middle of the storm. She couldn't get a hold of anyone, so she finally called her grandpa. Now here she was in his old truck, headed for the church to find her mom. Could her grandpa drive any slower? And did he ever talk about anything else besides Jesus? She was doing her best to be polite, but he was driving her crazy. On top of that, March was roaring in like a lion. It was another rainy day with tornado warnings blaring around the state. The power had gone out over an hour ago at the school due to high winds. She was sick of this weather and sick of Grandpa's Jesus talk. When they finally reached the church, she jumped out of his truck and made a beeline for the office door. Wouldn't you know it, the door was locked, and all the lights were out, even though her mom's and Pastor Sam's cars were still parked out front.

She was soaking wet from the rain by the time her grandpa got to the door and opened it for her. "I'm so glad you have a key," she said, and her grandpa just smiled. He was always smiling. Since he was one of the founders of this church and still on the church board, it didn't surprise Jill that he had a key. What surprised her was the locked door when her mom was still there.

When she stepped into the dark church with Grandpa right behind her, she knew something wasn't right. The wind was howling outside, but inside the church, it was completely quiet. Like nobody was there. Alarm tingled through her, but she headed for her mom's office anyway. Down the hall and to the right was the pastors' wing. Pastor Sam must still be here because his 300ZX was parked outside a few spots away from her mom's Mercedes, but it sure seemed like everyone had gone home, as was often the case here at church in these kind of storms.

Grandpa usually never shut up, but following in her footsteps, he was quiet, the smile gone from his face.

In her mom's office, a single candle burned on the desk, but nobody was in the room, and Pastor Sam's office door was closed. Jill thought she heard a noise, some kind of animal sound, but it stopped, and she turned to her grandpa. The look on his face in the candlelight scared her. He was tall and stooped with age, but in the moment, it seemed he straightened up and became stronger. His jaw was set with determination. There was a Bible on the bookshelf in the office, and her grandpa scooped it up before walking purposefully over to Pastor Sam's door. He didn't knock. Holding the Bible up in one hand, he barged into Pastor Sam's office, and Jill couldn't help herself. Even though she knew instinctively she shouldn't follow him, she did.

When Pastor Sam's office door swung open, two naked people jumped to their feet, trying to cover themselves.

"How did you get in here?" Beth demanded, grabbing her blouse off a chair and holding it in front of her pale body. A candle burned on Pastor Sam's desk; the scent of vanilla and something musky assaulted Jill's senses. She knew she should turn away, leave the room immediately, but shock froze her there, staring at her mom and Pastor Sam as they fumbled around, trying to dress themselves.

"I'm a board member. I have my key." Grandpa gave Beth a grief-filled glance and then turned to Pastor Sam. "How could you let the devil win this way, Samuel? You know better."

Pastor Sam was doing his best to slide into his pants. "Dear Lord, Adam, I'm sorry," he replied, shamefaced.

"Well, it's a good thing we're here." Her grandpa pulled out a cell phone and punched in some numbers. "You two have fallen into Satan's trap," Grandpa said as Beth was about to hurry past him with her clothes gathered in her arms. When her mom saw Jill standing beside the door, she cried, "Oh my gosh, Jill, close your eyes!"

Jill didn't mean to, but she laughed.

"Close your eyes!" Beth commanded.

"I've got a net here to fish you out," Grandpa said, holding up the Bible in front of poor Pastor Sam. "I'm calling Allen to come pick you up," he told Beth before she rushed past Jill and disappeared down the dark hall.

After one last look at Pastor Sam, now buttoning up his pants, Jill left the room. She didn't know what else to do, so she went out and sat in one of the padded blue chairs near the office door, where people waited to see the pastor.

Daddy arrived in record time. "Why didn't you get home before the storm hit?" he asked, all windblown from his walk from the parking lot to the church, when he saw Jill sitting in the chair near the door.

"My car wouldn't start. It's still at the school. Grandpa picked me up."

"Where is Dad? He called me and said to get over here right away. Is everyone okay?"

Jill didn't know what to say, so she said nothing.

"What's going on?" Daddy demanded. "Where's your mother?"

"In the bathroom," Jill whispered. Strangely, she felt like laughing again. This was so unreal. Beth and Pastor Sam doing the nasty in his office. Unbelievable.

"Why is she in the bathroom? Tornados have touched down in Memphis today. You girls need to get home. There's no decent shelter on the top of this hill."

"You better go talk to Grandpa." Jill stared at her dad, suddenly sorry for him. Reaping what you sow had come around to bite him. He was already married when he and Beth had fallen in love twenty years ago. She liked her older half-siblings, in their thirties now, raising families of their own. She remembered when she was little, Trudy bringing Daddy's older kids to the house to see him. Trudy didn't look like Beth. She was small and kind of dumpy, with brown hair cut short and messy on her head. Beth's legs were twice as long as Trudy's. Beth looked like a model, while Trudy looked like a mom. "She's a good mom. A good woman," Jill remembered Daddy saying one night in the kitchen when Beth was running Trudy down.

"Are you saying I'm not a good mom?" Beth had snapped back.

Jill had been in the second grade, and she kind of agreed with Daddy at the time. Beth wasn't much of a mom when she and Lily were little. Trudy would drop off homemade chocolate chip cookies when she dropped off her kids at their house on Saturdays. Jill had loved Saturdays when she was little. Homemade cookies and her older brother and sister at the house to play with all day. It was great.

Daddy disappeared down the hall, and pretty soon she heard him and her mom yelling. Actually, she heard her mom yelling at Daddy and Grandpa. She couldn't believe Beth was yelling. Pastor Sam came down the hall, putting his raincoat on as he neared the door. When he saw Jill sitting there in the chair, his face fell.

He stopped for a moment right in front of her. "I'm so sorry, Jill," he said, and her heart went out to him.

"It's okay," Jill said. "Beth is beautiful."

Pastor Sam looked so grieved, then he opened the door and stepped out into the storm. Wind and rain blew into the church before Pastor Sam got the door closed behind him.

Beth is beautiful. Why did she say that?

Jill sat there stunned, listening to the murmur of her parents and Grandpa in another office down the hall. Her mom was beautiful. Isn't that why Daddy left Trudy for her? Trudy wasn't beautiful, but she was faithful. She'd never remarried and still brought Daddy her homemade cookies from time to time on Saturdays.

"She still loves you," Beth had accused one day after Trudy dropped off her cookies.

"She's a good woman," Daddy had repeated.

That's what Jill remembered from her childhood. Trudy being good and her mother being beautiful. Beth wasn't a good woman. She was Miss Pasty's best friend. Who has sex with a best friend's husband?

But Beth had beauty going for her. And so did she. Tall, blond, and stunning, Jill was used to hearing that about herself and her mom. Ellie wasn't beautiful. Sure, she was cute, if you liked quiet, little brown-haired girls with stupid, big blue eyes.

When they'd gone shopping in Knoxville, Ellie had hardly said a word. What did Shawn see in her? And in that moment, it suddenly dawned on her. Ellie was good, like Trudy.

Jill stood up and went outside to stand in the rain. Her parents would probably get a divorce. She'd seen this coming, and it didn't surprise her. Of course, the affair with Pastor Sam surprised her. Not because of Beth, but because of Pastor Sam. She just never expected that from him. He was a good pastor who really seemed to know and love God.

No wonder people called Christians hypocrites. They were.

Jill raised her face and let the rain splash down on her. She didn't want to think about God. Didn't want to think about her parents divorcing. Didn't want to think about why Shawn chose Ellie over her. Talk about unbelievable. How could Shawn want a pregnant Gutterville girl? What was wrong with him?

What was wrong with her?

The rain felt like needles on her face. Wind roared in her ears and pushed against her body with the force of a person pushing someone. Maybe a tornado would come and sweep her away. That might be good. She'd never have to look at her mom again. Look at Shawn with Ellie again. See the outright regret on Pastor Sam's face again.

Why was life so hard?

Why were people so screwed up?

Was God really there?

Stop thinking!

The church door swung open, and Jill was relieved to see it was just Grandpa leaving. When he saw her, he walked right over, getting drenched immediately.

"Can I pray with you, honey?" Grandpa wasn't smiling. It made Jill sad.

"Sure." Jill bowed her head and stepped into her grandpa's arms.

He wrapped her in a warm embrace and said a prayer that actually comforted Jill. While he prayed, the wind seemed to die down, and the rain became softer. After he finished, he put his arm around her and said, "Let me take you home. Your parents need their time alone to sort this out."

Jill walked with Grandpa to his truck. She hadn't felt love for him since she was small, but now her affection for her grandpa returned like a flood.

In the truck, out of the rain, Jill strapped on her seat belt and said, "Do you think Daddy and Beth will get a divorce?"

"I don't know," Grandpa said as he started his truck.

He backed out of the parking lot with the trees blowing wildly at the edge of the pavement. The hill where the church sat had once been covered by woods. Trees still circled the sides of the hill, but Jill wasn't sure those trees, bowing before the storm, would survive the winds today.

"Why do you call your mom, Beth?" Grandpa asked.

Jill stared at the trees, nearly breaking in the wind. "I don't know." She turned to her Grandpa. "Were you sad when Daddy divorced Trudy?"

"Trudy was a good woman," Grandpa softly said as they headed down the hill in his old truck.

Jill couldn't help it. She laughed, and then she cried.

After a series of fierce March storms, spring had finally made her dogwood blooming appearance in Tennessee. Laughter and voices swirled around Shawn at high school. To his chagrin, he was sitting under a large maple tree during lunch period, waiting for his afternoon classes to begin. He missed homeschooling with Ellie. He was so glad it was Friday so he could spend the weekend hanging out with her. He didn't care that his classmates were eagerly planning their senior trip. He couldn't wait to graduate so he could get on with a life with Ellie. And hopefully E.J., if he could convince her to keep the baby, though he did feel bad for the McBrides about that.

Ellie was now eight months pregnant and waddled around the house looking tired and uncomfortable. Duncan never left her side. Ellie was always petting him, walking him, feeding him. She'd grown so attached to Duncan. Shawn decided when they moved out on their own, they needed to take Duncan with them. For Ellie's sake.

His parents were rarely home. Something had happened between his mom and dad in the middle of one of the big storms last month. His dad had come home that night and invited Mom to go upstairs. Pretty soon, he'd heard Mom yelling like he'd never heard her yell before. Something about Jill's mom. His parents had remained locked in their room for several hours. Everyone downstairs had fixed their own dinner and later went to bed, worried over what was happening upstairs.

The next morning his parents looked worn out and sad. Shawn and his brothers, along with Ellie, hadn't asked them a thing. Neither of his parents mentioned the fight from the night before. Mrs. Larson quit working at the church the next day. Shawn still didn't know why.

His mom began working more up in Sutterville at the woman's center. When she was home, she spent all her time with Ellie, talking endlessly about the baby. The other day he'd found his mom folding baby clothes on her bed. When she'd seen him standing in the doorway watching her, she'd hurriedly tucked all the tiny pink clothes in one of those clear rubber storage boxes and stuffed it under her bed.

"What are you doing with all those baby things?" he'd asked, wondering why his mom had baby clothes with the tags still on them.

"They're for the women's center," she'd said.

Shawn sensed she was lying, but he'd let it go. He'd never caught his mom lying before. "Ellie and I are going out for ice cream. Do you want us to bring anything back for you?" he'd asked.

"Milk," was all she'd said. He could tell her mind was on other things, which in a way relieved him because he and Ellie were still keeping their relationship a secret. And he'd been talking to recruiters: army, navy, air force, and marines. By joining the military, he would be able to provide for Ellie and E.J. His leg had become a major concern since he had to pass a physical exam to enter all the branches, and he didn't know if his leg would hold up for the tests. Dr. Larson said it was healing perfectly, but he told Shawn to refrain from sports for a few more months. Shawn wasn't about to ask Dr. Larson if his leg could handle a military exam this summer.

"Is that a Bible you're holding?" Jill asked, startling Shawn out of his thoughts under the maple tree.

"Your grandpa's Bible." He closed the book in his lap, wincing as Jill sat down beside him on the grass.

"Grandpa gave you his Bible?"

"For my birthday." Shawn slipped the old leather book into his backpack with his textbooks.

"Why aren't we back together?" She edged closer, looking intently into his eyes.

Shawn leaned back, trying to avoid the swirl of her perfume.

"Daddy says your leg is healing great. He says you'll be playing football for Vanderbilt before you know it."

"Your dad's been so good to me." Shawn meant that. Dr. Larson was an amazing doctor and an incredible man. He knew Dr. Larson would do anything for him. Even now that he no longer dated Jill.

"Daddy says I need to learn the world doesn't revolve around me. He says you broke up with me because I'm vain and selfish. Is that true?"

Shawn tried not to smile. "The world doesn't revolve around any of us, Jill. This world revolves around what God ordains."

"I don't want to talk about God. Let's talk about us." Jill rested her chin on her knees, gazing at him in that hungry way he no longer dreaded because they were so over.

"There is no us to talk about." He tried not to be cruel, but with Jill, you had to be blunt.

"Why did you take that ruined rose from Pastor Jerrod?" Jill stretched out her legs, resting back on her hands, finally giving Shawn some breathing space.

"I wanted it for Ellie." He saw no danger in telling her the truth.

Jill pinned him with her gaze. "Why?"

"Because I wanted Ellie to know Jesus loves the broken rose."

Jill's face twisted, and Shawn glimpsed what she looked like on the inside. It wasn't beautiful like her outside. "What's happened to you?"

"I don't know. God's changing me, I guess." Shawn just wanted to get out of there.

"Did you know our parents had an affair?"

Shawn stiffened. He could smell the grass. Freshly mowed and pungent. Everything slipped into slow motion. Like his life was about to stand still for a reckoning. "What are you talking about?"

"Why do you think my mom's no longer working for your dad at the church? My parents are getting a divorce. How are your parents handling it?"

The bell rang, signaling classes were about to begin. Shawn grabbed his backpack and jumped to his feet. He wanted to get as far away from Jill as possible. It felt like he couldn't breathe.

"Your dad is such a hypocrite." Jill was on her feet now too, but eager to go nowhere except where Shawn was going. "I saw him naked with my mom. I can hardly sit through his sermons without screaming 'you adulterer.' My parents want to keep it a secret. But the truth will set you free. Isn't that what Jesus says?"

Shawn headed for his truck. Jill strode after him. Students tumbled toward their classes, backpacks swinging, lunch garbage haphazardly tossed into trash cans and on the ground.

"Repent . . ." Jill taunted using a deep voice to mimic Shawn's father. "Your dad's sermon last Sunday made me sick."

"Shut up!" Shawn whirled around to face her.

"You're a hypocrite too. Your family thinks they're so high and mighty helping Ellie. I see what's going on, Shawn. You're after that Sutterville slut just like your dad was after my mom. You want to have sex with her, don't you?"

Shawn dropped his backpack. Grabbing Jill's shoulders, he shook her, trying to shut her mouth.

She screamed and laughed in his arms. Her laughter set all the little hairs on the back of his neck on end.

He released her.

Mr. Hartman was headed their way. "Mr. Klein, are you having a problem with Miss Larson?" the principal barked, striding toward them in a hurry.

"He assaulted me!" Jill became hysterical.

Shawn couldn't believe this was happening. "I didn't assault her," he insisted.

"Come with me. Both of you," Mr. Hartman said brusquely.

Shawn scooped up his backpack and strode toward the senior parking lot. He had to see his dad. He had to know the truth.

"Mr. Klein, if you don't come with me to my office, I will expel you right now for assaulting Miss Larson."

Shawn froze. *Expel?* This was insane.

He turned around. Jill glared at him from behind Mr. Hartman.

"I may press charges," she threatened.

"She's crazy!" Shawn was about ready to lose it.

"Mr. Klein, you're treading on very thin ice. I advise you to calm down and come with me." Mr. Hartman waved Shawn toward his office.

"Our parents had an affair," Jill announced.

"Shut up!" Shawn stepped toward her.

"Mr. Klein," Mr. Hartman moved between him and Jill, facing Shawn down, "you are a strong, athletic young man. I will call the sheriff for assistance if you do not settle down. Remember, you are eighteen now. An adult. Which makes this incident a very serious matter."

"Call my dad," Shawn said.

"Oh, I will," Mr. Hartman answered.

"Don't call my mom. I don't think it's a good idea to have our parents in the same room. They're still hot for each other," Jill said.

It took all the resolve Shawn could muster not to lash back at her.

"Miss Larson, you need to close your mouth." Mr. Hartman grabbed each of them by the elbow, leading Shawn and Jill toward the main school building that housed his office.

Chapter 35

A three-day suspension from school was his punishment for grabbing Jill. The whole time in Mr. Hartman's office, all Shawn could think about was his dad and Mrs. Larson. How could they have had an affair?

Mr. Hartman did not raise the affair issue at all. And he put Jill in a different office than Shawn. Once both their fathers arrived, Mr. Hartman went back and forth between the separate rooms, talking with them. Dr. Larson and his dad never spoke with each other. Shawn didn't even know if they were still friends.

"Mr. Hartman said you grabbed Jill because she made a serious accusation against our family? What was her accusation?" Dad asked once they reached the parking lot after leaving Mr. Hartman's office.

The 300ZX was parked beside Shawn's truck. Dr. Larson's Corvette and Jill's Mercedes were already gone, much to Shawn's relief.

"She said you and Mrs. Larson are having an affair." Shawn watched his dad's face for his reaction. Oh, how he wanted Jill to be lying. But somehow, he knew it was true. And the sickness in his stomach wouldn't go away.

"I'm sorry," said Dad.

"So it's true?" Shawn felt his guts being ripped out.

Dad leaned against the side of the car. Sunshine streamed around him, highlighting the gray in his hair. Shawn hadn't noticed gray there before. All of a sudden, Dad looked older. And sad. Really sad and humble.

Shawn tried to emulate Dad's calm demeanor. He had lost it with Jill. He didn't want to lose it with his dad too. Mr. Hartman might call the sheriff if he freaked out in the school parking lot. "Have you been sleeping with Mrs. Larson?" Shawn demanded to know.

Dad's eyes shone with regret. "Yes."

Shawn threw his backpack into the bed of his truck in disgust. "How could you? You're a pastor!" Shawn knew he needed to lower his voice, but disillusionment overwhelmed him. He wanted to punch his dad.

"I fell, Shawn. The good Lord sent Adam Larson to turn me around."

"Grandpa Larson knows about this?" Shawn slammed his hands against the side of his truck instead of hitting his dad, like he wanted to. The metal truck frame felt warm and unyielding under his palms. He leaned forward, pressing his forehead against the truck for a moment. Closing his eyes against the sting of hot tears.

"Adam is a man of God. He's forgiven me, just as the Lord has forgiven me. I'm hoping your mom will forgive me."

"So forgiveness is that easy?" Shawn shoved away from the truck. He took a step toward his father, then two steps back. He felt so betrayed. So confused. He blinked hard, not about to let his dad see him cry. "What about John Eldredge? You know all that *Wild at Heart* stuff you taught us? Does John Eldredge think forgiveness is easy?"

"No, forgiveness isn't easy. Forgiveness cost our Lord his life. Jesus died for my sins. That's more than enough for me." Tears flooded his dad's eyes.

"So I can go out and commit adultery and God will forgive me, just like that?" Shawn snapped his fingers. He wanted to snap someone's neck. Dad's. Jill's. Mrs. Larson's.

"Yes, like that." His dad snapped his fingers in return. Softly and gently without making a sound. "It's called mercy. You should try it, Shawn."

"I'm done with this conversation." Shawn climbed in his truck.

Dad nodded, and a tear streaked his cheek.

Shawn gunned his truck, squealing his tires all the way out of the school parking lot, leaving his dad standing there in his smoke.

A guy on a Harley fell in behind Shawn on the open road, trailing him down the highway away from the high school.

At first, Shawn didn't think much about the motorcycle behind him. He gassed his truck along, trying to outrun the truth about his dad. But the Harley hung with him for a long time. Shawn going fast. The Harley on his tail. When Shawn slowed down, the Harley slowed too. The guy seemed to be toying with him. Mocking him. Like he'd heard the conversation in the parking lot and was rubbing it in.

When the Harley finally roared past, the guy gave Shawn a scary look. Like the devil on a motorcycle. Shawn's hands trembled on the steering wheel. He turned toward home.

• • •

Shawn found Ellie on the couch watching the Food Network channel. Nobody else was home yet. Duncan lay on the floor beside the couch, Ellie petting him.

When Ellie saw him, she sat up on the cushions. "What's wrong?"

He shook his head, afraid if he opened his mouth, he would spew the story of his Dad and Mrs. Larson all over the place like vomit.

"Is everyone all right?" Ellie put her hand on her lower back. Her face appeared very pale. Duncan got up and whined, his eyes alert on Ellie.

"Sure. Everyone's okay," he fibbed. He crossed the living room to reach her. "Are you okay?" He petted Duncan. "Is she okay, boy?" Duncan whined some more.

Ellie lay back down on the couch. "I don't know. I think I'm getting the flu."

"Have you thrown up?"

"About an hour ago. And my back hurts really bad."

"Your back?" Shawn kneeled beside the couch, pushing Duncan over to get closer to Ellie. "Did you hurt yourself today?"

"No. I haven't done anything but hold down this couch all day. Poor Duncan is so worried about me. He won't go to sleep. All he does is watch me. I tried to get up to take him for his walk, but my back is killing me."

"I think I should take you to see Dr. Hammons."

"He doesn't work on Fridays." Ellie bit her lip but couldn't stop a sigh of pain.

Shawn was alarmed. "I'm taking you to the hospital right now."

He rushed out of the living room and returned with Ellie's hospital bag. She had packed it on Sunday because the *Week to Week* pregnancy book said she should have her hospital bag all packed now.

"It's not the baby. I'm not due for weeks." Ellie eyed the white leather duffel bag in Shawn's hand. Fear blazed in her eyes.

"I think we should take it just in case." After putting Duncan out in the backyard, he helped Ellie to her feet and out to the truck.

On the way to the hospital, the remaining color drained from her face. A patch of faint freckles stood out on her nose. Shawn had hardly noticed those freckles before. But now she looked white as a ghost. Terror replaced the rage inside him.

By the time they got to the hospital parking lot, tears were rolling down Ellie's face. Without a word, she opened her truck door and threw up. Shawn turned off the truck, jumped out, and ran around to her side to help her.

"Don't step in it," she told him.

"I don't care," he answered.

"I care," she said, trying to smile.

He lifted her out of the truck and into his arms.

"I can walk." She grabbed hold of his neck.

"I'm carrying you." He got a better grip under her knees, holding her cradled against his chest.

"Okay." This time she did smile.

Even pregnant, she wasn't that big, and he carried her into the hospital, his heart pumping like it did during a football game when adrenaline fueled him.

Inside the hospital, a nurse put Ellie in a wheelchair and took her directly to labor and delivery. Shawn trailed along without anyone questioning who he was.

The nurse guided Ellie into a room and told her to use the bathroom to remove her clothes and put on a gown. Ellie looked about to pass out, so the nurse followed her into the bathroom.

Shawn stood in the middle of that hospital room not knowing what to do. He heard a woman in another room across the hall groan in a frightening way. Fear flooded him anew.

The nurse came out of the bathroom in a hurry, leading Ellie over to the bed. "Her water broke in the bathroom," the nurse said.

"What?" Shawn was shocked.

"Wash your hands," the nurse commanded.

Shawn realized she was speaking to him. He went to the little sink in the room and scrubbed hands that trembled.

Ellie lay on the bed, looking as frightened as he felt.

The nurse rushed out of the room.

Shawn's eyes connected with Ellie's.

"I'm afraid," she told him.

He rushed over to her. "Don't be afraid," he said, though he was terrified himself.

"What if I die having the baby?"

"You're not going to die." Shawn stroked her hair back from her pale face. He kissed her on the forehead as the nurse returned, pushing a cart with a little bed on top of it.

"What's that for?" Shawn asked.

"The baby," the nurse replied.

"She'll have the baby in here?" The lump in Shawn's throat made it difficult for him to speak.

"We keep the mothers in one room throughout their labor. No more rushing to the delivery room. Every room is now a delivery room." The nurse smiled.

Shawn swallowed hard.

The nurse looked at Ellie. "Your doctor is off the schedule today. Dr. Blanchard is on call. I've informed him about your water breaking. He'll be here shortly to examine you."

The nurse busied herself preparing the room.

Ellie whimpered on the bed, squirming around, trying to escape the pain of a contraction.

Shawn stood beside her, holding her hand, feeling completely useless.

"I'm not due yet," Ellie told the nurse when she came near the bed.

"Some babies come early," the nurse reassured them with a smile.

"You're sure the baby's coming?" Ellie asked.

"No doubt about it. Your water broke. There's no turning back now." The nurse rushed out of the room again.

Ellie gripped Shawn's hand so hard she hurt his fingers.

The nurse returned, motioning to the chair beside Ellie's bed. "Make yourself comfortable, Dad. This is your wife's first baby. Her labor might take a while." The nurse left the room once more.

Shawn fell backward into the chair. Ellie did not release his hand when he plopped down. He scooted the chair closer to her bed so they didn't have to stretch to hold hands. "We should probably tell the nurse I'm not the baby's dad," he said.

"Please don't. She'll make you leave, and then I'll be alone."

"I need to call Mom," Shawn said. He wasn't about to call his dad.

"Not yet," Ellie pleaded.

He squeezed Ellie's hand, trying to calm her down. She had a death grip on him.

"If you call, your mom will come and take your place. I want you here with me. Nobody else."

The nurse returned. "I know you two are young and haven't done this before, but don't worry. I've helped deliver babies for twenty years. I'll take good care of you both." The nurse smiled again. She looked about Shawn's mom's age. Her confidence reassured him.

"Here comes Dr. Blanchard." The nurse welcomed the doctor into the room.

The doctor's age surprised Shawn. He looked young. Barely thirty. Hopefully, he was older than that. He wore green scrubs and washed his hands before walking over to Ellie's bedside.

"Hi, Ellie," he said in a friendly manner. "You're Dr. Hammons's patient?"

"I see on your charts you're a little early. I have you at almost thirty-seven weeks gestation. Is that correct?"

Ellie nodded.

"And your water broke about an hour ago?"

Ellie looked at the nurse.

The nurse smiled. "Her water broke."

The doctor smiled at Ellie.

"Well then, we should have a baby soon. Is there anyone you want to call before the baby arrives?" asked the doctor.

"Yes," Ellie replied, surprising Shawn. "I need to call the baby's parents. They live in Colorado."

"Colorado?" the doctor said in surprise.

"The McBrides from Colorado Springs will be adopting my baby."

The doctor glanced at Shawn and then returned his gaze to Ellie.

Shawn knew he looked like a deer caught in headlights. Ellie's mention of the McBrides had completely thrown him off.

"Why don't you let this young man . . ." the doctor waited for Shawn to say his name.

"Shawn," he rasped.

"Nice to meet you, Shawn. Why don't we have Shawn go make that phone call to Colorado while I examine you, Ellie? How does that sound?"

"I don't know the number," Shawn said, wanting so much to tell Ellie he would not make that call.

"The number is in the side pocket of my bag," said Ellie. "Please come back as soon as you can."

"Okay," he promised, letting go of her hand to follow the nurse from the room after retrieving the phone number out of Ellie's bag.

Shawn walked to the lobby in a daze. He didn't even know what time it was. He considered calling his parents but then remembered the afternoon at school. The last person he wanted to see was his dad. He thought it through and decided he didn't want to see his mom either. His perfect family blown to smithereens. The family he'd planned for himself falling apart now with this phone call he was about to make to the McBrides.

For a moment, he didn't know what to do. His eyes burned with tears he wouldn't let himself cry. What would they do without E.J.? Would Ellie still marry him? Nothing was going as planned.

Getting his act together, he left the lobby, found his way to his truck, and retrieved his iPhone. He also climbed up in the truck bed and collected his backpack. After taking Grandpa Larson's Bible out, he put the backpack in the cab of the truck and locked the doors.

Walking back to the hospital, it struck him that birds were singing all around him. Towering pines and maples shaded the hospital's sweeping lawns, the birds having a field day darting back and forth between the branches. The sun lay on the horizon, warm and rosy and reassuring somehow. A beautiful sunset tonight. In a few more seconds, that sun would sink behind the mountains. Again, it hit him he should call his mom. She would wonder where he and Ellie had gone when she got home, but he realized Ellie was right. There was no way his mom would let him stay in the delivery room. *Tell me what to do, God,* he prayed.

Back in the hospital, he felt he should call the McBrides. Ellie wanted that. And E.J. was her baby. *Hers and Number 33's.* His chest tightened. A man answered the phone on the second ring. At first, Shawn couldn't come up with the words he needed to say. He realized how much he loved E.J., though she wasn't even here yet. The last thing he wanted to do was give E.J. to the McBrides, even if Number 33 was her dad.

"Yes, hello?" the man on the phone said in a good-natured way.

Had the man been rude or impatient, Shawn would have hung up on him. But Mr. McBride sounded as friendly as Shawn remembered. "Mr. McBride?" he asked in a raspy voice. He blinked hard against the tears stinging his eyes.

"Yes, this is Ken McBride."

"This is Shawn Klein. I'm calling for Ellie. She's having her baby and wants you and Mrs. McBride to come to the hospital."

For a moment, Mr. McBride said nothing.

Shawn swallowed down his churning emotions. "Mr. McBride?" he finally said again.

"I'm here. Just a minute, Shawn."

Shawn heard the phone transfer over to a speaker.

"Jenny, you need to be a part of this phone call." Mr. McBride's voice deepened with emotion.

"Shawn, could you tell my wife what you just told me?"

Shawn closed his eyes, praying God would get him through this. "I'm calling from a hospital in Tennessee. Ellie's having the baby. She wants you to come to the hospital."

"Are you sure?" Mrs. McBride asked, sounding as shaken as Shawn felt.

"Pretty sure. We are kind of in shock right now," Shawn admitted. *Really in shock*, he realized.

"We'll be on the next plane out there," Mr. McBride assured him.

"We are at Tennessee East Hospital," Shawn clarified.

"We will find you." Mr. McBride sounded determined.

"Thank you, Shawn," Mrs. McBride said. "You don't know what this means to us."

Shawn knew what it meant to him. He was losing E.J. "You're welcome," he whispered and then hung up the phone.

Chapter 36

Shawn walked back to labor and delivery feeling much older than his eighteen years. Why couldn't he and Ellie just keep E.J.? They were young, but they weren't that young. Other kids their age had babies. He would tell Ellie that. He felt bad about the McBrides on their way here now, but things would work out. Things had to work out. The McBrides would understand. Giving up a baby wasn't like giving up a puppy. Everybody knew girls changed their minds all the time about keeping their babies.

When he arrived at Ellie's room, he found the place empty. Whirling around in a panic, he ran into a nurse he'd never seen before. "Where's Ellie?" He tried to calm down.

"Are you her husband?" the nurse asked.

Shawn longed to lie but didn't. "No."

"Are you the baby's father?"

Again, a lie hovered on his lips. "No," he managed to answer.

"Who are you, then?"

"I'm her . . . brother."

"Brother?"

"Sort of brother. Is Ellie okay?" he asked in frustration.

"The baby is in distress. Ellie's been taken to the operating room."

"What kind of distress?" He found it hard to breathe.

"We aren't sure."

"You're not sure?" Shawn's voice rose.

"Come with me," said the nurse. She led him down the hall and told him to sit in a waiting area outside the operating room.

He stayed there about five minutes and then went to the nearby lobby. Instead of calling his parents, he called Grandma and Grandpa Larson. He told them what was happening, and they promised to come to the hospital right away.

Shawn hung up the phone feeling a little better. He should call his mom now, but he couldn't bring himself to do it.

Returning to the waiting room, he sat back down in the same chair and began to pray for Ellie and E.J. The longer he waited, the harder he prayed.

Pretty soon he sensed a holy stillness and began to pour out his heart in prayer. Not just for Ellie and E.J., but for himself and his dad and mom too. And the McBrides. He even prayed for Jill and Dr. and Mrs. Larson.

Finally, the operating room's double doors swung open. Ellie lay on a gurney a nurse wheeled out into the hall. Shawn rushed to her side.

She was awake and smiled at him. The baby was nowhere in sight. The crushing thought that E.J. had died overwhelmed Shawn. At least Ellie was alive.

"You're okay," he said, then broke down into tears upon grabbing her hand.

"The baby's okay too." Ellie squeezed his fingers.

"Let's get Ellie to her room," said the nurse.

Shawn stepped back so the nurse could wheel Ellie down the hall. He followed the gurney as closely as possible, mopping his face. In the room, Shawn watched for a moment as several nurses worked to move Ellie to the stationary bed. He stepped out of the room to give them some privacy.

He was in the middle of regaining his composure outside her door when Grandma and Grandpa Larson arrived.

"How's Ellie?" Grandma anxiously asked.

"She's all right." Shawn motioned inside the room. "They're putting her in bed."

"How's the baby?" Grandpa asked.

"I think she's okay," Shawn said.

Grandma peeked inside the room. "It will take them a while to get Ellie set up in there. Let's go find the nursery."

The three headed down the hall. They found the big windows that looked over rows of glass cribs. Several babies slept peacefully. One infant cried like crazy. A nurse changed the crying baby's diaper. Shawn read the names on the cribs, but none said Ryan. He was about to panic, when a nurse pushed a new crib into the nursery.

"There she is," Grandma said.

"How do you know?" Shawn asked in wonder.

"I just know." Grandma smiled.

"She's a tiny thing," Grandpa pushed his bifocals higher on his nose.

The nurse noticed them peering in the window. She waved them around to a nearby door. Shawn and Grandma and Grandpa walked over to where the nurse met them with the baby in the rolling crib. "Are you the Ryan family?" the nurse asked, tucking the baby's bundling more firmly around her.

"Yes," Grandma said without hesitation. "How much does she weigh?"

The nurse pointed to the little sign on her crib. "Five pounds, thirteen ounces. She's a good size for coming early."

"Are her lungs developed?" Grandpa sounded like the doctor he'd once been.

"So far so good," replied the nurse.

Unashamedly, Grandma leaned over the crib, put her hand on the baby's head, and prayed out loud over the child. The nurse bowed her head in prayer with them.

Grandpa grinned at Shawn and then bowed his head as well.

At the end of the prayer, Shawn stared at E.J. She was so tiny and perfect. She looked just like Ellie with her full, rosy lips and that worried little scrunch between her delicate eyebrows.

"Where are your folks?" Grandpa asked.

"I haven't called them yet," Shawn admitted.

Grandpa and Grandma stared at him, wide-eyed with questions.

"They don't know the baby's arrived?" Grandma looked shocked.

"No," Shawn answered guiltily.

"Shawny," she softly chastised him.

Grandpa intervened for him. "We'll go call them right now."

"Why haven't you called them?" Grandpa asked as soon as they were out of Grandma's earshot.

"I found out about Dad and Mrs. Larson today," Shawn said.

Grandpa looked at him sadly.

"I feel betrayed, Grandpa. Dad's a pastor. How could he do that with Mrs. Larson?"

Grandpa walked slowly down the hall with his arm around Shawn's shoulders. "Remember that last chess game we played? When I told you about the war on this earth? Well, your dad, being a pastor, is kind of like a king down here. He's the enemy's number one target. If the devil can take your dad out, the smaller chess pieces are usually his for the taking too."

"Are you saying the devil made Dad do it?"

Grandpa squeezed Shawn's shoulders. "No. Your dad fell to temptation. That's his own fault. But he's doing the right thing now, trying to make amends. So you need to forgive him." They arrived in the lobby. Grandpa pushed Shawn forward. "Call your dad."

"What time is it?" Shawn and Ellie had left the house around three that afternoon. He had no idea how late it was now.

Grandpa looked at his watch. "Fifteen minutes to nine."

Shawn breathed a sigh of relief. His curfew was nine o'clock on school nights. His parents wouldn't really freak out until after that. He dialed the number. It rang once. "Hi, Mom."

"Shawn! It's Shawn," she called through the house. "Shawn, where are you? Is Ellie with you?"

"Yes, she's with me," Shawn answered, staring at Grandpa for moral support.

Grandpa nodded his encouragement.

"Where are you?" Mom asked again.

"At the hospital," Shawn tentatively answered.

"Why are you at the hospital? They're at the hospital," she relayed, probably to his dad.

"The baby's here." Shawn closed his eyes, praying his mom wouldn't go nuts on him.

"What? Ellie's had the baby? Ellie's had the baby!" his mom screamed on the other end of the line.

Shawn held the phone away from his ear. Mom kept on screaming. He handed Grandpa his iPhone and walked away.

Returning to Ellie's room, he found her there alone. She appeared to be sleeping. He walked over to the bed and stared down at her. Some color was back in her cheeks, and she looked beautiful. Never had he seen such a serene look on Ellie's face.

"I've given her pain medication." A nurse joined him in the room. "She's a little thing, and the way she's reacted to the medicine makes me think she's never done drugs." The nurse smiled. It was the same nurse who had assumed Shawn was E.J.'s father.

"I don't know if she's tried drugs," Shawn answered. He'd never thought to ask Ellie if she'd ever done drugs.

"Does the baby look like you or her?" The nurse checked Ellie's vital signs.

"Definitely Ellie." Shawn didn't correct the nurse's assumption that he was the baby's dad. He wished he was E.J.'s dad. Wished more than anything he and Ellie had E.J. together. If E.J. was his, they'd be a family now. He'd join the army, and they'd move far away. Maybe to Germany or Korea; he'd heard guys got stationed there.

"You two are starting out young." The nurse finished reading the machines and turned to Shawn with a smile. "But that's a good thing. My husband and I married young too. We had our first baby when I was eighteen and my husband nineteen. Daniel became a marine, and after a couple of kids, I went to nursing school. We've been married twenty-eight years next month. I wouldn't trade being a young bride for anything. Daniel and I've had so many good years together. Some hard years, but a good life."

Shawn smiled, and tears filled his eyes. It had been a long day. He felt so worn and raw. And scared of what would happen next. "After I graduate high school, I hope Ellie will marry me. I want us to have more kids together," he told the nurse.

"She'd be crazy not to marry you, honey." The smiling nurse walked out of the room.

Shawn sat down in the chair beside the bed, put his face in his hands, and cried.

Chapter 37

Jenny burst into laughter when she saw Joe jogging toward them at the airport. Her brother swung her up into his arms and then gave Ken a bear hug. "Let's go get your baby!" Joe said, and everyone within earshot looked their way.

"Can you believe it?" Jenny hugged Joe again. "Ellie never even called us. She never returned Ken's emails. We thought it was over until we got the phone call last night to come to the hospital to get our baby!" Jenny cried.

"God wanted to surprise you." Joe let her go and bounded over to scoop up Jenny's carry-on luggage.

Ken picked up his own carry-on, and the three of them walked as fast as they could to Joe's old truck.

"I'm beside myself. I'm going to be a mother today. I keep pinching myself to see if I wake up," said Jenny.

"It really does feel like a dream," Ken agreed.

Jenny and Ken hugged each other before climbing into Joe's old Chevy. They'd hugged about a hundred times since the phone call last night from Shawn.

It took about an hour to get to Tennessee East Hospital from the airport. They arrived just as the hospital opened for visitors that morning, having caught the first flight out of Colorado Springs before dawn. Neither Jenny nor Ken had slept a wink. Joe hadn't slept much either after receiving their call last night informing him that they would need a ride from the airport to the hospital today.

They went directly to the nursery, where through the viewing windows they scanned the row of cribs for Baby Ryan.

"There she is," Jenny said in a husky whisper when she saw the tiny girl bundled like a burrito in a row of other burrito babies.

"Boy, they wrap them tight," Ken said in appreciation.

Jenny knew he was thinking what she was thinking. Matthew had never been wrapped that way. Matthew wasn't put in a blanket at all. He'd been naked expect for a diaper, covered in tubes in an incubator that kept him warm and alive until the day he died.

Jenny waited for the grief to wash over her. She looked at her husband's face and saw what she felt today in her own heart. Pure joy. Pure and utter joy. The grief over losing Matthew had rolled away like the stone in front of Jesus's tomb on resurrection day. A future lay before them in that nursery crib. A baby girl God had created for them.

"Oh, Lord, thank you," Ken said with tears streaking his stubbled cheeks. "Look at her. She's so beautiful." He turned to Jenny, and they stepped into each other's arms, holding one another tightly.

• • •

Shawn, walking to the nursery beside his dad, found Pastor Joe and the McBrides standing in front of the nursery windows, looking at the babies.

"I'm so glad you're here," his dad said to the trio, stepping up to hug Jenny and then give Ken and Joe hearty handshakes.

Shawn stepped forward. He shook hands with Pastor Joe and then Ken and Jenny.

"Isn't she a beauty?" Dad pointed to the baby.

"Beyond beautiful," Ken answered.

Fresh tears streaked Jenny's cheeks.

"Can we see Ellie?" Ken asked.

"Of course," Dad said.

Shawn stepped in that direction, leading them down the hall to Ellie's room. He peeked into the room, making sure Ellie was ready for visitors before allowing them entrance.

Ellie was sitting up in bed. She smiled when she saw the McBrides with Pastor Joe.

"Hi, Ellie," Pastor Joe said.

"Hi. Have you seen the baby?" Ellie looked at Ken and Jenny when she asked the question.

"We have," Ken said with a wide smile. Jenny appeared too emotional to respond, though she smiled too.

"Do you still want to adopt her?" Ellie asked.

"Are you kidding?" Ken said. "That's like asking us if we want to breathe." Ken put his arm around Jenny, pulling her close.

Jenny wept openly now.

"The baby's yours," Ellie said without hesitation.

Shawn was relieved his mom had gone home in the middle of the night for some sleep after telling him and his dad she wanted to adopt the baby. Dad had put her off, saying he would think about it. Dad now shed tears along with the McBrides.

A nurse stepped into the room. Ellie asked her, "When can the baby go home with her new parents?"

The nurse stopped in midstride, donning a professional air. "Are these the McBrides?" she inquired.

"We are," Ken said, keeping his arm around Jenny.

"Where are the Kleins?" the nurse asked.

"I'm Samuel Klein," Dad said.

"Is your wife here?" the nurse asked.

"No. She should be arriving shortly."

At that moment, his mom stepped into the room along with a dark-haired man Shawn had never seen before. The guy looked worn in the face, like a smoker, maybe a drinker, but his arms were ripped with muscle. Not the weight-lifting kind. More like a hardworking body. He certainly didn't come from a comfortable life. The raw edge about the dark-haired man unnerved Shawn.

"Mrs. Klein," the nurse greeted her with a tight smile. Everyone was taken aback by the strange man with her.

"Hello," Shawn's mom said, smiling in return.

Ellie's face paled.

"Hi, kid," the man said to Ellie.

Ellie didn't answer him. Shawn stepped over to her bedside, grasping her hand.

"Miss Ryan," the nurse asked Ellie. "Is this your father?"

Ellie nodded.

"Have the two of you decided the McBrides are adopting your baby?"

Ellie looked at her dad, then at the McBrides. "Please give her to the McBrides," Ellie said, her voice trembling. Shawn couldn't believe his mom had brought Ellie's dad with her. And the guy was scary looking.

"No," his mom rushed over to Ellie's bed. "Samuel and I are adopting the baby." She gave Ellie a pleading glance before turning to Ellie's father. "Mr. Ryan and I have already made the decision, haven't we, Mr. Ryan?"

Dad stepped over to Mom. "The baby goes to the McBrides," he said firmly.

"Samuel," Mom begged. "Suzanna belongs with us. We can give her the best life possible." She was acting like the McBrides weren't even in the room.

Dad took Mom by the arm. "Come with me," he said.

"No!" She shook loose of him.

"Patsy, please, we need to speak about this in private."

"I'm not leaving this room so Ellie can give Suzanna to these people we don't even know!"

Pastor Joe intervened, "Patsy, these people aren't strangers. This is my sister, Jenny, and her husband, Ken. They love the Lord with all their hearts and will give Ellie's baby nothing but God's best."

"I want Mrs. Klein to have the baby," Ellie's dad said, smiling at Shawn's mom as if they were lifelong friends.

"No," Ellie cried from the bed. "You would have made me abort the baby. You have no say in where she goes."

"We all need to lower our voices," the nurse commanded. "This is a hospital. Women in the other rooms have had babies too. These patients are trying to rest."

"Ellie should be resting." Shawn did his best to remain calm.

"Ellie, please . . . give us Suzanna." Mom moved closer to Ellie's bed.

Tears filled Ellie's eyes, but she didn't back down. "I'm sorry, Miss Patsy. I've promised the baby to the McBrides."

"I took you in. I fed you and clothed you and loved you," Mom accused. "How could you do this to me? To Suzanna? To Shawn? You know he loves that baby." She turned to Shawn. "E.J. Isn't that what you call her, honey?"

"Mom, stop," Shawn rasped.

"I'm getting security," the nurse said, walking out of the room.

"Shawn. Patsy. Come with me," Dad ordered.

"No!" Mom cried.

"No," Shawn echoed. "I'm staying with Ellie."

"We will leave," Ken said, putting his arm around Jenny to lead her from the room.

Pastor Joe followed them out.

"I'm out of here too," Ellie's dad said. "I'll be back for you later, kid," he told Ellie as he left.

"They can arrest me. I'm not leaving." Shawn squeezed Ellie's hand.

His mom burst into tears. Dad put his arm around her. "Come on, Patsy. Let's go pray about this in the hospital chapel."

"I don't want to pray. I'm too hurt to pray." Mom glared at Ellie. "You've betrayed us."

"Enough," Dad said. "Shawn, take care of Ellie. Your mother and I need to talk."

"You don't have to tell me that," Shawn said as a security guard arrived with the nurse.

"Please allow my son to stay with Ellie," Dad said to the nurse.

"Is your son calm?" the nurse inquired.

The six-foot-something security guard waited beside the nurse with a frown on his face. He wasn't much older than Shawn but probably outweighed him by a good fifty pounds of muscle.

"As long as everyone remains calm and speaks quietly, they can stay during visiting hours. But we ask you to keep in mind that Ellie has just had a C-section. She needs rest."

"Certainly," Dad agreed. "We are not adopting Ellie's baby," he told the nurse. "Please allow the McBrides to bond with their baby."

"God is calling us to raise Suzanna. I've already bonded with her." Mom's eyes were full of desperation. "I have clothes, blankets, bottles. Formula. A bassinet. I'm ready to take her home."

"The only daughter we're taking home is Ellie." Dad appeared at his wit's end with Mom.

"Can't you see what she's done to our son? She's seduced Shawn, just like she seduced the poor boy who impregnated her."

"Patsy!" Dad took Mom by the shoulders. "Your desire for that baby is twisting your mind. You love Ellie. I love Ellie. Shawn and Stephen and Seth all love Ellie. She's a part of our family now."

"Suzanna is our daughter," Mom insisted.

"The baby's name is not Suzanna." Dad took a steadying breath. The nurse and security guard quietly stepped out of the room but stood by the door, looking ready to throw everyone out of the hospital if their voices rose again.

"Don't you do this to me, Samuel. If you deny me this child, I will divorce you. I swear I will."

"What?" Dad sounded flabbergasted.

"I'm serious. I will leave you if we leave this hospital without Suzanna."

"Patsy, please. Let's go pray about this in the chapel."

"No!" Mom jerked away from him. "I mean it. If you let the McBrides take Suzanna, I'll divorce you!" She spun around and rushed from the room.

Dad followed her out into the hallway.

"I'm going to try to talk to my parents," Shawn told Ellie.

She looked shell-shocked. And tired. So very tired.

Shawn kissed her on the forehead. "I'll be back soon," he promised before leaving.

Chapter 38

Alone in the hospital room, Ellie held her tiny daughter. The McBrides had chosen to name the baby Elizabeth Jenny. So they could call her E.J., they said. A fuzz of fair hair covered the baby's head, and her lips were full and pink. She had a rosebud mouth. Ellie couldn't believe how pretty she was. Staring down at the infant, she smiled through her tears. When E.J. waved her little fist around, Ellie offered the baby her finger to hold onto. She was delighted when the baby grabbed her finger and clasped it tightly. Ellie swallowed hard, trying not to break down in tears.

"You're going to a good home," Ellie assured E.J. "It's not a trailer. Don't worry, I checked. You'll have your own room upstairs near your mom and dad's room in a two-story house with a great big yard. Green grass and lots of flowers and trees there. You'll have a mom who doesn't drink or do drugs. She won't kill herself and leave you on your own in this world, I promise." Ellie bit her lip, her eyes burning.

Shawn stepped into the room. "May I come in?"

Blinking hard, she smiled. "Sure," she mimicked the way Shawn always said "sure."

"The McBrides are waiting in the lobby. They told me to tell you to take all the time you need with E.J."

When she kissed E.J.'s forehead, she fell apart and tears coursed from her eyes. "Give her to the McBrides," she told Shawn.

"I'll go get them. You can tell them you've changed your mind. That you're keeping her." Tears streaked Shawn's face too.

"No. Give her to them," Ellie said, kissing the baby one last time.

"Change your mind," Shawn begged.

Ellie handed E.J. to him. The baby still clasped her finger.

Shawn wouldn't take the baby from her. "We'll be a family. I'll take care of you and E.J. I'll enlist in the military right now. I'm eighteen. I'm old enough to join today. I'll have a paycheck in two weeks. We'll get married . . ."

"She belongs to the McBrides. Give her to them." Ellie pulled her finger free from the baby's grasp and held the tiny girl out to him.

Shawn pleaded with his eyes. He refused to take the baby.

"I mean it, Shawn. Take her." Ellie knew she had to do this. It wasn't just the baby she must let go of. Shawn had to go too. He was too good for her. Shawn deserved so much better. "I don't want to be a family. I don't want to be with you. Take E.J. and leave. I don't want to see either one of you ever again."

"You don't mean that." Shawn looked as if she'd just stabbed him in the heart.

"I mean it. I'm going back to Jamie when I get out of here."

Shawn took E.J. from her. He cuddled the baby to his chest with a crushed look on his face. Ellie thought she would die right then, she hurt so bad letting go of Shawn and E.J.

If only E.J. had been Shawn's child. If only the pregnancy had never happened. If she and Shawn had met like normal high schoolers in their senior year. Had fallen in love. Maybe after a football game with a million stars in the Tennessee sky. But that wasn't their fate. Someday Shawn would understand. Someday he'd thank her for cutting him loose this way. She pulled the bedsheet up over her face and sobbed as softly as she could so she didn't have to look at him holding E.J.

She wasn't sure when Shawn left the room.

He didn't come back. Not in five minutes. Not in ten. Not an hour later. Not even that night. Ellie wished she could take enough pain medication to commit suicide. In the depths of her heart, she even forgave her mom that night for doing that very thing. All the years of bitterness dissolved now that Ellie understood why her mom overdosed the way she did. Some pain was insurmountable. Some pain could kill you. She knew that now.

At first, Shawn could hardly function with Ellie gone. Putting one foot in front of the other, he went to school until his graduation in May. After grad night, his mom left for Georgia to see his grandma. Shawn had no idea how long she'd be gone, and he didn't care. These days he hardly spoke to either of his parents. To his surprise, they'd remained under the same roof. His dad studied the Bible all the time and preached endlessly about repentance. After gossip of the affair made its way around the church, half the congregation left. Shawn was one of those people. He couldn't stomach another day listening to a man who cheated on his wife and then had the audacity to stand on a pulpit and tell other people to stop sinning.

On Sundays, Shawn slept in until noon, then filled a blender full of protein powder, eggs, fruit, yogurt, and milk and hit the gym. His leg felt healed and strong, and he lifted weights every day. Working out took his mind off of Ellie.

Once he finished his workout, he showered at the gym, put on jeans, a T-shirt, and flip-flops and walked to his truck. After starting his pickup, he flipped on the radio, turning up the oldies station he'd been listening to that summer.

He was almost home when the song "The Rose" came on. The song hit him like a hatchet, cutting deep into his soul. Pulling into the driveway, he parked his truck but left the engine running. He found Duncan sleeping on the back porch and called him over. "Come on, boy, I need you today." Wagging his tail, the retriever trailed him to the truck. Shawn lifted the old dog onto the passenger's seat. Sutterville was a small town. Shawn figured it wouldn't be that hard to find Jamie Rivers.

When he arrived in the old mountain town, a thunderstorm clouded the horizon. Shawn could smell rain coming. He found an open gas station, where a tattooed guy worked on a car in the station's garage.

"I'm looking for Jamie Rivers, the Sutterville football player who got the UT scholarship," Shawn said without fanfare.

"He lives in the trailer park on the east side of town, but I think he's with a group of kids at the park right now having a barbeque." The tattooed man didn't stop wrenching on the car.

Shawn couldn't believe how easy it was to locate Rivers. "Where's the park?" he asked, adrenaline pumping through him.

"Keep on this road two more blocks. Turn on Blackberry Street and go one block north. The park is on the corner of Blackberry and Sugarland."

"Thanks." Shawn walked back to his truck, where Duncan waited for him, hanging his head out the window with a happy dog smile on his face. "Wish me luck, Duncan. Rivers might kick my butt today." Sitting in the passenger seat, Duncan wagged his tail in support as Shawn followed the guy's directions and arrived at the park five minutes later.

A volleyball game was underway. Here in the park, the June sun shone brightly, but black clouds blanketed the horizon. Shawn got out of his truck, leaving Duncan with the windows rolled down, and walked slowly over to the teenagers hanging around the volleyball court. He scanned the crowd for Ellie but didn't see her.

All the girls wore a lot of makeup, like Ellie used to wear when he'd first met her. And apparently, these girls thought they were at the beach in their little bikini tops and cut-off short shorts.

"I'm looking for Jamie Rivers," Shawn said loud enough to interrupt the volleyball game.

A big athletic-looking guy left the court and came over to him. "I'm Jamie Rivers." The guy didn't look mean without football pads and a helmet. In fact, he appeared pretty friendly until he recognized Shawn. "You're the quarterback from MVA."

"I need to talk to you." Shawn prepared himself for a brawl.

The volleyball game came to a standstill. Every kid stopped and stared at them.

"So talk, Sunshine."

"Alone," Shawn said.

Jamie glanced at his friends and then motioned for Shawn to follow him through the park. "I see your leg's good."

The volleyball game slowly resumed, but Shawn could tell the group's attention remained on him and Rivers rather than the ball bouncing back and forth.

"Where's Ellie?" Shawn asked.

"Probably packing for Nashville, if she hasn't left already."

"You going with her?"

Jamie stopped walking. He turned to face Shawn without saying a word.

"Aren't you back together?" Shawn kept his hands loose, ready for a punch when it came.

"Why would I take her back? I heard she put your kid up for adoption." Jamie smirked, but his eyes appeared wounded.

It took a moment for Shawn to comprehend what Jamie was saying. "My kid? What are you talking about?"

Jamie clenched his fists. His mouth hardened.

Shawn's heart skipped a beat, but not because he felt threatened by Jamie. Was Jamie saying he wasn't the father of Ellie's baby?

Jamie's eyes widened on him, and then his hands opened at his sides as all the fight went out of him. He stood there looking beaten.

"Ellie was pregnant when I met her," Shawn told him.

Jamie adjusted the orange UT ball cap on his head, looking as baffled as Shawn felt. "I didn't knock her up," Jamie said. "She never let me touch her that way. I thought she was a virgin."

"What do you mean it wasn't you?" Shawn's heart raced faster.

"I thought she dumped me for you. I thought you got her pregnant."

"Ellie was three months along when I met her."

Jamie fiddled with his ball cap. "I don't know what to tell you, man. I thought she was pure until that night I found out she was pregnant at the game when I broke your leg. Sorry about that, dude."

"It's okay." Shawn shook his head to clear his thoughts. Nothing made sense about Ellie's pregnancy. "Have you talked to her since she got back here?" he asked Jamie.

"No. I stay away from her, and she stays away from me."

"Who got her pregnant?"

"I have no idea." Jamie crushed his hat in his hands.

Shawn felt for him. He knew what it was like to love Ellie but not know her secrets. "She told me she was coming back here to be with you."

Jamie smacked the wrinkles out of his hat before putting it back on his head. Shawn could feel his frustration. He felt the same way. "She lied to you, man. I haven't talked to her since she left here last fall."

"Where does she live?"

"Stay away from her. She'll mess you up."

"I need her address." Resolution steadied Shawn. He had to know the truth.

Jamie told him how to get to the trailer park where she lived, then walked back to the volleyball game. He stepped into his old position in front of the net, and on the next round pounded the ball into the other court. The opposite team didn't even try to return the spike.

The scent of coming rain filled Shawn's nostrils as he strode back to his truck. Duncan greeted him with a wagging tail.

Shawn gave him a pat on the head as he got behind the wheel. Jamie said Ellie's trailer was only ten minutes away. He wanted to get there before that darkening sky cracked open.

Chapter 39

Thunder rumbled, and the flash of lightning illuminated the horizon as Shawn pulled into the trailer park. The place looked deserted. He was shocked by the decay and filth here. Beat-up cars without tires rested in front of old, run-down trailers. Weeds grew in abundance. A flock of crows had settled in a big dead tree, the barren branches hosting the birds' nervous party. Shawn was taken aback. Ellie had grown up in this place. No wonder she constantly told him how beautiful his home was. How much she admired the immaculate yards up and down his street. How she made a big deal over the dogwoods when they bloomed all around his neighborhood.

Their last evening walk together came to mind. They'd taken Duncan out for a stroll, the dogwoods flowering like crazy the day before Ellie went into labor. "I love it here," she'd said, looking at him with a softness in her eyes that left him longing to kiss her right there on the sidewalk in front of everyone, even with her big belly between them. "I love being here with you. I wish we could live here forever with dogwoods in bloom," she'd said.

"People don't randomly just have a life. They make a life one choice at a time," Shawn remembered telling her. It was something his dad always said. "You choose to plant dogwoods. You choose to surround yourself with beauty. You choose God's goodness instead of a life of sin and death."

"Sometimes other people's choices make your life," Ellie had said. "You have a perfect life because you have perfect parents. It wasn't my fault I never had that." They'd finished their walk in silence, Ellie holding her pregnant stomach as if in pain. Shawn understood that walk much better now. How arrogant he must have sounded talking about choosing beauty and goodness instead of a life like this. How stupid and self-centered, just like his cheating dad.

Looking around at this run-down trailer park, he understood Ellie a hundred times better now. Understood she'd grown up without dogwoods. Without choices. Not everyone was given choices the way his dad always said they were. Dad was an adulterer. His mom had flipped out over not getting E.J., saying all those things about Ellie. Both his parents falling apart.

Unbelievable.

This place was unbelievable too. And Ellie had lived here her whole life.

Shawn found himself praying before knocking on her trailer door. As his knuckles connected with the thin aluminum, he realized he hadn't prayed since Ellie handed him E.J. and made him carry her to the McBrides.

Ken and Jenny now sent pictures of E.J. through Facebook, telling him how great she was doing. E.J. looked more like Ellie every day with her pretty eyes and rosy lips. Bolts of pain hit him—those thoughts of what might have been whenever he looked at that beautiful baby.

If Jamie hadn't fathered Ellie's baby, then who had?

When she opened the trailer door, Shawn didn't know what to say.

She looked as shocked to see him as he was to see her. Her hair was wet from a shower. Long and dark and tumbling down her back, free from her normal ponytail. She wore faded jeans ripped at the knees and a white T-shirt with holes in it too. Dark eyeliner edged her eyes. She looked skinny and frail. "Shawn," she said as if she could hardly believe he stood there on her rotting porch.

"I talked to Jamie," he said quietly.

Ellie stepped past him out of the trailer, closing the door behind her. Without a word, she walked off the porch, down the steps, and over to a nearby pine, where she sat down on a large stump beside the tree. The stump was wide and old, table-like. A tree cut down in the trailer park some years back, Shawn supposed as he went to the truck, let Duncan out, and then followed the retriever over to Ellie at the stump.

She jumped off her perch, grabbing Duncan around the neck when he reached her and burying her face in his fur. For several minutes, she stayed that way, Duncan wagging his tail like mad with Ellie hugging him like crazy.

Again, Shawn was struck by how thin and fragile she looked. It was hard to believe she'd been pregnant just months ago. She seemed so small now. Duncan probably weighed more than she did. When she finally took a break from loving on Duncan, she asked, "What did Jamie tell you?"

"Not what I thought he would tell me." Shawn glanced at the sky. He was surprised the storm hadn't unleashed on them yet.

"So what did he say?" Ellie pressed.

Shawn studied her and just couldn't figure her out. "Jamie thought I got you pregnant."

"I figured that when he tried to kill you at that football game." Thunder boomed in the distance. Ellie jumped, and so did Duncan. She whispered something to the retriever and stroked him as he settled down on the ground beside her. On her knees, she kept her arms around his dog. The wind picked up. Rain was coming. They didn't have long to talk out here without getting pounded by the storm. He hated that black eyeliner back on her eyes and her pale lipstick. "Why are you wearing all that makeup again?"

"You're judging me. Like everyone else has judged me." She turned toward the flashing lightning. She didn't jump this time when thunder boomed.

"I'm not judging you. You look better without makeup is all I'm saying." He tried not to sound bitter, but he was.

Ellie motioned to the trailer, then around the park. "Now you know where the broken rose comes from. I told you the rose was dirty, but you wouldn't believe me."

"Who are you really, Ellie Rose?" He stared intently into her eyes.

"Do you really want to know?" The way she said it scared him.

"Are you a prostitute?" The thought had come to him out of the blue. In a place like this, any girl might turn to prostitution.

She laughed, and then tears slipped down her cheeks. Duncan licked the sadness from her face, trying to comfort her like Shawn wouldn't. Couldn't.

"I'm serious," he said, a lump in his throat because he still loved her.

"I know you are." She hugged Duncan, refusing to say anything else.

The sound of a motorcycle brought both their heads around. Ellie's dad drove through the trailer park on his Harley, frightening off the crows. He pulled up, parking in front of the trailer as lightning flashed in the distance. Shawn recognized that Harley. It was the guy who had mocked him on the road after he left his dad in the high school parking lot the day he found out about the affair.

Mr. Ryan turned off his bike and ignored Shawn, talking to Ellie as if Shawn wasn't there. "What's he doing here?"

"He just stopped by to let me see Duncan. He's not staying." Ellie held on to Duncan, streams of black mascara marring her cheeks.

"Tell your rich boyfriend to take his dog and leave. I'll bury him in the mountains if he comes here again." Clive went into the trailer.

Shawn's heart pumped wildly. "Your dad's a scary guy."

"Jamie was never afraid of him." Ellie pushed Duncan away. The retriever leaned back against her, thumping his tail. "You gotta go home," she told Duncan, scratching his head and then gently pushing him away again.

"Did he ever tell Jamie he was going to bury him in the mountains?" Shawn kept his gaze on the trailer door.

"All the time. He's been drinking. You really should go." Ellie kissed Duncan's head for a long, tender moment and then pushed the dog away again.

Shawn glanced at the trailer and then searched Ellie's face. "Tell me the truth, and I'll go." He called Duncan to his side. The retriever came to him slowly, reluctant to leave Ellie.

Shawn petted Duncan when the dog reached him. "Who is E.J.'s father?"

Ellie slowly rose to her feet. She wiped her cheeks, staring up at the darkening sky. She was about to speak when the trailer door burst open.

Clive came out with a gun in one hand and a beer in the other. He waved the beer and then the pistol at Shawn. "Get out of here, rich boy."

Adrenaline slammed through Shawn's veins. "I'm not leaving until I finish talking with Ellie."

Clive shot the pistol in the air. "Get out of here, or I'll shoot your dog." Clive downed his beer, then crushed the can and threw it from the porch.

Shawn's legs trembled, but he wasn't leaving Ellie.

"Take Duncan and go." Ellie sounded terrified.

"Come with me," Shawn pleaded with her.

"Get out of here!" she screamed at him.

Stepping down off the porch, Clive took aim and fired at Duncan. The old retriever yelped and then flopped over on the ground.

Ellie screamed, raw and wild.

Shawn sprinted past her and tackled Clive. The two sprawled in the dirt together. They tangled on the ground until the gun went off between them. The gunshot stunned Shawn.

He couldn't believe it. How had the gun gone off? Mr. Ryan let go of him. He didn't feel any pain. Was he shot?

Jumping to his feet, Shawn now held the gun in his hand. Blood was smeared across the front of his T-shirt. He looked around for Ellie.

She was nearby, cradling Duncan's head in her lap, sobbing like her heart was broken. Duncan wasn't moving. Blood matted his golden fur.

Shawn looked at Mr. Ryan lying on the ground. Mr. Ryan's eyes were closed. He was holding his stomach. A bright red blotch was spreading under his hands. "I think I shot your dad," Shawn called to Ellie. He turned away from her and threw the gun as far as he could as the first drops of rain fell from the tumultuous sky.

Chapter 40

Feeling as if her world had come apart, Ellie placed Duncan's head gently on the ground. She crawled across the dirt on her hands and knees to Clive.

"Kid," he said, reaching for her.

"I'm here." She took hold of his hand.

His gaze locked with hers. "I want you to know something before I die."

"You're not gonna die." Ellie shook all over, feeling so cold, though the rain fell surprisingly soft and warm upon them.

Shawn knelt down beside her. He pulled off his bloody shirt to hold against the bullet wound pumping blood from Clive's stomach.

"I'm not your real dad." Clive focused on Ellie, ignoring Shawn doing his best to stop the bleeding by pressing his shirt to Clive's wound.

Ellie squeezed Clive's hand, trying to take in what he was saying. Her tears mingled with the rain on her cheeks.

"Your mom left me for a while. When she came home, she was pregnant with you." Clive clung to her hand. "I wish you were mine. Jana was my kid. You're better than your sister. And you sing so pretty."

Clive closed his eyes, resting for a moment before he spoke again. "Your mom sang backup for Johnny Jones when Jones was a nobody in Nashville. He's still a nobody." Blood slipped out of the corner of Clive's mouth and mingled with the rain on his face.

Ellie tenderly wiped the rain and blood away. "You did the best you could after Mama died. You took care of me when you didn't have to if I wasn't your kid."

Clive smiled. "You never did belong with me and Jana. You belong in a mansion. Jones is your real daddy. But you take after your mama. You look and sing just like her. Raising you was the best thing I ever did. I got even with Jones. I got you."

Ellie kept wiping the rain from his face and the blood from his lips.

The howl of sirens filled the air. Several police vehicles pulled into the trailer park. Uniformed men rushed over. More sirens screamed in the distance. The deputies had their guns drawn. Ellie knew these men's faces. Knew their names. Even liked some of the cops that ate at the diner all the time.

"The gun's over there." Shawn pointed to the pistol lying near the stump. He nodded toward Clive. "He shot my dog. I tried to take the gun from him, and it went off. I'm sorry. I didn't mean to shoot Mr. Ryan. I don't know how it happened."

Two deputies grabbed Shawn, hoisting him to his feet none too gently. Another deputy, after quickly putting gloves on, took over trying to stop Clive's bleeding.

Ellie jumped up to defend Shawn. "It wasn't his fault! Let him go," she cried as they handcuffed him.

The Dunburgers stood on their porch watching the whole affair. "Did the Dunburgers call you? Did they see what happened?" Ellie asked the deputies, waving toward the old couple across the street.

The officers tried to calm her down.

She wouldn't have it. One of the deputies took Ellie in his arms like a father, holding her as he would his own little girl.

Paramedics arrived and put Clive on a stretcher. "He's critical. We need to move fast," one of the paramedics told the officers, rushing Clive into an ambulance.

The fatherly deputy took Ellie over to his squad car, helping her into the backseat. Shawn was shoved into the backseat of another cruiser.

Several deputies climbed the Dunburgers' porch steps to speak with the couple. Two more squad cars arrived on the scene. The cruiser carrying Shawn backed out of the driveway first. The car with Ellie followed a moment later.

At the sheriff's station, Ellie was allowed to make one phone call. A deputy named Raymond who ate regularly at the diner looked up the Larsons' phone number for her.

Grandma Larson answered on the second ring. "I'm sorry, Mrs. Larson, but I don't know who else to call," Ellie began in a trembling voice.

Grandma Larson recognized her right away. "Where are you, Ellie?"

"I'm at the Sutterville sheriff's station. Clive's been shot, and Shawn's in jail. Can you come help us?"

"Grandpa and I will be there fast as we can." Grandma Larson prayed for Ellie there on the phone before hanging up.

The Larsons arrived at the Sutterville sheriff's station an hour later. Grandpa Larson insisted on driving Ellie and Grandma back to the farm and then turned around and went back to Sutterville. Nobody could reach Shawn's parents. They weren't answering their phones.

Grandma Larson found some dry clothes for Ellie. A pair of pink sweats and a matching sweatshirt that were baggy on Ellie since Grandma, though small, outweighed her. Grandma Larson warmed up fried chicken and mashed potatoes from supper that night, encouraging Ellie to eat. She threw Ellie's blood-and-mud-spattered clothing in the washing machine and then dried them once they were washed. Ellie still couldn't believe Johnny Jones was really her dad. How could the famous singer be her father? Johnny Jones was a huge country star.

Ellie told Grandma Larson as they sat at the kitchen table late into the night that her mom had written one of Johnny Jones's songs. "I used to get mad when the radio played her song," Ellie confessed. "I know Clive used that royalty money to buy the diner after he buried my mom in Nashville."

Ellie told Grandma just about everything. Starting with growing up in the trailer with Jana and Clive. To her credit, Grandma Larson didn't act surprised about a bit of it. She just handed Ellie tissues as she talked and cried. They moved to the living room couch, where they stayed until the middle of the night, speaking and praying over Ellie's life, first with Clive and then with the Kleins. Duncan's death broke her heart. He'd been such a good dog. The dog of her dreams. The only thing Ellie didn't tell Grandma Larson was how she got pregnant. She just couldn't bring herself to relive that too.

Grandpa Larson called and said he wouldn't be home until sometime tomorrow. He was staying with Shawn at the sheriff's station in Sutterville.

In the guest room where Grandma Larson tucked Ellie into bed, a wooden cross hung on one wall and a tapestry of flowers and scripture decorated another wall. *Come to me, all you who are weary and burdened, and I will give you rest. Matthew 11:28*, the tapestry with flowers read. A Bible lay on the nightstand beside the bed. After Grandma Larson left, Ellie couldn't fall asleep. She finally picked up the Bible and turned to Matthew, chapter eleven, reading the same text that was on the tapestry before finally falling to sleep with the Bible clutched to her chest.

She woke in the morning just before daylight with birds singing outside her window. At first, she had no idea where she was, but the peace in the room overwhelmed her. Realization dawned slowly, yesterday unfolding in a matter-of-fact way that didn't frighten her. The Bible lay next to her in the bed. Picking it up, she opened to Matthew, chapter eleven again.

Come to me, all you who are weary and burdened, and I will give you rest.

Those words sank in as the bedroom flooded with daylight. The rays of morning sun shooting through the windows proved more beautiful than Ellie had ever seen before. Looking at the light, she knew God was real, more profoundly than she'd ever known anything in her life. Amazing white light filled her soul like she'd never imagined anything could. Peace filled her too.

A little while later, she found Grandma Larson in the kitchen making muffins. "I feel God here," Ellie told her.

Tears filled Grandma's eyes. "I prayed all night that Jesus would be with you." They hugged and cried together in front of the kitchen sink.

Ellie then helped Grandma Larson prepare a breakfast of fruit and muffins, which they ate on the porch in the sunlight, watching the road for Grandpa Larson's old truck. That summer morning couldn't have been prettier. Last night's rain had left everything clean and fresh and new. The sun shone soft and warm on Ellie's face as she stared out at the green fields where horses grazed and the woods behind the fence that circled the meadow.

Grandpa's old Chevy came up the drive before Grandma and Ellie finished their tea.

After walking up the porch steps, Grandpa hugged Grandma and then Ellie too. He held Ellie by the shoulders, staring at her for a moment with a smile on his face. "You look different. You're shining."

"She certainly is shining," Grandma Larson said.

They hugged some more, and then Grandpa sat down, and Ellie went to get the muffins and fruit set aside in the kitchen for him. When Ellie returned, Grandma and Grandpa were talking about Shawn.

"Is he still in jail?" Grandma Larson asked.

"Yes, and it looks like he'll be there a while." Grandpa Larson turned to Ellie. "Come, sit with us, Ellie," he gently said, his gaze soft and tender upon her.

Ellie placed the breakfast tray on the table in front of him and then took a seat in the comfortable old wicker chair beside Grandma Larson.

Grandpa Larson said a breakfast prayer, and after the prayer, when Ellie opened her eyes, he said, “Honey, your dad didn’t make it. He died during the night at the hospital.”

Ellie blinked. It took a few moments for her to comprehend it. “Clive wasn’t my real dad,” she said, and then she wept.

Chapter 41

Jamie knew what he had to do before he left town. Everything he owned, which wasn't much, was packed into the two old duffel bags in the back of Uncle Charlie's truck. He'd said good-bye to his mama and little brothers. Only Jenner was left, and he dreaded seeing his big brother.

The University of Tennessee had Jamie all set up. Where he'd sleep. Where he'd eat. Where he'd train. All he had to do was get there. Uncle Charlie was hauling him down in his new Ford pickup that stood out in Sutterville.

Uncle Charlie had finally sold his hillside land for more money than Jamie could ever fathom to city bigwigs hoping to mine it. Uncle Charlie was leaving town too, promising to make every one of Jamie's home games at UT since Uncle Charlie had bought his retirement estate close to there just so he could go to Jamie's games. "You can live with me and Ruth if you want," Uncle Charlie had offered yesterday.

Jamie had laughed and grabbed Uncle Charlie in a big bear hug. Since his dad ran off, Uncle Charlie was the closest thing to a father Jamie had besides his coaches. There was some kind of special bond between his dad's brother, Uncle Charlie, and his mama, but neither Uncle Charlie or his mama had ever explained it to anyone. He suspected the bond included a long-ago fling between the two, but that wasn't his business. Most folks knew each other in Sutterville better than they should—trading bedbugs, Grandma called it. All Jamie knew was Mama never once looked sideways at another man once she settled on Pa. Now Pa looking sideways was a different story. Jenner got that skirt-chasing habit from him.

What Jamie couldn't understand was why women fell for men like his daddy and Jenner. Jenner went through girls the way he went through toilet paper, crapping all over them, and then just flushing them away. The only girl Jenner had treated halfway decent was Jana. But like Ellie, Jana was more than beautiful, she was smart and wanted out of Sutterville in the worst way. Jenner couldn't hold onto a girl like that. Jana saw Jenner for what he was, and so did Ellie. Or so he'd thought. In spite of it all, Jenner had always been Jamie's hero. Until that day in the park when Shawn Klein had opened up his eyes to the truth.

A shiver ran down Jamie's spine, though it wasn't cold as the sun rose over the mill parking lot. He remembered what Jenner had said last summer after that night at the lake when he had gotten so drunk he'd passed out in Jenner's truck and couldn't remember a thing after leaving the party.

"Ellie thinks she's better than us, better than anyone up here in Sutterville. I taught her a lesson. Now you need to cut that high-and-mighty girl loose," said Jenner.

Ellie hadn't been the same since Jenner drove them home from the lake.

The night shift at the mill let out at seven a.m. Jamie asked Uncle Charlie to wait in the truck while he said what he needed to say to Jenner. This wouldn't take long, he told Uncle Charlie, all that needed saying could be said with one punch.

"Hey, little bro, what are you doing here this early in the mornin'?" Jenner called ten minutes later, walking toward Jamie, carrying a small ice chest that held his lunch. "Aren't you leaving tomorrow for UT? You should be sleeping in right now. You're gonna need sleep after we party it up tonight at the lake."

Jamie didn't bother to tell Jenner he'd decided to skip out on his going away party. He never wanted to see that lake again anyway.

"You might want to set down that lunch box," he warned his brother.

Jenner came to a halt in front of him. Since he'd moved home, his older brother had put on weight. Once all muscle playing football, Jenner now looked like a bale of hay with the center strand cut. "Did Mama send you here? All her cookin' is makin' me fat. I don't want no breakfast."

"Mama didn't send me. And it's not her cookin' makin' you fat. You's makin' you fat cause you're a loser." Jamie squeezed his hands into fists.

"You on somethin'?" Jenner stared into Jamie's eyes. "They'll give you a piss test when you get to UT. You better be livin' clean, little bro."

"I've always lived clean, unlike you."

Jenner tossed his ice chest in the back of his truck. "I can see you're fit to be tied. Tell me what's got you all twisted up, Jam Man." Jenner had called him Jam Man since they were little because he'd always loved jam sandwiches. No peanut butter, it was too expensive, just jam.

"I know what you did to Ellie after I passed out on the Fourth of July."

Jenner froze there beside the truck. The sun rising in the sky shone on his face, and he looked old and tired. Hard living did that to a person. "She was askin' for it," Jenner defended himself.

Jamie threw the punch before his brother saw it coming. The blow knocked Jenner to the ground. "Did you rape her?"

Jenner rubbed his jaw. He didn't get up, but stayed on the ground, which frustrated Jamie. He wanted to fight. One punch wasn't enough. He'd loved Ellie, and Jenner had ruined it.

"I ain't fightin' my little brother over some high-and-mighty Ryan trash."

"Ellie's not trash. I was gonna marry her. She was saving her cherry for me."

"Is that what she told you?" Jenner tested his jaw for damage.

"You better get up. Because I'm gonna kick your—"

"Ellie deserved what she got," Jenner interrupted him. "I did you a favor popping her cherry. She'd have gotten herself pregnant, and your football career would have been over at UT. You'd be workin' at this mill with me for the rest of your life. You want to end up livin' like that? Workin' all night at this mill, doin' time like you's in prison?"

"She had your baby." Tears streaked Jamie's cheeks now. He couldn't stop his feelings from showing and hated Jenner for it.

Jenner scooted back against the tire of his truck. He didn't deny he was Ellie's baby daddy as Jamie had desperately hoped he would. He kind of just smirked about it.

Jamie let out a string of curses. "Get up and fight me," he cried. He'd lost the only girl he'd ever loved because of his stupid brother.

Jenner put his head in his hands as if he was finally ashamed and wouldn't look at Jamie anymore.

"You gonna do what's right and take responsibility for your kid?" Tears dripped onto Jamie's UT shirt.

"I hear she put the kid up for adoption. I'm good with that."

Furious, Jamie punched Jenner's truck, leaving a dent in the side, nearly breaking his hand in the process.

"Hey, don't go busting anything. You got a football scholarship to keep, little bro."

Jamie couldn't stop crying. His hand throbbed, but his broken heart hurt far more.

"Little bro, listen to me." Jenner gazed up at him as if he really cared. "I did you a favor. No Sutterville girl's gonna end up with you. You're far better than that. You're gonna make our family proud. And just wait. Those UT girls are gonna be all over you. Pick the prettiest one and make sure she comes from money, you hear me."

Jamie couldn't take anymore of Jenner. Rubbing the tears from his cheeks, he walked away, holding his injured hand against his chest.

Chapter 42

Shawn sat in his jail cell listening to the Sutterville sheriffs plan for their community picnic this coming Saturday. The sheriff's department was in charge of overseeing the dunking booth. A dangerous endeavor, being dunked by children, Shawn was tempted to tell them.

Grandpa Larson had left after spending all night waiting to see if he would be released so Grandpa could drive him home. When Clive Ryan died during the night, the prospect of him walking out of this jail cell was gone. Grandpa said he'd gotten a hold of Shawn's parents. His mom was on a red-eye home from Georgia, and his dad was picking her up at the airport. They'd be up here to see him by late morning, Grandpa had told him before he finally went home.

A deputy brought Shawn's mom to his cell a few hours later. "How could this happen? You killed Mr. Ryan?" his mom asked, all red-eyed from crying when she saw him.

"I didn't mean to kill him." Shawn was shocked to hear someone actually say he'd killed Ellie's dad. "The gun went off when I tried to take it away from him."

His mom looked frightened and tired and about to freak out on him. He hoped his dad would come and calm her down like he always did. "Where's Dad?" Shawn asked.

"I wouldn't let him come with me. We're separated."

"How can you separate when I'm in jail?"

"I warned your father, if he let the McBrides take Suzanna, I'd leave him."

"You mean Elizabeth? The McBrides named her Elizabeth, Mom." Shawn didn't hide his frustration with her.

"Her name should have been Suzanna. She was meant to be our baby. Your little sister."

"Dad didn't give the baby to the McBrides. Ellie gave them E.J. It wasn't Dad's fault."

"Your dad should have supported me. He could have changed Ellie's mind, but he didn't want another baby with me. He wants Beth." Mom pulled a tissue out of her pocket and mopped her teary face.

Shawn closed his eyes, still unable to believe this had really happened to his family. His mom sniffed loudly, and he opened his eyes to look at her. She was a wreck. Had been a wreck since the night of the big storm when Dad had confessed his affair with Mrs. Larson.

Shawn held up the Bible Grandpa Larson had left with him in the jail. "I've spent the past six months reading this Bible. All of it. In here it says, 'Do not commit adultery.' In here it says, 'Do not divorce.' In here it says, 'Pick up your cross and follow me.' You and Dad say you're Christians, but I don't see you living like this Bible says you should live." Shawn waved the Bible in her face.

"I never should have brought Ellie home. She ruined our lives," his mom said as if she hadn't heard him.

Shawn laughed incredulously. "Are you kidding me? Ellie didn't ruin us. You and Dad ruined us."

Mom pressed a tissue to her nose. "How can you say that, Shawn?"

He shook the bars in frustration. The metal rods didn't budge in his hands. "You're so blind!" he yelled at her. "You and Dad are both hypocrites!"

A paunchy deputy came to his mom's defense. "Lower your voice, boy. Give your mother some respect, or I'll come in there and teach you some respect myself."

Shawn banged his head against the bars. The rush of pain calmed him down.

Two more deputies stepped into the room. Captain Dickerson was in charge. Unlike the other Sutterville deputies, Captain Dickerson kept himself in shape. He was maybe in his forties and looked fit as any bodybuilder at the gym.

"Why did you murder Mr. Ryan?" Captain Dickerson asked Shawn.

His mom rounded on the deputy. "My son says it was an accident. He didn't mean to shoot Mr. Ryan. " His mom's voice broke.

Chomping on his gum, Captain Dickerson narrowed his eyes on Shawn. "Tell me again what happened, boy. We got your mama here to keep you straight now. Give me your story one more time."

Shawn sat back down on his cot. He'd talked till he was blue in the face with Captain Dickerson yesterday. It hadn't done any good. The captain's mind was made up. But he gave it another try anyway because his mom was there. "Mr. Ryan shot Duncan, so I tackled him. I wasn't trying to kill Mr. Ryan.

I was just trying to take the gun away from him. He was drunk and acting crazy. I was afraid he'd shoot me too."

"What?" his mom cried. "Our Duncan? " her voice rose in hysteria.

"Duncan's dead." Shawn looked at Captain Dickerson. "What did you do with our dog?"

"How could someone hurt Duncan? He was such a good dog!" His mom's shoulders shook, and she buried her face in her hands, weeping brokenly.

Captain Dickerson motioned for the paunchy deputy to give him the keys to Shawn's cell. "Please escort Mrs. Klein to her car," he said. "And don't let her drive until she calms down. The kid and I are going to do some more talking."

"I'm not leaving my son with you!" his mom yelled.

Captain Dickerson raised his eyebrows at her. "Mrs. Klein, you have no choice. A man is dead, and your son pulled the trigger. This is the state's affair now. You need to calm down."

"I'll hire a lawyer," his mom threatened.

"I highly suggest you do." Captain Dickerson chomped his gum and then smiled.

Deputy Raymond took his mom by the arm. "Come on, ma'am, I'll walk you to your vehicle." Appearing in a state of shock, his mom docilely went with him.

After they left, Captain Dickerson opened Shawn's cell. "Come with me, boy," he said tensely.

Shawn followed the captain into the department's main office. He looked longingly at the front doors. Through the glass, he could see his mom getting into their black Suburban.

"Sit down," Captain Dickerson commanded when they arrived at his desk.

Shawn took the same chair he'd occupied for endless hours the night before.

"Tell me about Ellie's relationship with her father," Captain Dickerson said.

"Which father?" Shawn made himself comfortable as best he could in the hard wooden seat.

Captain Dickerson stuck another piece of cinnamon gum in his mouth. Shawn knew the man chewed cinnamon because he could smell it. "She only had one father. Don't get smart with me, boy."

"Mr. Ryan wasn't Ellie's real dad. He told her that after he was shot. Her real dad is Johnny Jones from Nashville."

"Johnny Jones? The famous country singer?" Captain Dickerson threw back his head and laughed.

Shawn squeezed the arms of the chair in frustration. He sure didn't like this deputy, and prayed he could remain polite and respectable with him.

"You're just full of stories, aren't you, boy?"

"I'm not telling stories. I'm telling the truth."

"Tell me more." Captain Dickerson worked his gum.

"Ellie never asked me to kill Mr. Ryan, like you said last night. Ellie and I haven't even spoken since she had the baby. I went to her trailer to see her on my own. I took Duncan with me because Ellie loved him. Ellie told me she'd worked in the diner for five years with Mr. Ryan." Shawn thought for a moment. "I'm pretty sure she said five years."

"I'm aware she worked at the diner."

"Did you eat at the diner? Did you know Ellie before this?" It was a small town. Everyone ate at the diner, Shawn supposed. If the sheriff knew Ellie, he'd certainly know she'd never ask him to kill Mr. Ryan, no matter how mean or crazy he was. Ellie wasn't that kind of person.

Captain Dickerson stopped smacking his gum. "I'm asking the questions, Mr. Klein. Your job is to answer them, not ask me questions."

"Sure. You ask the questions, sir." Shawn blew out a big breath, reminding himself to stay calm and polite and quiet.

"How did you meet Ellie Ryan?"

"My mom runs the crisis pregnancy center in Sutterville. Ellie joined our church's Mother Keeper program through the crisis center. Our family took her in until she had her baby."

Captain Dickerson jumped to his feet. "Raymond," he bellowed. "Bring Mrs. Klein back here!"

Shawn was relieved when Deputy Raymond, huffing and puffing, returned from outside. "She already drove away, sir," he said apologetically.

Captain Dickerson squished his gum between his teeth. All that gum chewing was really bugging Shawn. "Call the husband. Tell him I want to speak with both of them at nine a.m. tomorrow morning."

"Will do, sir." Deputy Raymond crossed the room to his own desk to make the phone call.

"So Ellie got herself pregnant. That's pretty common up here. You come up here often, boy? You been sleepin' with our Sutterville girls?"

"No, sir. I've never slept with anyone. I'm a virgin, sir."

Captain Dickerson leaned back in his chair, kicking a booted foot up on the desk. He grinned at Shawn, a smile that didn't reach his eyes. "Now I know you're lyin', boy. I know for a fact Ellie Ryan was real thick with Jamie Rivers, but he ain't had nothin' to do with her since she left here. I'm wonderin' why. Did some rich boy from the valley start knockin' boots with Ellie behind Jamie's back? Some rich boy decided Miss Ellie Ryan was so good in the sack he'd kill to keep her. But Clive Ryan didn't like that. Poor old Clive didn't want some snot-nosed rich boy takin' his daughter from him." Captain Dickerson leaned forward in his chair, smacking Shawn hard under the chin with a ballpoint pen. "You listenin' to me, boy?"

Shawn refused to give the captain the satisfaction of rubbing his stinging chin. "I'm listening, sir."

"I've watched Jamie Rivers play football since he was eight years old. I don't believe for a minute he didn't bang his girlfriend before you came along. And I don't believe you didn't bang her either. Sex and murder. That's what we got us here. That's the real story."

Dickerson hollered across the room. "Raymond! Call up Jamie Rivers. Get that boy down here for an interview."

Captain Dickerson turned back to Shawn. "I believe you and little Miss Ryan hatched yourselves a plan to get rid of her old man." Captain Dickerson did that thing with his gum, biting it between his teeth in a way that drove Shawn nuts.

He realized with a sinking feeling that the interview had taken a very wrong turn. "How could we have hatched a plan to kill Mr. Ryan? I haven't talked to Ellie since she was at the hospital having the baby. I didn't see her until yesterday afternoon at the trailer."

"Ellie Ryan couldn't get Jamie Rivers to kill her old man, so she found some stupid rich kid from the valley to commit the crime. It all makes sense to me now. She wanted to get rid of her drunken daddy, and she used you to do it." Captain Dickerson stood up in front of his desk and rubbed his hands together. "Raymond!" he yelled. "Find Ellie Ryan. I think we got us a murder in our jurisdiction."

Shawn spent the night in his cell reading the gospel of John. Chapter three particularly spoke to him. *For God so loved the world that he gave his one and only Son, that whoever believes in him shall not perish but have eternal life. For God did not send his Son into the world to condemn the world, but to save the world through him. Whoever believes in him is not condemned, but whoever does not believe stands condemned already because he has not believed in the name of God's one and only Son.*

Worn out from a night of no sleep, he shut the Bible and closed his eyes. No longer could he say he wasn't a real sinner. Self-defense or not, he'd killed Mr. Ryan.

The weight of the realization crushed him.

Raymond came to Shawn's cell a while later. "Boo hoo hoo," he said, making fun of Shawn when he found him crying.

Shawn flipped over on his stomach and buried his face in the stale mattress.

"I can see you ain't ready to face the morning yet. I'll turn off your light for a spell." Raymond switched off the light and returned to the morning news on television in the other room. Shawn could hear the weather report, all sunshine for days.

He sat up on his cot, and suddenly all the hair on his arms stood on end, and his neck hairs prickled too. His heart began to beat so hard he thought he might pass out. He realized he was afraid. He knew the Spirit of God was there as surely as he knew the hands he clasped together in prayer.

Ask to be forgiven, came to him as a gentle suggestion.

"Please forgive me, Jesus," he said out loud. Warmth and peace engulfed him, and he wasn't so afraid. His skin began to tingle, like his body and the air around him was electrified. His heart pounded thick and steady now.

You are forgiven.

He didn't hear the words with his ears, but never had a thought so invaded his mind and heart and soul. Mostly his soul. Fresh tears splashed down his cheeks. His cell was so dark he could hardly see a thing. The sound of the news no longer drifted from the other room. He realized until that moment he'd been nothing more than a cultural Christian, like being Irish or Italian, having inherited a religion from his parents, but not having a real relationship with Christ. The need to forgive his dad suddenly overwhelmed him. What was adultery compared to murder? What was murder compared to grace?

Fresh love for his mom washed over him too. Words of scripture poured through his mind. *Forgive and you shall be forgiven. Blessed are the merciful, for they will be shown mercy. Ask and it will be given to you; seek and you will find; knock and the door will be opened to you.*

In the dark cell with his mind full of light, Shawn lay on his cot, recalling every word he could from reading the Bible. God was absolutely real to him, and he'd never felt so grateful in his life.

Chapter 43

At the trailer, Ellie gathered what evidence she could to prove to Captain Dickerson that Clive wasn't her real father and she certainly hadn't wanted him dead. She'd already had one interview an hour ago at the sheriff's station and was amazed at how Captain Dickerson was twisting things. The evidence she found consisted of a photo album with pictures of her mom and Johnny Jones. Grandpa and Grandma Larson were with her in the trailer. Grandpa Larson had driven them up to Sutterville in his old truck without air-conditioning. Ellie was incredibly thankful for the Larsons. They'd offered to let her stay at their farm for as long as she wanted to live with them. So at the trailer, she packed some clothes along with the photo album.

Before returning to the station, she finally reached Jana by phone out in California. It was the first time they'd spoken in over a year. Jana said she was really busy in Hollywood and wanted nothing to do with the details of Clive's demise. Ellie had arranged to have Clive buried in the cemetery beside his older brother, Jerry, who died from drinking too much about ten years ago. There would be no funeral. Clive wouldn't have wanted one anyway. Jana's lack of emotion about the whole thing left Ellie sad.

She stopped by Turner's gas station and told Clive's only friend, Carl, that the antique pet was his. Clive would have wanted that too. Carl promised to pick up the motorcycle and keep an eye on the trailer until Ellie and Jana decided what to do with it.

At the police station, Captain Dickerson interviewed Ellie again. This time he asked her all kinds of questions that were hard to answer, but Grandma Larson sat right there for it all, sometimes interrupting things, sidetracking the sheriff with her sweetness. Obviously, Captain Dickerson liked Grandma Larson. He was nothing but kind and respectful with her, though he wasn't like that with anyone else. At the end of the interview, Ellie discovered why Captain Dickerson liked Grandma Larson. He said she reminded him of his grandmother he'd dearly loved as a boy.

During Ellie's interview with Captain Dickerson and Grandma, Grandpa Larson was with Shawn in his jail cell. Ellie had not seen Shawn since the shooting and wanted more than anything to talk to him, but after the interview, Captain Dickerson said she had to go home.

"You're lucky you're not in the pokey with your boyfriend," he told her. "I've got plenty more to do to sort this mess out. Consider yourself under house arrest at your grandma's, young lady." Then Captain Dickerson put his arm around Grandma Larson and walked them out into the sunshine.

"Our young lady is a victim, not a perpetrator," Grandma Larson reassured Captain Dickerson. "She will be in our care. If you need to speak with her, just call me." Looking up at the tall captain, Grandma Larson wiggled her finger at him. "God has entrusted you to keep the law and protect the innocent. You need to take this honor very seriously, Captain Dickerson."

He nodded his head like a chastised schoolboy.

"I also expect you to let my grandson go soon. You know that boy was only acting in self-defense, which is not a crime. Every one of us has the right to stop someone from shooting us and from shooting our beloved animals."

Again, Captain Dickerson nodded his head for Grandma Larson as if he agreed with her.

Grandma Larson gave up being stern and grinned at him. "You are a wonderful man, doing your utmost to protect good citizens. I know you will do the right thing by these young folks." Then Grandma hugged the captain.

Ellie was amazed at how Captain Dickerson softened with Grandma Larson. "Do you think they will release Shawn soon?" she asked once they were outside alone together.

"I hope so, honey." Grandma Larson took the photo album from her hand. "May I look at your pictures?"

Sitting on the brick steps side by side in front of the police station, they gazed at the photos while waiting for Grandpa Larson to finish his visit with Shawn.

"Your mom sure was pretty, just like you." Grandma Larson pointed to Johnny Jones. "And there's your eyes, honey. Right there, I see you in that man."

Ellie looked at the country singer's eyes. He had lots of lashes for a guy, and really nice eyes. "You think so?"

"I do."

"What if Clive lied? What if Johnny Jones isn't really my dad?"

Grandma Larson studied the photos. "Look here," she said, pointing to a picture of Johnny with his arm around her mom.

The star was grinning. "When you smile big like that, showing all your teeth, you look just like him."

Hope washed over Ellie. She'd always wanted someone else besides Clive for a dad.

"You know what? Your grandpa owes me a trip to the Grand Ole Opry. We'll go tomorrow. You bring this photo album along, and we'll pray God opens the door for you to meet your daddy."

"But he's a big star. I don't think it's possible to meet Johnny Jones."

"All things are possible with God," Grandma Larson said with a great big smile.

"Johnny, we've got an elderly couple here at the gate with a girl. She claims to be your daughter. I wouldn't have bothered you, but the girl has a photo album with pictures of you and a woman she claims is her mother."

Johnny laid aside his guitar. He was working alone in his home studio. He preferred to write songs all by himself in the mornings and then work with his band during the afternoon. The band preferred it that way too. They liked sleeping in late. Johnny was a morning person and at his most creative before lunch time. "Ask the girl her mother's name," Johnny told the gate security.

It only took a moment for security to reply, "The girl says the mother's name was Rose Grayson."

Johnny's gripped the phone tight. "Let her in," he said on a deep breath.

"I'll have Logan escort them on over to your studio," security answered him.

"Thank you." Johnny clicked off his cell phone. The last he'd heard of Rose she'd overdosed on alcohol and sleeping pills. The news had saddened him immensely. He calculated how old the girl would be now. Eighteen, if she was really his daughter. She also would have her birthday in May, most likely. His affair with Rose hadn't lasted very long, especially when he found out she was already married. He wondered if the girl had a birth certificate on her. Even a driver's license to prove her date of birth would be helpful.

He went over in his mind what Rose had looked like, petite with dark hair, real pretty. A voice that had stopped him in his tracks. The fact that she wrote her own songs—songs that left him speechless—made him hire her on the spot the day she auditioned for his band. Just a few days later, they'd ended up in the sack together. She was the sweetest thing he'd ever known. For years, he'd compared other women to her and they always came up short. The problem with Rose had been her sensitivity. She felt things so deeply. That came out in her songs. But she was like a finely tuned instrument; if you didn't handle Rose just right, she came apart on you.

He hadn't handled Rose right at all, especially when one of his other backup singers, Mary who was supposed to be Rose's friend, but probably wasn't, told him Rose was married. That she'd left a husband and a baby back in her hometown. As soon as he accused Rose of this, coming down hard on her about leaving her child behind, Rose unraveled on him. He would never forget what she said that terrible night. "You don't know what it's like to watch your dreams die. You don't know what it's like to be stuck in Sutterville singing to the pines with no one to hear you. No one, but the pines, whispering to the wind like spirits making you crazy."

After that, Johnny not only broke it off with her, he fired her from the band as well. He had to. She was married with a child. She needed to go home and be a wife to her husband. A mother to her little girl. Their love didn't matter. He felt betrayed by her secrets.

Letting go of Rose the way he had never sat well with him. Those months with her had been some of the best and worst days of his life, and in the end, he'd been harsh with her. Yet, one of her songs had launched him into the big time. It had taken several years to find a singer with a voice like Rose's to perform that duet she'd written for them. That singer was now as famous as Johnny thanks to Rose's song, "Holding On."

Through the years, other kids had come forward claiming he was their father, but those claims all proved false. Johnny felt in his bones this wasn't a false claim. He hadn't used condoms with Rose.

Knowing Rose, she probably hadn't used birth control either. After he discovered her secret marriage, she left Nashville, and he didn't know where she'd ended up until Mary told him Rose was buried in a Nashville cemetery. Just like his relationship with Rose of highs and lows, that day he hit a very deep low. He went to Rose's grave and apologized for the way it had ended. She had no tombstone at the cemetery. "The husband can't afford it," said Mary. "I'm surprised he even buried her here. Maybe the husband had really loved Rose. And she left behind two little girls."

That haunted him. Two little girls. And a husband who had loved Rose enough to bury her in the city of her dreams. Good ole Nashville. The town that makes or breaks you.

After he made it big with "Holding On," he paid to have a large, rose-colored marble headstone carved into an angel and placed on her grave. When he went to see the angel, he'd wept. That angel reminded him of Rose.

Logan, one of his security guards, walked into the studio with an elderly couple and the teenage girl. Right away, Johnny knew she was Rose's daughter. The girl looked just like her.

"This is Mary and Adam Larson. And this is Ellie," Logan introduced the visitors.

Johnny shook all their hands. He couldn't take his eyes off the girl. She stared at him the same way, all wide-eyed and full of angst. "So you think you might be my kid?" he asked for lack of something better to say. He tried to keep smiling, but his mouth felt dry. He could no longer slide his lips over his teeth to form a smile. He felt like he'd been to the dentist and his face was numb from Novocain.

"The man who raised me said you were my real father," she said. When she talked, she sounded just like Rose. Johnny wondered if the girl could sing like her mother.

Thinking hard, he calculated again when the girl's birthday would be. Focusing on two weeks in May, he went ahead and asked her, "Do you have a birth certificate with you?"

"No." She looked at the older couple. "We should have tried to get that before coming here," the girl said.

The elderly couple kept smiling. They were sweet-looking people.

"Are these your grandparents?" Rose had been an orphan, so if this couple was Granny and Granddad, the gig was over.

"No. They're . . ." She looked at the couple fondly. "My spiritual family."

"So they're not actually related to you?" Johnny fingered the silver cross he'd worn around his neck these past five years. He counted on his Savior to show him the truth here.

"No, I'm not related to them," the girl admitted. "I don't have any grandparents."

"You got a driver's license?" Johnny's heart was pounding hard.

"No." She sounded so disappointed.

"When's your birthday?"

"May 20th," she said softly and finally smiled all hopeful. When she smiled, there it was, his little dimple under her eye. Just like his mama's dimple. Mama would hit her knees and howl hallelujah if this girl turned out to be her grandbaby. She'd always wanted a grandbaby out of him.

His heart beat even faster if that were possible. He looked at the girl more closely, hoping he wasn't having a heart attack. He'd always regretted never having children and didn't want to die at her feet.

Could she really be his? "Would you be willing to take a paternity test with me?"

She smiled bigger, reminding him so much of Rose, except for his little dimple high on her cheek right under her eye just like Mama. Just like him.

He took out his iPhone and made the call right there. As soon as he could arrange it, they would take a DNA test together.

Chapter 44

Opening his jail cell, Captain Dickerson led Shawn to the front office. Chomping madly on his gum, Captain Dickerson told him to take a seat at his desk. He got straight to the point. "There's insufficient evidence for a capital murder charge. The DA in Knoxville decided not to waste anymore taxpayer money on you. It's your lucky day. You're free and clear. Get out of here, boy."

Shawn jumped to his feet. He hadn't expected this at all. "Thank you, sir!" He reached out his hand for a handshake.

Remaining seated, unwilling to shake his hand, Captain Dickerson kicked his feet up on the desk, rolling his gum between his teeth. "Don't thank me. Thank that valley girl throwing her weight around down in Knoxville."

Shawn strolled out of the sheriff's station into bright sunshine. Because his dad and mom were in the middle of the ten o'clock Sunday worship service, he called Grandpa Larson to pick him up. Grandpa and Grandma always attended eight a.m. service. They should be home by now.

When Grandpa pulled up in front of the station in his old Chevy an hour later, Shawn was waiting on the steps, watching two little sparrows building a nest in a nearby shrub. Seeing Ellie in the truck, Shawn's heartbeat accelerated. He hadn't talked to her since the day Mr. Ryan died. He waited until they parked the truck to walk over to them. The scent of sweetness floated in the air. Some kind of tall pink flowers he didn't recognize bloomed along the station's brick walls. Summer had settled firmly upon Tennessee while he was in jail. Walking out into all that sunshine, full of forgiveness, Shawn felt like a new person.

A gentle breeze blew through Ellie's hair, a rare day because her hair wasn't in its usual ponytail. A big smile lit her face. There was something different about her. A spark that hadn't been there before. Grandpa and Grandma followed Ellie over to greet him.

"Hey," he said, his throat tight with grief.

"Hey."

"I'm sorry your dad . . . Mr. Ryan died. I didn't mean for that to happen." Shawn needed to say it straight out.

"It was an accident," Ellie assured him.

Shawn held out his arms, and she eagerly stepped into his embrace. He hugged her fiercely, loving her so much. There was no dark makeup on her eyes, and her countenance shone with a brightness he'd never seen before.

After hugging her, he embraced Grandpa and Grandma. He couldn't speak for the emotions churning through him. He hugged Ellie again, holding her for as long as he dared with Grandpa and Grandma there.

"I've missed you," she whispered, straining on her tiptoes to say it in his ear.

"I've missed you too," he whispered back, kissing the top of her head, her silky hair warm under the sun.

They drove back to Mountain View with the four of them crowded in the truck's single cab. Ellie told him that Johnny Jones was really her dad. The paternity test came back 99.9 percent certain of that. Good enough for everyone involved. In two weeks, she was going to Nashville to stay at Johnny's mansion for a while to get to know her father.

"What are your plans, Shawny?" Grandpa asked him.

Shawn looked at Ellie. "I'm not sure. I was thinking about joining the military."

"What branch?" Grandma asked.

"I've heard the air force is good for families, but I've always thought the army would be cool." Again, he looked at Ellie, hoping she'd like his idea. Hoping with all his heart she'd want to be with him. "If I go into the military, I can do ROTC at Vanderbilt," he explained. Vanderbilt was in Nashville. And there was still the offer to play football there. He didn't really want to go the football route, but if it paid for his schooling, he'd consider it so he could live near Ellie.

"Johnny Jones has asked Ellie to sing a duet with him," Grandma said proudly.

"Really?" Shawn could see by the look on Ellie's face that she was terrified and delighted at the same time.

"Do you know Ellie's mom wrote that song 'Holding On'? Can you believe it?" Grandma couldn't stop smiling.

"Your mom wrote 'Holding On'? Wow." He was really surprised. "Holding On" was a huge song.

"Thanks, it is an amazing song." Ellie said.

"When will you be singing with your dad?" Shawn wasn't sure he should call Johnny Jones her dad, but he went ahead and tried it anyway.

"My dad? That sounds so strange." Ellie smiled. "Johnny says we'll rehearse it together when I stay with him. If I can sing it like my mom, we'll do the song at one of his concerts this fall when he tours."

"Your Nashville dream is coming true." Though he was happy for her, the fear of losing her forever hit Shawn hard.

A few days later, Grandma Larson helped Ellie pack a beach bag. "Where are we going?" Ellie wanted to know.

"All Shawn told me was that you need a towel and a swimsuit and casual weekend clothing." Grandma Larson was all smiles as she helped Ellie pack.

Shawn picked her up a short while later at the farm. His destination was a surprise. And a whole day in his truck gave them plenty of time to talk.

Ellie knew she had to tell him about E.J.'s father. She'd tried so hard to forget that night had happened, but now she closed her eyes, and remembered it all, exhaling a prayer before telling Shawn the truth. "We went to the lake, Jenner, Jamie, and me. Jenner is Jamie's older brother. A lot of girls wear bikinis at the lake, but I never did." Ellie stared straight ahead, tangled in the pain of the past. "I was wearing shorts and a T-shirt. Maybe those Levi's were too short. I threw them away." Blaming herself for what had happened wasn't something new. It was something she lived with. She glanced at Shawn, but he was staring at the road in front of them, his knuckles white on the steering wheel.

"Jamie got really drunk," she continued. "He passed out in Jenner's truck that night. Jenner said he'd take me home."

Feeling cold, Ellie wrapped her arms around herself as they drove down the highway with trees speeding by along the roadside. Shawn turned down the air conditioner when he noticed her hugging herself.

"Did Jamie's brother take you home?" he quietly asked.

"He took me to a friend's trailer. Jenner said his friend owed him money. Jenner was headed back to college to play football on a scholarship. I told him I'd just wait in the truck with Jamie, but Jenner said his friend had a puppy. Maybe Jamie told Jenner I wanted a puppy."

"Did Jenner's friend really have a puppy?" Shawn's question was cautious.

Ellie bit her lip. Hard. The pain helped her keep talking. "I'd never seen Jenner's friend before. He looked like a football player. Big. Tattoo sleeves on both arms. It was a pit bull puppy." Ellie looked out the passenger window, praying, *God help me. Help Shawn. Please get us through this.*

"So what happened?" Shawn kept his eyes on the road.

"Do you really want all the details?" She could hardly breathe.

"I'm sorry. I need to know."

Ellie could hear the strain in Shawn's voice. She trudged ahead. "I walked into that trailer with Jenner that night. I guess it's my fault."

He glanced at her, and their eyes connected in shared grief.

"When I was younger, I kind of liked Jenner. Every girl had a crush on him." She begged Shawn with her eyes to understand.

"Did you want to be with him that night?" Shawn looked back at the road. His jaw was clenched, and he appeared as distraught as Ellie felt.

"No. I knew something was wrong, but I kept telling myself Jenner wouldn't hurt me. I was Jamie's girlfriend. Jenner would respect that. Jamie looked up to Jenner. All his life, Jamie wanted to be just like Jenner.

"Jenner and his friend started doing shots of Jack Daniels. I asked if I could see the puppy. 'It's in the bedroom,' Jenner's friend said. So I walked into the bedroom."

Ellie closed her eyes. Why on earth had she walked into that bedroom? Why on earth hadn't she run out of the trailer as fast as she could? Why on earth had she gone to that party at the lake to begin with?

She knew better.

"I was petting the pit bull puppy when Jenner's friend came into the bedroom and took the puppy from me. He threw the puppy outside the bedroom and locked the door."

"It wasn't Jenner. And it wasn't what you wanted." Shawn slowed down, looking for a place to exit the highway. Ellie could tell he was really upset now.

"After the friend forced me, he left, and Jenner came into the bedroom." Ellie's chest ached so badly. It physically hurt to keep talking. "I felt so dirty. So used. I should never have gone to that Fourth of July party. Should never have gotten into Jenner's truck. I set myself up for it all."

Shawn stopped the truck on the side of the road.

Ellie was trembling all over. She stared at Shawn. They both sat there in the shock of this together. She'd done everything she could to forget about the Fourth of July until she missed her period two months in a row and dragged herself to school each morning sick to her stomach. The pregnancy made her finally face something she still couldn't quite see as rape.

Rape was violent. Sometimes women were killed while being raped. Jenner's friend hadn't tried to kill her. He'd ripped off her shorts, and took her virginity as she pleaded with him to stop. It happened so fast.

Shawn reached across the seat for her hand, his eyes holding hers. "Nothing you say will change how I feel about you, Ellie. I'm not going anywhere, no matter what you tell me about that night."

"Jenner got busted for selling drugs at his college a few months later. I think Jenner traded me to his friend for drugs that night."

Shawn tried to pull her close. Ellie resisted him. "Please," she said, struggling to breathe. "I'm not ready for you to touch me." She just couldn't look into Shawn's eyes anymore. She felt so dirty. So shamed and dirty. She let out a low moan and leaned her forehead against the dashboard, warm under the summer sun.

The truth will set you free. She'd had this exact same thought—*the truth will set you free*—the day she'd put her hand on the door of A Woman's Hope, the day she'd forced herself to face her greatest fear, that she was pregnant.

"Ellie," Shawn pleaded, "let me hold you."

She clung tighter to her knees. "I'm not done telling you what happened. When Jenner came in after his friend left, he started trying to kiss me, saying he was sorry. I kept telling him 'no,' but he said, 'My friend likes virgins. He promised not to hurt you. Did he hurt you? I won't hurt you.'

"'What about Jamie? How can you do this to your brother?' I asked Jenner.

He said, 'I'm setting Jamie free.'"

Shawn reached out and touched her hair. "It's okay," he whispered.

Ellie pressed on. She had to tell him all of it. She was sick of her secrets. "Jenner did it to me too. I don't know which guy got me pregnant that night." Tears finally washed Ellie's cheeks.

Shawn touched her wet face. He was crying too. "You didn't deserve that, Ellie."

"I thought it was the worst thing that could ever happen to me, but if I hadn't gotten pregnant, I wouldn't be here with you."

Shawn opened his arms to her. "E.J. brought us together. A baby wasn't the worst thing. It was the best thing." Shawn held her for a long time, whispering prayers into her hair as they sat beside the road. Finally, he nudged her back toward the passenger seat. "We better get going. I really want to reach our destination before the sun goes down."

Chapter 45

Shawn and Ellie walked out onto a North Carolina beach right before sunset, holding hands with no more secrets between them.

"Take off your shoes. You need to feel the sand between your toes." Shawn got down on his knees, reaching for Ellie's tennis shoes.

She nervously started laughing.

He wrapped his arm around her knees and tumbled her down into the sand with him.

As they stared into each other's eyes, Ellie stopped laughing.

Shawn was serious. "I love you, Ellie Rose."

"I love you too, Shawn Sherwood." She was so relieved that she'd finally told him the truth about the baby's father. She thought he would kiss her.

Instead, he untied her shoe laces. Slipped her shoes off. Then both socks. "I like your nail polish."

"It's Blooming Rose." Ellie leaned back on the sand as he held one of her feet in his hands, inspecting her toenails.

"Blooming rose fits you." He finally grinned at her. "I've missed watching you paint your toenails."

"I've missed you watching me paint my toenails." She leaned forward. Surely, he would kiss her now.

Instead, Shawn took off his own shoes and socks. "Our family came here a few years back. I love this beach. Want to look for seashells with me?"

"Okay." She was a bit disappointed he didn't kiss her. Was he afraid to kiss her after she'd told him the truth? She tried not to worry about it. They hadn't gone far when Ellie spotted a snail-shaped shell. Large enough to place to her ear for listening. The shells on this beach would echo the sound from around them. It really was the ocean you heard in these shells. Ellie was about to put the shell up to her ear when she saw little brown legs tucked up inside it.

She handed the shell to Shawn when he stepped up beside her. "What's that?"

He examined the legs for a moment and then, squatting down, set the shell on wet sand. Shawn put his finger to his mouth, warning Ellie to remain quiet for a while. Soon the little crab appeared, rushing across the sand into the sea.

Ellie started laughing; the little crab racing away with his shell made her happy.

Other folks walked the beach, but Shawn and Ellie hardly noticed them. "I'm the first guy to see the ocean with you, Ellie. There's all kinds of firsts in life," Shawn told her. "Together, we have a lifetime of firsts ahead of us." Shawn finally lowered his lips to hers.

With the sun sinking into the sea, Ellie had never been so ready for a kiss in all her life.

After kissing for a while, they went to dinner on the pier, peeling shrimp and drinking strawberry lemonade, talking about their future.

After walking the beach under a full moon, they found the hostel Shawn had booked for them. The place was full of college kids. Ellie slept in the girls' dorms, Shawn in the guys. For three days, they did this: the beach, the pier, and the hostel for sleeping. It was the best three days of Ellie's life.

Shawn adjusted the black beret on his head for the tenth time, standing in his army uniform backstage in Nashville, where he waited for Ellie and Johnny Jones to finish singing, "Holding On."

Ellie didn't know he was there.

They hadn't seen each other since their beach trip.

He'd spent the rest of that summer at Army Basic Training. He was now enrolled in Vanderbilt's ROTC program, and if he excelled there, graduating at the top of his class like he planned, the army promised to send him to flight school at Fort Rucker, Alabama. He hoped to fly helicopters for a living.

He reached into his pocket and found the tiny box that held the ring he'd bought for Ellie. It was a simple solitaire, nothing fancy, but the best he could afford. Johnny had offered to give him the money for a really nice ring, but Shawn said no. He wanted to do this himself.

When he'd asked Johnny if he could marry Ellie, Johnny said certainly, but under one condition. "You have to ask her onstage during my opening night in Nashville after we sing our duet together."

Shawn would have asked Ellie on the White House lawn with the whole world watching on the national news if he had to. He loved her and wanted more than anything to marry her, hopefully while he was still in college here in Nashville.

Onstage, Ellie and her dad ended the song. With Ellie standing beside him, Johnny told the crowd she was his daughter, and that her mom had written the song. Then Johnny gave the signal for Shawn to join them.

His knees shaking, Shawn walked out into the bright Nashville lights.

Ellie looked completely surprised to see him. He hugged her.

"I didn't know you were home from boot camp," she whispered.

"I wanted to surprise you," he said.

"This handsome soldier has a question for my daughter," Johnny announced over his microphone.

The crowd quieted. Amazing how silent thousands of people could get while waiting for something special.

"I've got to do this on my knee," Shawn said.

"He says he's got to do this on his knee," Johnny repeated into the microphone for the audience.

Shawn's fingers shook as he took the ring from his pocket. What if Ellie said no in front of all these people? He breathed a prayer and then got down on his knee in front of her.

Johnny held a microphone to his mouth.

"Ellie, will you marry me?" The sound of his own voice echoed across the building.

"Say yes!" a woman screamed from the crowd.

Johnny held the microphone to Ellie's lips. "Yes," she answered, smiling from ear to ear.

"Did you hear that, folks? My little girl said yes to her handsome soldier." Johnny sounded delighted.

The audience went wild. Clapping like thunder. Hooting and hollering and whooping as if he'd made a touchdown.

Shawn slipped the ring on Ellie's finger and rose to his feet. He took her into his arms and kissed her. It didn't matter that they stood in the middle of a bright Nashville stage. For a moment, it felt like just the two of them there.

In the front row, Seth and Stephen clapped enthusiastically. Shawn's dad leaned over and put his arm around his mom. They'd been trying to work things out. Grandma and Grandpa Larson held hands, beaming smiles on their faces. Beside Grandma and Grandpa sat Dr. Larson and his first wife. It was such a surprise when Dr. Larson introduced the first Mrs. Larson to Shawn an hour ago. "Please, just call me Trudy," the smiling woman said to Shawn. She was short and kind of round and looked nothing like Jill's mom.

"What do you think of Ellie singing a solo for us?" Johnny asked the crowd.

The crowd roared its approval.

Ellie looked at Shawn.

"Go ahead," he urged. "Sing 'The Rose.'"

Ellie glanced around, spotting the piano. A band member sat there, smiling at them. Ellie waved to him, and he waved back. "I'll sing if Shawn plays the piano for me," she told her dad.

It was Johnny's turn to look surprised. "Your soldier plays the piano?" he asked over the microphone.

Ellie nodded.

Shawn took a deep breath. He sure was nervous. So many people watching them.

"Well, let's do it!" Johnny pumped his fist in the air, and the audience clapped some more.

He motioned for his band member to give Shawn his seat at the piano. Shawn walked over and settled himself there.

Ellie sat down on a stool onstage, and her dad adjusted the microphone to her mouth. "Sing your heart out, honey," Johnny told her.

That's exactly what Ellie did.

Epilogue

Jenny watched Ken lead Elizabeth by the hand around the Easter egg hunt. Their baby girl was toddling now and determined to carry her own Easter egg basket today. The basket was nearly as big as she was, and their tiny daughter kept falling down because she wouldn't let go of the basket. Such a determined little girl. Jenny wondered if Ellie was that way, unwilling to give up on anything, or did that determined streak come from Elizabeth's biological father?

She and Ken had held their breath, waiting for the biological father to come forward during the adoption process, but he never did. It had been over a year now, and the only one they ever heard from was Shawn. "The good news," she told Shawn this morning on the phone, "is that Elizabeth loves carrying a basket. She'll make a perfect flower girl for you and Ellie this summer."

Shawn and Ellie's wedding was set for June 21, the longest day of the year, at Johnny Jones's Nashville estate. They'd hardly spoken with Ellie since the adoption was completed. It was always Shawn they exchanged pictures and information with, mostly through private Facebook messages.

In the beginning, social media had scared Jenny to death. "What if the father finds us through social media?" she'd asked Ken. "What if he comes and takes Elizabeth away from us?"

"That's in the Lord's hands," Ken had said. "God gives and takes away. We've already learned this lesson, honey. Let's just trust the Lord, okay?"

Trusting the Lord wasn't easy. Before the accident, she thought she completely trusted God. Wasn't she a woman of faith? Didn't she go to all those Christian women's conferences and run the children's ministry at church? She'd been a Christian nearly all her life, and it had been so easy to trust God when everything was going her way. It was the dark valley of suffering that had shown her just how firm her faith was, and to her shame, she'd found her faith wasn't firm at all. Ken's faith had proven more solid than her own. Her husband, who refused to follow church rules, yet in the valley of great suffering had been absolutely unwilling to give up on God.

"I just want to curse God and die," Jenny had railed one day at Ken. Her pain was so great, she couldn't see straight after Matthew died. How could God take Matthew from them? How could God take her womb away as well? How could God do this to her when all she'd ever wanted was to be a mother and a wife and a good Christian woman? What on earth was wrong with wanting these things?

It had taken the past several years of being shattered for her to realize she'd put so much of her hope in this world instead of hoping in God alone. She'd wanted good things from the Lord but didn't want to share in his suffering. Didn't want to pick up her cross and follow the Lord into a dark valley, but Jesus had led her there anyway, teaching her just how small her faith really was. Humbling her with great sorrow, to the point she no longer judged girls like Ellie Ryan for getting themselves pregnant. It happened. It was life.

Before losing Matthew, she would have looked down her nose at a pregnant teenager like Ellie. Why was the girl having sex outside of marriage anyway? Why couldn't people just follow God's rules?

Of course, she wouldn't have said any of this out loud. She would have gone with the Christian thing to say, like, "Praise Jesus, Ellie Ryan didn't get an abortion. Praise the Lord she chose life for her child," but this judgment on pregnant teenagers was hidden in Jenny's heart. Great suffering had exposed her heart and also her real lack of love for the Lord. Before the accident, she hadn't really loved Jesus; she'd loved being a Christian, counting on God to give her a good life, a happy family, children blessed by the Lord. Now the only thing she counted on was humbly learning the lessons God taught her, keeping her eyes on the Lord, and trusting even in the darkness, especially in the darkness.

Elizabeth had brought so much light back into their lives. She'd finally had enough of dragging around her pink wicker basket that got heavier with each egg placed there. The toddler plopped down on her bottom, beginning to cry, and raised her hands to her daddy.

Of course, Ken immediately scooped her up, and her basket too, holding the Easter eggs they'd gathered within Elizabeth's reach. Elizabeth grabbed a plastic egg, her tears subsiding, and the smile returned to her face. She was such a pretty little thing with wispy golden-brown curls and a dimpled grin that melted everyone who saw her. Especially melted Ken. Elizabeth was the apple of his eye.

You are the apple of my eye.

The thought came to Jenny, and it wasn't really a thought, more of a whispered kiss from God. Watching Ken with their daughter, she realized her heavenly Father really did love her the way Ken loved Elizabeth in spite of it all. Would she have ever known the depth of God's great love without the dark valley? Probably not. She certainly wouldn't have known how much she could love God instead of just loving the good things he gave her.

Ken walked over and placed Elizabeth in her arms. "I'm going to get the car. E.J.'s ready for a nap, and so am I." Ken kissed her lightly on the lips and then strode across the wide church lawn, carrying Elizabeth's pink Easter basket full of eggs. His limp was showing, even in his special shoes. He was tired. They both were tired. With Elizabeth teething and fussing all night long, none of them were getting enough sleep. Plus, they'd arrived late to the Easter celebration, having to park down the road and around the block from the church. As soon as her daddy left with the basket, Elizabeth began to cry. It was a beautiful spring day, no reason not to walk with Ken to the car. "Hey, wait up, Easter Bunny," she called after him.

Ken swung around, and as she crossed the wide church lawn to reach him, Jenny realized how much grace they'd been given. Easter was the perfect time to celebrate God's grace. To celebrate new life. They were a family—not the way she'd imagined her family would someday be, but the way God intended it to be. And it was good.

THE END

A Note From Paula

The Mother Keeper has ended up surprising me. When I first wrote the story eight years ago, I didn't realize I was the mother God would be keeping. I didn't know I would pull this book out of my computer vault to publish it in 2017 because my own teenager would become a daddy.

Children are always a blessing from the Lord no matter how they get here.

"Mom, please don't blog about this," Luke said when he first told me his girlfriend, Alex, was pregnant.

I just want to say, "I didn't blog about it, Luke. I published this story instead. I'm so proud of you for joining the Army to take care of your baby and Alex. God has good plans for you. I love you, and I can't wait to meet my grandbaby in October."

I also didn't know after writing this story in 2009, that a perfect spiritual, physical, and emotional storm would hit my life. I added the breakdown scene with Jenny falling apart at the church with tears streaming down my face. I had a breakdown at Mount Hermon's Christian Writers' conference in 2013. I left that conference under the redwoods half out of my mind and entered a hospital the next day. Doctors said it was an exhaustion breakdown. And it was. I had given birth to four baby boys in eight years during my late thirties and early forties, with three kids already. I love my children, and I can't believe all seven came out of my scrawny body, but I was beyond tired in 2013, with our youngest just two years old, and our hardest baby yet.

Scott is my amazing husband and a magnificent father, but he couldn't save me from wearing myself out to the point of nearly dying in 2013. I was very good at pushing myself well beyond my physical limits. And I was exhausted, especially of church. In December 2012, I was diagnosed with melanoma. Someone I dearly loved at our church, when I told them I'd just been diagnosed with melanoma, said, "Maybe you got that cancer for judging our pastor. You need to repent and just love our pastor in his sin."

The truth is, I had judged our pastor, and I wasn't the one who needed to repent. Our pastor needed to do the repenting. He needed to end his affair and stay with his wife. Instead, he left his wife and carried on with his girlfriend right in front of God and the rest of us. And I was so mad. Not just at this pastor, but at the Lord for letting it happen even though I'd prayed my heart out for this to stop.

And then I got melanoma. I had surgery to remove it from my leg right after New Years that year. I couldn't walk for two months, but I still went to Mount Hermon writer's conference in spring 2013, because I'd already paid for the conference before knowing I had cancer.

I was in no condition to be at that conference. My sweet daughter, Lacy drove me down, because I couldn't drive yet. My husband was due to pick me up four days later. Fortunately, Scott came down early and was there the morning I collapsed in James Scott Bell's mentoring class. I'm not sure what happened, but Jim was having us do a meditative type of writing exercise. He said to close our eyes and try to relive three events from our past. I can't remember what two of those events were, but the third I remember clearly. Jim said, "Remember something powerful that happened to you during your 16th year."

I'd already fallen apart in Karen Ball's early morning worship service before Jim's class that morning. For some reason, I was having flashbacks. Things long forgotten from my childhood that I didn't want to remember. Karen was so kind to let me cry on her shoulder, now here I was an hour or so later in Jim's class, feeling like the walls were closing in on me.

I couldn't remember something powerful from my 16th year, but my 17th year hit me hard. That year, I was sexually assaulted by an older boy who drove me home from a high school party. I didn't lose my actual virginity in the assault, it's too gross to explain what occurred, but I told my best friend, Christy, and she called the pregnancy hotline for me. "Was it possible to get pregnant from what had happened?" Christy asked after explaining things to the nurse.

"Probably not," the nurse assured Christy. "But with sperm involved, there's a slight chance it could be possible. If your friend misses her period, she needs to see a doctor."

I had nightmares about getting pregnant from that assault, and I sobbed in relief when my period finally came.

Christy and I kept my secret for years. I thought the assault was my fault because I let that boy drive me home because I'd drank several wine coolers at the party. Instead of driving me home, he drove me to an orchard. After the assault, I felt so dirty. So ruined. I became bulimic, and was so ashamed of what had happened.

And I was ashamed again when that person from church told me I got cancer from judging our pastor. Affairs happen in the church. People are human. But I wasn't ready to forgive these men. That pastor and that boy who assaulted me in high school were so much alike. Selfish butthole human beings, excuse my language, but that's how I felt in 2013 in Jim's mentoring class.

I actually made it through the powerful, teenage memory part of the exercise where I remembered that sexual assault in such vivid detail I thought I might throw up. I'd begun to sweat and tremble in my seat as Jim told us to now write a powerful scene in our WIP, which is a work in progress. I was working on two novels while attending the conference that year. *Until the Day Breaks* and *The Mother Keeper*. I chose to write a scene for *The Mother Keeper* that morning.

Jim quietly waited as we all typed our scenes out on our computers. It came to me that Duncan had to die in the story. Originally, Clive had fathered Ellie's baby in the first version of the book, but Christian publishers didn't want to touch incest. So I was trying to change the plot.

Clive was still a bad guy. He still needed to do something bad that would lead to his death because I wanted him to die. The scene played out vividly in my head, and when Clive shot Duncan, I lost it. I literally lost it. I don't know why. I don't know how the mind and the human heart come together to undo a person the way I was undone. But when that scene unfolded like a movie in my head after our meditative writing exercise, I absolutely came unglued.

So unglued that when Jim tried to calm me down after I'd collapsed on the floor and got back up, I called him a jackass and slapped him. I don't remember this happening. A pastor in the class told my husband it happened. *I know.* Talk about shame. After that breakdown, I was filled with such shame. A few years later, I was able to apologize to Jim. We laughed a little about it and hugged each other.

But that morning, nobody was laughing in Jim's class. A dog getting shot wasn't new to me. Several of my beloved dogs had died from gunshot wounds. When I was in high school, my daddy shot Gidget, a dog I'd dearly loved since I was little, to put her out of her misery after accidently running her over in our driveway. A neighbor shot my beloved dog Evie because she wandered onto his property when I was twenty-three. Daddy also shot my horse Soda Pop because Soda Pop got sick and was dying down at the barn. I was there at the barn holding Soda Pop's head in my lap as Daddy waited by his truck with his deer rifle. Soda Pop was the best horse I ever had. Daddy didn't want to shoot these animals I dearly loved, but he did. Daddy's a cowboy, and this is how he takes care of sick or wounded animals on the farm.

So I had a breakdown. Not because of those animals my daddy shot, or that sexual assault in high school, or because our pastor cheated on his wife. Or that I got melanoma, or was a physically exhausted mother who weighed hardly a hundred pounds soaking wet in 2013, and on it goes. We all have wounds. We all have scars. We all have these powerful experiences that shape our lives and shape us and shape our souls.

And we all have a healer.

A soul healer.

Jesus.

I've experienced so much healing through Jesus.

I want to thank Pauline Berry and Gene and Barbara Siemens for mentoring me when I was a baby Christian. I modeled Grandpa Larsen after Gene Siemens, and Grandma Larsen was a mix of Pauline and Barbara, godly people who taught me so much about loving Jesus. Gene passed away in February. He was the most godly man I ever met. I can't remember how many times Gene prayed over me for healing at the altar. After one of my pregnancies, I'd torn my placenta and it was a life-threatening situation for me and my unborn baby. Gene anointed me with oil at the altar and I stopped bleeding that very day. A few weeks later, on an ultrasound, they couldn't find the tear in my placenta at all. God had healed it.

I also want to thank Pastor Matt Chandler of The Village Church for all his podcast sermons that have so encouraged our family through the years. The rose scene with Shawn and Ellie at youth group came from Chandler. When he told that story during a sermon, it so touched me, and I knew I had to include it in Ellie's journey. Chandler was outraged that a youth pastor had used two roses, one perfect, one broken, to encourage purity in a youth group. "The whole point of the Gospel is that Jesus wants the broken rose," says Matt Chandler.

Amen Pastor Matt, says this broken rose.

If you are a broken rose too, you can trust your Lord. He has healing for you. A new life for you. Jesus loves you. And he'll bring you through every dark valley and over every high mountain if you let him.

Let him.

Love,
Paula

Made in the USA
San Bernardino, CA
25 November 2017